DEAD OR ALIVE

"I don't know anything about all of this," Perkins pointed out, "and none of it is shedding any light on those corpses we found today."

"You have to understand, Detective Perkins," said Fallows, "when the tire tracks at the site matched those of the stolen car found this afternoon, Tracey became the only shred of a lead that we have to Bryant."

Montgomery shot her a cold look that warned against any further unilateral disclosures.

"Who's Bryant?" asked Tracey.

The cat was at least halfway out of the bag, so Montgomery conceded more of his hoarded information, "David Julian and the unidentified girl were murdered, we feel sure, by Calvin Peter Bryant, also known as 'the Prince of Darkness.'"

The name meant little to Tracey.

It was a different story with Perkins. "That bastard is dead. One of your people killed him, a Taskforce man."

"I shot him," Montgomery admitted quietly.

IDENTITY

STEVE VANCE

LEISURE BOOKS NEW YORK CITY

A LEISURE BOOK ®

January 2005

Published by

Dorchester Publishing Co., Inc.
200 Madison Avenue
New York, NY 10016

ISBN 0-8439-5483-3

IDENTITY

Prologue

The house was quiet while they ate. Milton didn't like distractions when he was at the table, so there was no annoying, midday nonsense from the radio or television and very little conversation in the dining room.

"What time would you like to have supper?" Peggy Davis asked in a low tone. Sometimes it seemed that all they ever talked about were the schedules and contents of their meals.

Her husband ate on in silence for a time, as if he had failed to hear her. Though it was still April, spring had come very warm here in Washington, as it had over most of the nation. A breeze drifted through the open windows and rippled along the fresh-scented curtains. Finally, Milton paused in his chewing to reply, "Late. Eight, eight-thirty."

Peggy sighed, though only to herself. "That's after dark. Jimmy will be in bed."

1

Milton Davis nodded slightly, allowing her permission to feed and bathe their eighteen-month-old son and put him down before he returned from the fields.

"What will you be doing so late?" she asked.

Another few moments passed. "Clearing out down by the lake. With that money we got for selling Granddad's place, we can irrigate down there and put in barley."

All this was news to Peggy. "I thought that we were going to use that money for a newer car."

Milton regarded her coolly. "Can a car put food on this table, Peg? Can you and the kid live in a car?"

The young woman was wise enough not to reply, and the meal concluded in silence.

As Peggy cleared away the dishes, Milton iced down a sixpack of beer in a small cooler and carried it with him as he left the house. Peggy took a moment to watch him leave, a slim, muscular figure in the unusually harsh sunlight, his blue baseball cap bobbing away from her with a jaunty air that she seldom saw in the man himself.

He was a good man. A hard worker and a good provider. Peggy loved him, really, but he wasn't the easiest person to live with sometimes.

When Milton was out of sight in the overgrown field to the south of the house, she put Jimmy down for his nap, left her chores where they stood, and curled up on the couch to catch the last half of "The Young and the Restless."

He returned at five in the afternoon.

Knowing Milton's habits as well as she did, Peggy was a little shocked to see him walking slowly across the front yard so much earlier than he had told her. He was moving slowly, natural enough after hours of heavy work, but there was something more, something in the limpness of his carriage that somehow alarmed her.

Peggy had been watching his approach from the picture window in the front room, absently wiping her damp hands with a dishcloth. Without thinking, she tossed aside the rag and rushed to the porch to meet him. Jimmy was playing at the door, and she swept him up as she went.

"Milton?" she almost whispered as the screen door thumped closed behind her. "You're back early. Is something wrong?"

Typically, he said nothing. He was halfway across the yard, and his head was tilted so far forward that the bill of his cap obscured his face and neck. An icy sensation began to swell in Peggy's stomach. Her eyes searched frantically for blood or any other indication that he'd hurt himself. Out there alone, driving the tractor or using the chainsaw . . .

"*Milton,*" she repeated with more insistence, "what's wrong?"

He reached the steps and climbed them, slowly. When he looked up, she could see that there was nothing wrong with his face . . . at least, no injuries. But, God, his eyes, his eyes were so wide and empty.

Peggy tried to say his name again, but nothing came out. The ice in her stomach had climbed through her chest and into her throat. Milton tromped across the wooden porch as if his feet were made of cement. He stopped only when he reached the doorway.

For a long and unbroken moment, the two people stood there in the already fading sunlight, saying nothing, but each understanding that something had happened. Something so awful that their lives together could never be the same again.

Now Peggy didn't want to know.

Jimmy squirmed in her arms, trying to slip back to his toys on the floor.

Milton reached out and took the boy from her numb arms before he seemed to sleepwalk into the house. Once there, he sat in the overstuffed reclining rocker that was his private island in the den and hugged his son in a way that Peggy had never seen before. His eyes remained vacant and cold, but it was a coldness that appeared to come from too much emotion to express rather than too little.

Peggy knew that she had to find her voice. "Miltie?" she asked hoarsely. "What happened, baby?"

Her husband began rocking their child slowly. "Call the sheriff," he whispered. "For God's sake, call somebody."

The heat of the day failed to linger with the night. Though it was just a little past nine when Special Agent Russell Montgomery arrived at the crime scene, he could see his breath forming momentary cotton puffs in the luminous air that was encased by the local authorities' portable lamps.

The scene itself was quite ugly in its rural commonness. A lake just large enough to merit that description lay some two hundred yards from the nearest road wrapped by thin woods and heavy undergrowth. No good for fishing or other forms of recreation, it had rested in its anonymity for most of the memories of the local residents. Montgomery had seen this tableau all too many times.

He parked on the dark, isolated highway, which drew a southern border across the Davis property as straight as a surveyor's line. An ancient two-rut path led to the lake, and after flashing his badge for the deputy stationed there, Montgomery followed it into the night-thickened forest. He was aided a little by the battery of portable lamps, which had been set up by the sheriff and his people. The surroundings were so dark otherwise that he was within fifty feet of the lights before he caught sight of the three patrol cars, positioned like predators just beyond the intersecting cones of radiance.

Of course, by then his attention was fixed on the large blue van captured by the lights.

Montgomery sighed. The pieces were beginning to slip into place. It was going to be a bad night.

There seemed to be a dozen or more uniformed officers in and around the van, but the pungent smell that was emanating from the vehicle told Montgomery he would find what he expected within it. He thought he could hear someone retching in the darkness.

One of the deputies spotted his approach and jogged from the van to intercept him. "Hold on, sir. There's an investigation underway—"

Montgomery flipped the badge again, a little surprised that the lookout on the highway hadn't radioed his presence.

The deputy, a tall guy who looked very young and pale in the stark lighting, nodded shortly. "Uh, you're the Fed Shelby called about?"

"Yeah," Montgomery answered with a private grin. There were all kinds of Feds. "Who's in charge here?"

The deputy took a short breath and then grimaced, as if actually tasting the vile smell. "That'd be the sheriff, Sheriff Page."

"I'd like to speak with him, please."

The young man nodded again and trotted back to the van.

Page proved to be a gray-haired man who carried a little too much gut for his uniform. As he stepped gingerly from the rear of the vehicle, his expression read not much more composed than had those of his men. This was probably the worst thing he'd encountered in this quiet back yard of a generally quiet state. At least he wasn't vomiting in the dark.

"Page, Carl Page," the big man said, extending his hand.

Montgomery accepted the handshake. "Special Agent Russell Montgomery, Federal Serial Incident Taskforce. Glad to meet you, Sheriff."

Page removed his hat and used a forearm to wipe away the chilled sweat on his brow. "You sure got here fast, Agent Montgomery."

"Russ."

"Russ. 'Serial Incident.' That sounds like you might have investigated Tyson's butt-grabbing sometime back."

Montgomery smiled. "We tend to concentrate on matters a little more serious than that." As if to end the forced casualness of the moment, an owl called loudly from a nearby tree. Both men started and then grinned with embarrassment, before Montgomery asked, "What's the situation here, Sheriff?"

Page took a heavy breath before replying. "Bad as anything I've seen since the Army. Inside of that van's a goddamned slaughterhouse. Three, maybe four bodies, a couple of them little girls. Torture and dismemberment."

"How young?"

"Hard to say. Late teens, early twenties."

"Locals?"

"Can't be sure, yet. It ain't going to be easy to identify what's left. Nobody in that age range has been reported missing lately, and from the looks of them, I'd say these kids have been dead for several days, anyway." He shook his head. "The son of a bitch left all of the doors open, so the bugs and vermin could get at them."

"Forensics been here?"

That sparked a brief flicker of offended pride in the older man. "The report came in at five-thirty this afternoon, Montgomery; we've got all of the pictures and prints you'll ever need."

Montgomery raised a hand in an appeasing fashion. "I certainly don't mean to insult you or question the competency of your department, Sheriff, and I'm sorry if it sounded that way. But I'm going to have to ask that you leave the scene as nearly untouched as possible until the Taskforce can fly a team in. I'm sure your people have been thorough, but with our special equipment—"

Page waved him quiet. "Sure, Russ, I understand. Don't worry about stepping on any toes. The inside of the van is pretty much as we found it."

"Good. Mind if I have a look?"

As the two men moved through the blazing light toward the rear of the van, Page noted again, "You sure got here damned quick, Russ."

"I was in California when the call came in. Santa Rosa."

"Checking another serial report?"

Montgomery shrugged noncommittally.

"Goddamned freak assholes are springing up like weeds."

"Amen, brother."

The situation was everything Montgomery had expected and feared. The local authorities had established that the van had been stolen a week before in upstate Washington, and the outfitting that had taken place within it was sickeningly familiar.

Chains and cuffs had been expertly spot-welded to the floor, walls, and ceiling, and a number of instruments as commonplace as a tire iron and as esoteric as a surgical clamp lay scattered throughout it. The body of one girl lay spread-eagle on the floor, while the second sat, almost lifelike, by the right side of the first's head. What remained of the boy dangled above them.

Montgomery knew this. He knew that these kids had died slowly over a long period of time. He knew that the animal who had done this was entirely capable of sudden and brief episodes of violence when it suited his purpose, just as he was instinctively required to periodically give himself over to these intervals of studied, sadistic, and drawn-out horror.

Following each "interval," the creature invariably left behind the bodies, the vehicle, and the tools.

Montgomery knew these things, though he once had

been sure that he'd never have to acknowledge them again.

The atmosphere inside the van wouldn't allow an extended examination, so Montgomery and Page backed out after less than half a minute. They walked well away from the spot before pausing. Page lit a cigarette and offered one to the Fed.

"Thanks, no," Montgomery responded.

Page took a few drags. "Pretty bad, ain't it?"

"Bad enough." Montgomery's voice was almost inaudible even in the quiet night.

"But I suppose you've seen worse. In your work, I mean."

Montgomery answered with another slight shrug.

The sheriff didn't press the issue and silently concentrated on his cigarette. After finishing less than a third of it, however, he dropped the glowing butt to the ground and crushed it with a heavy boot. "Russ," he said slowly, "I know you're the expert here, but I think maybe I have an idea about this son of a bitch."

Montgomery was a master of maintaining a working rapport with the local authorities in all of his cases. "Glad to hear any new perspectives on the problem."

Page licked his lips slowly. "Well, taking into account all of the evidence . . ." He coughed and snorted through his nose, as if attempting to cleanse himself of the stink from the van. ". . . everything, I'm reminded of that crazy bastard they supposedly tracked down and killed two or three years back, the guy who called himself 'the Prince of Darkness.'"

If Montgomery were an expert in departmental relations, he was just as much the captain of his own emotions. There was not a flicker of concern in his expression when he said, "Calvin Bryant. He was about the sickest animal I've ever encountered, and God knows I've seen just about anything you can imagine in this business. But there's a problem with that theory. Bryant's dead."

"That's what they tell us."

Montgomery smiled slightly. "You don't buy it?"

"Russ, when that asshole was slaughtering people, the federal cops were getting their butts roasted every damned day. They had to kill somebody and hand his head over to the public. Sometimes it's best to believe only what you see with your own eyes, and then just half of that."

"Then I know Bryant's dead."

Page had a deceptively quick and incisive mind. "You saw them kill him?"

Montgomery's smile became a laugh. "Shit, man, I personally blew his spine through his breastbone."

The two men fell silent. Page lit a second cigarette and glanced back at the brilliantly illuminated van before finally saying, "This guy must be one sick mother of a copycat, then. You really shot him in the back?"

Montgomery winked. "Damned straight."

The night was even colder by the time Montgomery made his way back to the highway and his car. He knew that it would get hotter, though. By sunrise, with the local and state boys, the media ghouls, and the inevitable civilians buzzing around the pathetic corpses like flies, this area would be frying.

He caught the up-link to D.C. and filed his report. It wasn't an encouraging one.

"No, it's *Wallula*, Washington, not Walla Walla. This is due west, forty-fifty miles. Right. Yes . . . the signs are classic," he stated into the receiver, "mouths sewn shut, ritual slashes on the buttocks, no preliminary evidence of semen . . . a load of markers that weren't released to the public. The kills are at least thirty-six hours old."

He looked back into the dark forest and the miniature aurora of police lights that marked the van's location. He sighed.

"Don't blame the messenger, but all of the signs say that the Prince is back at work."

Chapter One

"It's almost like there was no life before the accident."

The center of the large room floated in darkness isolating it from the May sunshine that seeped through the blinds covering the windows. It was a warm and protective darkness that existed for the benefit of the eight people assembled there.

"Would you like to elaborate on that, Jessica?" asked Harrison Stafford quietly. He leaned forward in the cool leatherette chair that formed one-eighth of the injured circle; the doctor felt it to be important that his patients be able to see the concern and support in his expression even in the helpful darkness.

Jessica Simpson sighed, immediately sorry that she'd found the courage to speak up. Her thin body seemed to radiate tension. "Well . . . I didn't mean that . . . um, I mean, sometimes when my family is together, talking about something that happened before the accident—

13

like a birthday or a holiday or anything—it feels like . . ."

"Like they're talking about someone else entirely," Wally Gaithers said. He knew the sensation intimately.

"Exactly," Jessica said, nodding. "It seems like your parents are remembering something that happened before you were born. But when it's your own kids, it's like that's another lifetime, another person, and you were born when the car wrecked and the first 'you' died."

Several sympathetic voices responded to the woman's admission. In this group, it was not an uncommon feeling.

"Perhaps that is part of the solution," Dr. Stafford ventured, "regarding the point of injury not as an event that took something away from you but as an opening to a new phase of life, an opportunity to be reborn."

"For Christ's sake, I'm thirty-seven years old," Jessica responded. "I'm a mother and I can't even remember giving birth."

This once, Stafford was glad that his patient couldn't see the full extent of his own reactions. At least she was talking.

Wally Gaithers, ever the peacemaker, quietly came to the rescue again. "Jessica, you know that no one here doubts the depths of your pain and your sense of loss—how could we? It's been much the same for many of us; that's the purpose of our sessions together, isn't it?" He glanced at his own thin, slightly twisted legs. His accident had left him a paraplegic. "But actually, sometimes it can be best not to recall the old days."

A sailor of the psychic seas, Dr. Stafford thought,

what I spent a fortune and a decade of life to learn, you grasp intuitively.

And a second after, his assistant produced another reprieve, the end to a long afternoon: "Doctor, it's three-forty-five."

"Thank you, Miss Lund," Stafford said, sliding his chair out of the circle in a very decisive act of conclusion. "Nonnie, dear, would you get the blinds?"

The young woman hurried to readmit the sunlight.

"And that, ladies and gentlemen, is that for today's session," Stafford continued. "See you all Thursday, same time, same place."

Naturally, that wasn't all, as many of the six regular members of these twice weekly talk and support gatherings crowded about the doctor with various questions and comments that couldn't wait until Thursday. It was a common reaction to a session's end—there was even an extremely intimidating scientific name for this reluctance to break the patient-doctor bond, however temporarily—so Tracey Lund paid little attention to the grouping about Stafford as she gathered up the doctor's materials for him. After slipping the papers into his brief bag, she joined Nona Bartlett at the wide front window.

"Wow, I'd call that a sunny afternoon," she said, smiling and blinking in the radiance as she patted the woman's shoulder.

Nonnie's smile was due partially to her newly developed facility with the Venetian blinds rod (every small triumph drew this reward) and mostly to the childlike joy she felt as she bathed in the warmest day of the year. "It *tastes* good," she whispered happily. Though she was twenty-three years old, in a very real way this was Non-nie's first spring.

Tracey understood the visceral feelings that the afternoon sun was inspiring in the girl and she felt more than a touch of the same response herself. But in certain cases, it was best to be rather unwavering about the rules of grammar. "It is beautiful, honey, but you know that we can't really taste the light, don't you?"

Nonnie answered with a mischievous grin. "When I let it touch my tongue . . ."

"Nonnie." Tracey's tone was good-humored but stern.

The other woman sighed. "No, Tracey, we don't taste light."

Tracey laughed. "Ready to go home?"

Her excitement returned. "Yeah! *Saved by the Bell* is on today!"

"*Saved by the Bell,*" Tracey repeated to herself as Nonnie darted toward the main hall.

An employee in the records department of the Madison (Virginia) Facial and Cranial Surgery Center, Tracey's hours were eight A.M. to four P.M., five days a week. But on Tuesdays and Thursdays, she assisted Dr. Harrison Stafford with his conference sessions and generally left at their conclusions a few minutes before four. She was a good worker and popular with her superiors and coworkers, so these minutes were forgiven her.

"If that's all, Doctor, I'll be going," she told him.

Stafford thankfully turned away from an aggressively unhappy Jessica Simpson. "Oh, of course, Tracey. As always, thank you for your help. See you in a couple of days."

That woman needs a lot of work to come to terms with what's happened to her, Tracey thought. "See you then. Now, I'd better get out to the parking lot before Nonnie decides to hot-wire the car and take off without me." Snatching up her purse, she made tracks before Jessica could refocus her anguish.

Nonnie was waiting in the hall. "Ready."

Tracey struggled into her jacket with one arm at a time. "You bet we are. Want to drive?"

Nonnie giggled as the two young women walked quickly toward the exit.

They didn't quite make it. Standing at the door, as if posted there by royal decree, was the huge figure of David Julian, another Madison Center employee. Julian's duties ran to the moving of heavy objects and the occasional security obligation, tasks for which his hulking form was well suited.

"Leaving so early, little ladies?" he asked with a smile that, in Tracey's eyes, contained a wealth of leering threat.

She and Julian had crossed paths before. "It's five till, David. I think you could hold your breath until quitting time."

"Maybe." He remained stationed before them, leaning casually on his push broom, but his gaze shifted from Tracey to Nonnie. With her shining red hair and green eyes, it was not difficult to understand his interest in the younger woman. "What are your plans for the rest of the day, Sweetpea?"

Embarrassed, Nonnie lowered her eyes and said nothing.

17

Tracey put an arm around the girl and stepped forward. "We really need to leave now, David."

The big man ignored her. "Be nice. What are you going to do when you get home?"

"Watch TV," Nonnie answered in a shy voice barely loudly enough to be heard.

"You like to go to parties?"

She nodded.

"If you'll move out of the way, we can—" Tracey began.

Julian faced her with a piercing look. "You're not my boss, Lund, so don't try to be." His immediate supervisor was a woman, and he regularly vented his frustration on others with no power over his job status. Glancing back to Nonnie, he continued, "You need to come to my parties sometimes. Would you like that? To come to my place? I'd show you a real good time, one like you never had before."

Rage exploded within Tracey and flared outward to envelop her. It was almost more than she could contain. But, with a terrific effort, she kept her expression clear and her voice even when she said to Nonnie, "Run back to the conference room and see if Dr. Stafford has left yet, okay?"

Still uncomfortable under Julian's gaze, the young woman rushed back down the hall.

For the first time, Julian's demeanor seemed to crack a little. "There's no reason to bother any of the doctors—"

Tracey quickly stepped close to the orderly and thrust her face as near his as was possible under the circumstances. "Listen to me, you big slug," she stated in a low

18

but furious voice, "I know you don't like me, and the feeling is mutual, but if you have any brain function at all, you'll keep your few filthy thoughts to yourself. And don't you ever try to push your crude desires on that girl again."

Julian was startled and intimidated by the sudden offensive, but his sullen insolence quickly resurfaced. "I think that's up to the girl, isn't it? She's an adult."

"You know that's not true, not legally and not morally since her surgery, so you keep your damned hands the hell off of her."

"And maybe it would be smart if you watched your mouth, lady," he whispered.

Tracey heard Nonnie approaching behind her. "Are you going to move and let us leave, or do you want to have your ass on the unemployment line tomorrow morning?"

Julian curled his upper lip. "You don't have the pull."

"Try me."

Nonnie arrived, but Tracey refused to take her own gaze from David. After another tense moment, he coughed slightly and followed his broom toward the nearest corner of the hallway, leaving the door clear. Tracey quickly grasped Nonnie's elbow and steered her into the parking lot.

Once in the car, Tracey settled back behind the wheel, closed her eyes, and allowed her swollen tension to dissipate through a long sigh. She hated scenes like that. Julian was a thug and an animal, and his vulgar advances on an innocent like Nonnie had to be deflected by someone more responsible, but Tracey felt disgusted with her own ugly response. She should have been able to handle the situation in a more mature, reasoning manner, rather than giving in to the same sort of base instinct as Julian had shown.

Sometimes her own capacity for rage frightened her.

Nonnie picked up on her mood immediately. Maybe the fact that she hadn't yet cranked the car was something of a giveaway.

"That man didn't like us, did he?" Nonnie asked softly, staring out of the passenger window.

Tracey opened her eyes. "Honey, what that man likes or dislikes doesn't make one iota of a difference to you or me."

The girl didn't turn to look at her.

Tracey laughed. "Will you lighten up? Let's go watch *Saved by the Bell*!"

The Madison Facial and Cranial Surgery Center actually was a more multifaceted institution than the name implied. In addition to performing the actual surgical techniques that each case required, the Center was set up to provide comprehensive care both before and after these operations, whether the case happened to be a tiny child with severe skull deformities or a middle-aged executive trying to reclaim a life that had been shattered by head injuries.

Part of this care was evinced by the existence of the Marian Rosewell Apartments. The Center owned this four-story building and regularly accommodated recovering patients at income-based rates that often amounted to virtual rent freedom. An efficient system of private fundraising complemented by substantial federal grants allowed the institution to perform its medical miracles with little thought to the patients' financial conditions.

Tracey had lived in the Rosewell building since coming to Madison, Virginia, from New York nearly three years before. In fact, many of the employees of the Center resided in the modern and secure complex due to the rent break they received and its proximity to the hospital grounds. Tracey often resolved to park her car and jog the two miles from the apartments to work and back, but so far this had received no more attention than any of her other frequent resolutions.

By the time she and Nonnie arrived, the younger woman appeared to have already forgotten the ugly encounter with the orderly. She sprinted upstairs to the apartment she shared with a Center nurse, and Tracey had to wonder if all of her childlike mental disabilities were really so awful.

Personally, she knew that she would carry that afternoon's confrontation with her into her dreams.

She reached her apartment just in time to encounter Delia McKenzie on her way out.

"Hi, Trace, 'bye, Trace," called Delia as she opened the door. Delia was tall—well, at five-nine, tall to Tracey, who was a couple of inches shorter—blonde to Tracey's light brown, and, if not classically beautiful, certainly rather aggressively attractive. Delia acted attractive, though still accessible, so it was easy to picture her that way.

Despite the fact that Delia and Tracey had been best friends in college and now were reunited as roommates, Tracey had to admit to a certain feeling of intimidation when comparing their looks.

21

"Where are you off to in such a rush?" she asked.

"Date," Delia answered. "You know, Phil, that guy I met last week in D.C." Delia always had dates.

"At four in the afternoon?"

"That's right. We're driving to Baltimore for an early dinner, and then he's doing a part in *Phantom* at eight. You know how long the makeup takes."

Tracey rolled her eyes. "An actor? Delia, you're never going to meet the right guy doing soft-shoe in a dinner theater."

"So who's looking for 'the right guy'? Maybe I'm just pursuing a personal avocation."

Tracey nodded in a resigned fashion. "Well, have fun."

"Always. Don't wait up!" When she reached the hallway, however, Delia stopped as a sudden thought struck her. "Oh, Trace, a package came for you about three."

"A package?" Tracey repeated.

"Yep, Federal Express. I signed for it and put it in your room. 'Bye!"

"Later." With that distracted reply, Tracey dropped her purse and jacket onto the sofa in the den and continued on into her bedroom. A package? Federal Express? She wasn't expecting anything. Maybe it was something from Mom and Dad, though it was not her birthday . . .

Yeah, right, hissed a repressed but angry and painful portion of her mind, *like they'd send so much as a card if it were*.

Confusion aside, the package definitely was there, resting comfortably in the center of her bed. It wasn't large, about the size of a boxed sugar bowl, and it was covered in heavy brown shipping paper. She picked it up only to be surprised by its unexpected weight. A fluid shifting sensation caused her to think of a bottle of something liquid.

"The newest in mail order scams: the Tapwater of the Month Club," she muttered, reading the typewritten shipping label.

Actually, it wasn't addressed to her. It simply said, "Brown Eyes, Marian Rosewell Apartments, 2-E, 115 Thomas Jefferson Road, Madison, Virginia," with a terse return address of "Coeur d'Alene, Idaho." Since Delia had striking blue/gray eyes, she naturally had assumed the package was for Tracey, whose eyes were a darker brown than her hair.

It sounded rather mysterious and romantic. She smiled to herself and ignored the fact that she'd never been farther west than Ohio, much less Idaho, as she began to tear open the thick paper. Perhaps it was expensive perfume . . . in an uncommonly large quantity.

After several seconds, the wrapping slit along a side and came away from the glass in a ragged, cocoon-like piece, so that Tracey suddenly was holding the bottle in the palm of her left hand. She was still smiling during the instant it took for her mind to register what her eyes were seeing. Then she hurtled the object away from her with a strength that was magnified by her horror and revulsion and began to struggle for a breath that had been snatched from her lungs. The jar would have been smashed had it not landed on her bed.

There it sat . . . cold and staring, a sealed round bottle that held in its formaldehyde-filled interior a floating human eyeball.

* * *

His hair had grown long while he was inside, and he let the California wind race through it like the fingers of a woman. It plucked at his ragged beard and licked down his neck beneath his collar.

Bobby Preston had been in a Canadian prison for the past eighteen months, real-time, which worked out to about six years, jug-time, at an exchange rate of one to four. It had been a long while since he'd felt either a woman's fingers or the wind running through his hair, and that was why he chose to ride helmet-less through the brilliant May sunshine, even though he carried a permanent metal plate in his skull from a previous impact with the paving.

He had been on the road for eight days, and his lean body was weary with the exertion, spotty meals, and general lack of rest. In his saddlebag most of the ten grand, U.S., that the Canadian government had paid him to forestall any litigation nestled comfortingly, promising good times to come. But there was something he had to do first.

Bobby had forgotten how beautiful the Pacific Ocean was during his vacation in the Iron Bar Hotel. It rolled in, blue and endless, to his right, riding the coattails of the wind, and kissed the white sands of the beach. Someday, when he had the time, he would have to walk down to that waiting vastness and see how far into it his arms and legs would carry him. Sometime.

He had to get his bearings. It had been over three years since he'd been in this part of the country, and just the one time then. Leslie and Leland had just moved in, and he was in the area, so they'd celebrated with dinner.

Since Bobby never stayed in one place for very long, he hadn't been back before today.

He pulled the bike to the side of the road for a break. Venice Beach stretched before him, with its bronzed bodies in postage stamp bathing suits, playing in the snowy sand and waves with a sort of fevered abandon. Kids and dogs romped amid the dunes, while surfer boys and girls paddled out toward Hawaii, searching for the perfect wave to bring them back. Everybody seemed lost in a kind of joy that Bobby Preston couldn't remember ever having experienced.

Airheads. Cotton candy disguised as life: bite it and there's nothing there.

Standing above it all in his road leathers and stringy black hair and beard, Bobby could hardly have looked more out of place. He surveyed the happy panorama from behind the safety of his dark riding glasses, and he tried to feel only disgust for the emptiness of it. But there was something that he couldn't deny deep in the middle of himself, a certain faint longing. As if he'd once been a part of that absurd scenario.

If their lives were empty, what did he have?

After a moment longer, Bobby turned back to his motorcycle and kicked it up. As he rode off, he repeated to himself that he didn't belong there and never had, that he was too smart to blow his life the way those jerks were blowing theirs. There was more for him, and all he had to do was find it out there somewhere.

But it took a lot of miles just to get the dazzling vision of it out of his mind.

The house was simple and neat. Located on a quiet street in a residential neighborhood more than fifty miles from Venice, it was a single floor, white-siding suburban fantasy with attached garage. About half an acre of beautifully tended green lawn buoyed it like a smooth sea. The security of this side of town was evident in the fact that the garage doors were open all along the street, even those belonging to the simple, neat house where his sister once lived. Its two-car interior was empty.

Bobby couldn't imagine living in this '60s wet-dream of a place, and he couldn't understand how Leslie had wound up here, either. But the name on the colorfully decorated mailbox still matched.

There were probably a lot of suspicious eyes monitoring his progress down the quiet street, which had never seen a motorcycle cruising along its length at three P.M. on a Tuesday.

But even though he realized this, Bobby also knew that it would have been poor etiquette for any of the owners of those eyes to act upon his discomforting presence before he did anything more incriminating than just wheeling down their lane. They watched but stayed away from their 911 buttons for the moment.

Bobby coasted from the street onto the paved drive that was as white as the Venice Beach sand. It didn't look as if a rubber tire had ever touched it. When he rolled into the garage, it was no shock to find a pair of lightly stained oil pads positioned neatly side by side, right where Leland and Leslie would have parked their twin BMWs. Preston characteristically kicked the stand on his bike between the pads.

Several rings at the side door brought no response, so he dug the key that Leslie had made for him three years ago out of his wallet. It still worked, and there wasn't even a deadbolt to screw with. Nice neighborhood, all right.

The inside of the house was shadowed and cool, the air scented just a touch with a hyacinth deodorizer. Bobby's main priority at the moment was a pit stop, and after calling out Leslie's name a couple of times just to be sure he was alone, that was first up.

Next in order of importance was the kitchen. On his way there, however, he passed through the den, where he paused for a moment at a huge, floor-to-ceiling set of bookshelves covering most of one wall. Leslie had always loved to read.

And write. Thirteen hardcover volumes boasted her maiden name, two more than when he had last been in this room. It was simple enough to figure who had gotten the brains in the Preston family.

Bobby smiled grimly. And who got the jerk genes.

Apparently, the master of one pair of those suspicious eyes that tracked Bobby's arrival made a telephone call, though it hadn't been to an emergency number. Leland Salter's white car glided into the driveway no more than twenty minutes after Bobby's own arrival, while he was still in the kitchen, sucking down cold cuts.

Bobby observed the arrival through a window, and he could read Leland's expression even at a distance. It didn't look good. He had no doubt that Salter was trendy enough to have the BMW outfitted with a phone, and the image of the black motorcycle upsetting the ambiance of his all-white haven would be more than enough ammunition to trigger a frantic call to the police.

If there was anything that Bobby Preston didn't need at the moment, it was the presence of any of those assholes in blue.

To prevent this possibility, the young man stepped to the side door through which he'd entered and stood just far enough into the garage for Leland to see him. His hair was longer than it was three years ago, but otherwise he didn't feel that he'd changed too much for his brother-in-law to recognize.

Salter had stopped before entering the garage so that he wouldn't risk marring his car's pristine finish on some awkward projection from the cycle. He opened his door and slowly stepped out while keeping his eyes glued to the man who had invaded his perfect home. Recognition fought with alarm in his expression. And lost.

Bobby spoke first. "How's business, Leland?"

That faintly rang a bell for the other man. "Bob?"

Bobby responded with a marginal smile that might not have made it past his beard. "Yeah."

Salter's grin was equally as tentative. "I thought you were . . . well . . ."

"I was." Bobby turned and stepped back into the kitchen. He knew that Salter would follow him.

He was working on the submarine sandwich and beer at the kitchen table by the time Leland made it inside, looking an uneasy mixture of confused, upset, and embarrassed homeowner. "This is a surprise, old man," Salter said.

"I'll bet."

"I mean, we haven't heard from you in some time."

"About a year-and-a-half."

Salter laughed hesitantly. He was a big man, at six-one and two-ten a couple of inches taller and forty pounds heavier than Bobby; he still looked like the California college athlete he'd been ten years ago, though his glory probably had come in water polo rather than football. Despite his size and home court advantage, he seemed nervous in this situation, possibly because Bobby so obviously fell outside of his suburban limits of propriety.

An uncomfortable silence simmered in the room, with Bobby casually eating his sandwich and Salter stationing himself between the doorway and the table. It wasn't exactly a homecoming sentiment to be found on a greeting card.

Finally, Leland broke the quiet, "Well, Bob, I hate to be blunt, but when were you released?"

"Last week," Preston answered. With a cool stubbornness, he didn't elaborate.

Leland sighed slightly with the effort of extracting information. "You were released, weren't you? I mean, Leslie and I didn't think you would be eligible for parole for another—"

Bobby interrupted with a genuine smile. "Don't worry, Leland: nobody's on my ass. A couple of weeks ago, the RCMP busted a French separatist group in Quebec and found all of the evidence they needed to prove that they were the bunch who pulled the bank robbery in Alberta."

"The one you were convicted of? That's great! But why would a radical gang in Quebec go halfway across Canada to knock over a bank?"

Bobby shrugged. "So the law would drop on some

dumb sons of bitches far, far away, I suppose. Which it did." He drained the last of the beer. "How much does a refill cost?"

Leland relaxed visibly. "No charge at all." He patted the tall, glistening white refrigerator at his side. "Right in here, Bobby boy. So, when the Canadian Feds found out they'd railroaded you and the other guys, they reversed the convictions?"

"About as fast as you got here when you found out that some scuzz on a bike was prowling around in your spotless kitchen." Preston stood and opened the refrigerator to pluck another Heineken from its interior. He remained standing, facing his brother-in-law. "The career politicians didn't want the shit in the fan, so they rammed through four pardons and paid us ten grand apiece just for signing documents that guaranteed we wouldn't sue the government and would get the hell out of their country."

By Salter's look, it was obvious that he was impressed, but he had to add, "You could have gotten a lot more than ten thousand with a good lawyer."

"I was more interested in getting my butt out of jail."

He nodded sagely. "I can imagine. Leslie and I were planning to visit you soon, but now, thank God, we—"

"Where is Leslie?" Bobby asked, closing his eyes and leaning against the door of the top-loading "tallboy" freezer. "Work?"

Leland coughed a little. "Uh, no. She's away, on a sort of working vacation. Gathering material for another book. But if we'd known you were coming—"

"I called maybe twelve times the day I got out. Didn't even get the answering machine."

Any sense of relaxation Salter had gained during the last few moments evaporated, and he found himself standing face to face with this smaller but still threatening hoodlum. He tried to think Zen. "We were out. The machine's broken."

Bobby opened his eyes. They were different now, deep gray pits of cold rage locked in the center of that coal-black hair and beard. He stood away from the refrigerator with his left hand hooked over the top of the freezer compartment. "You know, I got a lot of letters from her when I first went inside, but they stopped coming, oh, more than a year ago."

Prison's really screwed him up and he somehow blames me, Leland thought. Look for a knife; they always carry knives.

"When did Leslie leave on that 'working vacation,' Leland?"

Salter set himself, weight right, response series alive in his brain and hands. If this little shit thinks he's going up against me, he was better off in jail. The bigger man took a step forward.

"Is that the phone?" Bobby asked, and Leland instinctively turned toward the wall-mounted telephone.

Bobby whipped the freezer door open. It smashed into Salter's face and sent him to the floor like two hundred pounds of wet sand. There was an instant welling of blood from his nose and mouth and more of it had splashed about the floor and the refrigerator. It contrasted starkly with the white decor.

"Is that what your sensei taught you, Leland?" Bobby whispered, staring down at the man. "How to beat up your wife?"

Leland tried to say something, only to choke on his own blood.

"Sorry, old man, I didn't catch that." When Salter tried to sit up, Preston shoved him down with a foot to the center of his chest.

"You son of a bitch," Salter gasped weakly. "I think you broke my nose."

The core of rage that Bobby Preston had lived with throughout his life rumbled deeply. When he thought of this big prick slapping around his sister, he knew that he could turn this rage to good use and beat the jerk to death. And then spend the next four or five decades rotting in the joint, naturally.

"Where's Leslie?" he asked tightly.

"I'm going to pull your spine out," Leland said, again trying to rise.

Bobby thrust his right boot into Leland's throat and forced him to the floor. "I guess that makes you some kind of hardass, doesn't it? I met a lot of hardasses in the jug." He applied an ounce of pressure to the man's neck.

"Okay!" Salter hissed. "Let up!"

Instead, he leaned forward. "I thought you were going to break my back, Kung Fu Charlie."

"All right . . . God . . . you're strangling me!"

Bobby eased up a little. "Where's Leslie?"

"I don't know."

"Wrong number." He stiffened his leg.

Leland lashed at the younger man's legs with his own arms and feet. But Bobby had learned how to keep his emotions harnessed and how to use their energy to his benefit. He stepped easily away from Leland's flailing attack and kicked him once in the right side, just below the ribs. It was enough.

When Salter had regained his breath sufficiently to allow speech, Bobby said calmly, "We'll try once more: where's Leslie now?"

"I don't know . . . I don't even know why she left me," Leland replied in a thin and raspy voice.

"You don't know why?" the younger man repeated with disbelief. Those harnessed emotions very nearly burst their confines. "What in the hell do you think she wrote in her letters? You beat her, you bastard! That's why!"

"Wait!" Salter responded frantically. "I mean, I mean she left . . . I don't know, a year ago, I guess, when she stopped writing you. I woke up one morning, and she was gone, that's all."

"I'm glad to see that one member of the family has some brains." Bobby sat on the corner of the table and opened the beer he'd taken from the refrigerator. Where would she go? With a memory that had been fractured like a china bowl in a motorcycle crash, there weren't that many places he could recall that Leslie might have fled to. They had only one another for a family, and in spite of her greater success in the socialization process, Bobby knew of no close friends to whom she might have turned. Of course, he knew little enough about his own life these days, much less his sister's.

He took a swallow of the beer. "She didn't leave a note or anything?"

"Go screw yourself," Leland whispered.

"The less you cooperate, the longer this is going to take," he coldly reminded the other man.

Salter took a deep breath, though he remained on the floor. "She . . . didn't leave anything for me, but there was a letter for you. I found it in the box before the carrier ran. I burned it."

"What'd it say?"

"How am I supposed to remember something I glanced over a year ago?" His mildly defiant attitude lasted until Bobby seemed to slip toward the edge of the table. "All right. I really can't remember all of it, but it said something about wanting to get a new start, a new life. She said you got one, so maybe she could."

A new life? Bobby thought. What's so damned new about getting locked up for a year and a half? Then, with a clarity that seldom visited him since the accident, the answer came. He nodded to himself. "I guess I'll be moving along, too," he said aloud.

By then, Salter had struggled into a sitting position, huddled against a row of oaken cabinets. "Go," he spat. "Get your filthy body out of my house!"

Bobby took his time finishing his second beer. When he was through, he pulled a twenty-dollar bill from his pocket and dropped it next to the empties. "Whatever's left over is your tip."

Leland had watched his deliberate actions from the floor, and he tried to awaken his self-esteem when he repeated, "Screw you."

Bobby stood from the table. "It's a little late for that. Just one more thing, brother." He stooped next to Salter and clutched a handful of the man's carefully styled hair, including the ponytail that was supposed to make him resemble Steven Seagal. Bobby's voice went low and as close to uncontrolled as he could afford to allow it. "If you never remember anything else, remember this for me, Leland: what goes around comes around. Leslie told me in her letters how you threatened to hunt her down and kill her if she ever left you. If you decide to look her up or if she should ever exercise the poor judgment to come back to you someday . . . for whatever reason, should you decide to take up where you left off playing macho man, I'll kill you."

Salter twisted his bleeding lips in an attempt at a defiant sneer.

Bobby jerked his head back sharply. "I'm not joking, Leland. I'll kill you. Do we understand each other?"

Salter coughed through the blood. "Yeah . . . okay. Just go."

Bobby patted his shoulder in an outwardly friendly way and left the room without a look back.

It was several minutes after he heard the motorcycle leave that Leland Salter painfully stood and made his way to the bathroom.

Chapter Two

Tracey wanted nothing more than to put the day completely out of her mind, everything from the stupid face-off with Julian to the sick joke that had been waiting for her in the apartment. But the police had to be notified, of course, and *they* weren't inclined to let the matter drop.

Questioning began before five P.M. and ran straight through dinnertime into early evening. In fact, as the examiners graduated from uniformed patrolmen to detectives, the perimeters of the questioning expanded far beyond the supposed human organ in the glass jar to virtually every facet of Tracey's private life and background. This was the point at which she began to lose her enthusiasm for cooperation.

When finally the investigators decided to end the grilling, she almost collapsed with relief. It was now after eight, and hunger was galloping through her system like a disease. Somehow, she maintained a civil exterior while showing the men to the door. But the ordeal wasn't going to end there, not without a last jab.

"Oh, yes, Miss Lund," said the senior member of the team, a man named Bledsoe, as he paused at the door, "when did you say your roommate would get in from Baltimore?"

Tracey sighed. "I'm not sure, really. Late, though. You won't need to talk to her, will you?"

The detective smiled professionally. "We can't afford to pass up any source of information, can we? This may be a prank—probably is—but when a possible human body part is involved, it's best to cover all of the bases."

What could Delia tell them, she wondered, how cute the Federal Express guy had been? Damn, they're not even sure it was a real eye. "Do you want me to have her call when she gets in?"

The cop shook his head. "It can wait until morning. The two of you can come down to the Fifth Precinct on Patterson Way at ten tomorrow; here's my card."

Tracey took the card automatically. "Both of us? Aren't you finished with me?"

He shrugged. "We'll know more by then: whether the organ is real, what the Fed Ex people in Idaho have to say, fingerprints, like that. And you may have remembered something useful by then."

"But I have to be at work at eight."

He responded with the cool certainty that develops through years of functioning as the ultimate immediate authority in peoples' lives. "Tell them it's an ongoing investigation."

So, at ten the next morning, Tracey and Delia arrived

at 108 Patterson Way to enter a bland, single story building that looked much more like a small library or a stationery store than any of the police precincts they'd seen on television. Neither woman was particularly enthusiastic.

"Why do I always get caught up in your wake, Lund?" Delia asked. Her tone was lighthearted, but there was an undercurrent of real exasperation to it.

"*My* wake?" Tracey repeated. "Who decided this was my problem? That little package was addressed to our apartment, and *you* signed for it."

Delia fluttered her lashes. "Who has the right-colored eyes, Brownie?"

"Someday I'm going to catch you with your contacts out."

The reception desk was just inside the front door. The officer behind it was cordial enough as he read the card Tracey presented to him and phoned Detective Bledsoe, but a purely natural sense of intimidation settled over both women. Delia had never been in a police station before, and Tracey's previous visits all created unpleasant connotations for her.

Even the visitors' badges they were given by the desk sergeant to clip to their jackets felt more like targets than civilian identification.

Bledsoe himself arrived at the desk within a couple of minutes to collect the women. The squad room was relatively quiet at that time of the morning, so even though the two had prepared themselves to confront hookers, murderers, thieves, and all sorts of loud and ugly sights (just as they'd witnessed dozens of times on *NYPD Blue*), the only really offensive elements that faced them was the haze of cigarette smoke that permeated the room. It seemed that every person in the large, desk-cluttered area was puffing away like a chimney.

"Jeez Louise, haven't any of these Sherlocks heard of secondhand smoking liability?" Delia whispered none too quietly.

"I guess the lure of life-threatening danger is hard to resist," Tracey answered.

Bledsoe apparently chose not to overhear. Coming to his own desk, tucked away in a corner, he motioned to the single empty chair before it and deftly produced a filter-tip from his jacket with one hand and a lighter with the other. "Miss McKenzie, if you'll have a seat, we'll make this as quick as possible."

Tracey stood next to the desk, feeling about as awkward as a loser in a musical chairs game.

"And, Miss Lund, we have a fellow waiting to meet you right in this office." Bledsoe took a couple of quick steps to a door that Tracey had hardly noticed.

"Someone else is going to interview me?" she asked, confused.

"A topflight mind. If you don't believe me, just ask him." He rapped shortly on the frosted glass, which read, "Perkins," in stenciled black lettering. "Hey, Braniac, she's here," he called before opening the door and stepping aside.

When Bledsoe returned to his desk, Tracey was left again with that fool-in-the-spotlight sensation. She looked to the detective. He nodded toward the door.

"Either come in or shut the door," said a man's voice from within the office.

So she went inside.

In complete contrast to the cluttered and smoky atmosphere of the squad room, the interior of the office was clean and well kept, and Tracey couldn't see the air she was breathing in here. A humidifier hissed industriously on a corner table.

"Close the door, please," said the man behind the single desk in the room. "Some of us have a certain regard for our lungs."

"Oh." Tracey pushed the door with her elbow.

Without rising, the man behind the desk absently nodded to one of the two swivel chairs before it. He was a black man whose close-cut hair was sprinkled with gray. Sitting as he was, Tracey could only guess at his height, but he looked tall. His nameplate read: "Det. Ivan Perkins."

She sat down.

Perkins stared at the screen of his desktop computer terminal, occasionally tapping a key or two, for a long moment, while Tracey sat in silent impatience. Finally, the man seemed to reach a pause in his search and looked toward her.

"Um . . . Ms. Tracey Gale Lund, twenty-five of the Marian Rosewell Apartments on Thomas Jefferson Road?" he asked, reading from a printout sheet.

"That's right," she answered.

"Ivan Perkins." He extended his hand across the orderly desk. "Don't let the authoritarian first name throw you, Ms. Lund; I use it because my middle name is Carl."

Tracey shook his hand. "I thought Detective Bledsoe was in charge of my . . . this case."

Perkins leaned back in his chair. "From an official

standpoint, he is. An investigation is a collaborative effort. If a particular case appears to warrant significant attention, additional people are brought on board."

"This is a 'significant' case, then?" This simple confirmation made Tracey feel suddenly cold.

"Possibly. Let's see what facts we have to work with." He continued to consult the readout sheet. "First, that organ you received yesterday was, indeed, a human eye. Blood type O, most common in the U.S., almost certainly from an adult or near-adult male, apparently of relatively recent vintage, though the preservative fluid it was shipped in makes this hard to pinpoint."

"Oh God," Tracey whispered, hardly aware that she was speaking.

Perkins continued, unperturbed, "We've been in touch with the Federal Express office in Coeur d'Alene, and they have a record of the fellow who shipped it to you—"

Tracey looked up. "They know who sent it?"

"We're not that lucky. The name and address are fakes, and the employee who handled the matter can say only that he was a medium height and build Caucasian man wearing what appeared to be a false beard and wig. Don't panic just yet, Ms. Lund." He casually laid aside the sheet and shuffled through a small collection for another. Obviously, this wasn't causing him any concern. "After all, we're not sure that you were the intended recipient."

"It was addressed to my apartment, right down to the zip code."

"True enough, but there was no name. You have a roommate."

"Whose eyes are blue. Mine are brown."

"So was the one in the bottle."

This hadn't occurred to Tracey. "I didn't know. I mean, when I saw it, the color didn't register . . . do you think that 'brown eyes' referred to the contents and not the occupant of the apartment?"

Perkins smiled in a private way. "I think that it's just possible that this incident was meant as a prank rather than a threat."

That's what Bledsoe had theorized. "A prank?"

"You work at a hospital, don't you?"

"Madison Facial and Cranial Surgery Center," she answered. "But what does that—"

"A hospital is a good place to pick up a ghoulish souvenir to scare a coworker."

Tracey sighed. "After first taking it to somewhere in Idaho and then sending it back, I suppose. Detective Perkins, I'm not trying to tell you your job or anything, but I think you've got this all wrong. First, I don't know anyone with that kind of sick sense of humor. My friends would be offended by something like this.

"Second, Madison isn't the type of hospital where a person could just 'pick up' a body part. We're not a teaching hospital or a pathology lab."

Surprisingly, Perkins didn't appear to be offended by her layman's assessment of his investigation. Instead, he abruptly shifted his line of questioning. "What kind of hospital is the Center, Ms. Lund?"

The switch confused Tracey a little. "Madison is, well, just what the name says, 'facial and cranial surgery.' People who have suffered head and brain injuries are the primary patients, and some of the most delicate, intricate surgery in the world takes place there. The doctors are wonderful."

"Then the majority of the work done there involves people with some degree of brain damage."

"A large portion of it, yes." Tracey wasn't sure that she liked his inference. "But nearly half of the cases are devoted to reconstruction of facial deformities, either due to birth defects or accidents or disease. And then just as much effort is directed to the recovery of—"

"But you deal regularly with men and women who are unbalanced," he said, pushing his chair away from the desk and standing. Tracey had been right: he was quite tall, over six feet. "Could be that an unbalanced mind would see the humor in mailing an eye to a hospital employee. A former patient, maybe?"

In Tracey's mind, this was going nowhere. "Detective, I'd like to cooperate with you in any way that I can, but it's ridiculous to even . . . speculate that one of those poor, injured people is trying to pull some elaborate joke. Unless you have some more relevant questions to ask, I don't see how I can help you."

"Who are your enemies?"

"What?"

"If none of your friends would do something like this to you, that leaves your enemies, doesn't it?" Perkins walked to the corner humidifier and stood before it for a moment, allowing the moist air to billow about his face. "So, who are your enemies?"

"Well . . . I don't really have any that I know of."

He looked over his shoulder at her with a slight smile. "None?"

For an instant, she considered the brief ugliness that

she had experienced with David Julian. But that had been their initial clash, and it had occurred only yesterday afternoon, much too late to have anything to do with an eye mailed from Idaho. "Sorry, I can't come up with a name for you."

"Then you're a luckier woman than you know." He returned to the desk but remained standing. "Maybe it was meant for Ms. McKenzie. Whatever, we'll come up with something sooner or later."

Tracey felt relieved that the interview seemed to be coming to an end, and she started to stand. "You know, this is just a thought, but maybe it was meant for someone who lived in the apartment before Delia and I."

"The apartment you've lived in for three years?"

It seemed an innocuous question, asked casually enough, but it froze Tracey in her chair. "How did you know that? I never told you that."

"I don't like mysteries, Ms. Lund." Perkins leaned onto the desk. He didn't look so amiable now. "It doesn't bother me to admit that I'm probably the best investigator in the city. Bledsoe, Crocker, and the others are good cops, professionals, but they're nothing more than that. They do their jobs, they handle the politics, and they leave it all right here in the precinct. I can't do that.

"Questions without answers eat at me. In thirty years, I've come across maybe three cases that offer me nothing, no hints, and they're with me every night. I will figure them out, because I hate mysteries. Since I have adequate but not exceptional intelligence and none of the psychic gifts of fiction, I have to rely on old-fashioned work. The ground floor for me is all of the information that I can gather about all of the participants. That includes you, Ms. Lund."

"The police have a file on me?"

"Not in the sense that you might fear. Yes, I checked you for the standard red flags: traffic tickets, complaints, arrests."

"I've never been arrested in my life."

"I know that. But you do have other public records, including employment. That's how I discovered the length of your stay at the current address."

"Then you knew all about my work at the Center even before you asked, didn't you?"

He grinned. "Young lady, I knew all about that hospital before you left Peekskill, New York, where you were born twenty-five years ago last November sixteenth. I just wanted to get your impressions of the place to match them against my own." He slipped back into his chair. Tracey realized that this meeting was far from over. Perkins continued, "Why'd you leave New York for Virginia, Ms. Lund?"

Instinctively, Tracey began to close up. "I was ready for a change," she said.

"And your family? How'd they feel about your leaving?"

"How do you suppose they felt? They hated to see me leave, but they want me to be able to make my own way in the world."

He nodded slowly, sagely. "Why Madison? Why not New York City or Boston or Philly?"

"Well, I worked in a hospital in Peekskill that served much the same purpose as the Center, and I find the work fulfilling, so, naturally, I gravitated to a similar institution—"

"Someone at the first hospital recommend Madison, then?"

"Yes, the director, Dr. Ansel Heywood."

"Anyone at this other hospital have a . . . an unusual sense of humor?"

"No one from Peekskill sent me that jar, Detective," Tracey stated firmly.

"Not even this Dr. Heywood?"

Tracey remained silent.

"Ms. Lund?"

"Dr. Heywood is dead. He was killed in the crash of his private plane last year."

This information had no visible impact upon the policeman. He began to shuffle the computer readouts into a neat stack. "I believe that should do it for this morning, Ms. Lund. Thank you for your cooperation."

Eager to get out of the office, Tracey stood.

"And there's no one who comes to mind who might be behind this?" Perkins obviously was a master at dragging out the moment.

"No one," she answered.

"Well, don't worry unduly. I'm more than half-convinced that this is simply a sick joke that won't go any further." In a sudden reversal of his previous offhanded manner, the detective stared up at her intensely. "As I told you, Ms. Lund, I'm a real hound when I get the scent of something. I push and probe at it, I take it home with me. I dream about it. So far, this obsessive personality trait of mine has cost me a mar-

47

riage and a good chunk of my stomach, and the doctors tell me it probably will cut years off of my life. But as long as I'm in this job, that's how it will be. We will find out who sent this thing to you, Ms. Lund. I will."

Perkins' quiet and level delivery made the statement very easy to accept. Somehow, that wasn't comforting. Tracey turned to leave.

"Oh, and, Ms. Lund," he added with impeccable timing, "mind if we get your fingerprints while you're here?"

She stared at him.

He shrugged slightly. "Just to eliminate them from any others we may pick up on the jar."

Chapter Three

The only identifiable prints on the jar were Tracey's. This fact led to just two possible conclusions in Ivan Perkins' estimation: either the person who had bottled and mailed the excised human eye to Tracey Lund had been extraordinarily careful throughout the procedure, or, for some reason, Ms. Lund had gone to the trouble of carrying out the episode herself.

Perkins wasn't ready to dismiss either possibility.

For her part, Tracey tried to convince herself that she hadn't been the target of the twisted prank and to put it securely in the past. Certainly, her job at the Center was more than enough to keep her mind off of ugly surprises, and Dr. Stafford planned to add to her workload by admitting four new members into the twice-weekly recovery meetings.

Yes, it was more work for her, more responsibility, with no corresponding raise in pay, but there were times—like now—when Tracey felt sure that the job was in large part necessary to the salvation of her sanity.

The first time that Special Agent Russell Montgomery of the Federal Serial Incident Taskforce saw Boulder, Colorado, he fell in love. Even from the air, he could see his future in the clean lines and pristine atmosphere of the city as it slipped beneath him. It was so powerful a realization that he decided not to keep it to himself.

"In ten years, I'll have my thirty in," he told his partner as they walked through the airport toward a waiting rental car. "I'll be fifty-three, and with any luck, I'll have my health. This is where I'm coming."

"Colorado?" asked Michelle Fallows. "What are you, a Broncos fan or something?"

Their car was a two-year-old, off-blue Tercel. So much for the unlimited expense accounts.

Relatively familiar with the area, Fallows drove. She was a tall woman in her middle-thirties who had worked well with Montgomery on a number of previous investigations. The two were compatible coworkers rather than friends. Few real friendships were formed in their line of operations.

"Where are we meeting Cavella?" Montgomery asked.

"At a local TV station. He's guest of honor at a mystery convention over the weekend, and the chairwoman of the planning committee has set up an interview on an afternoon current affairs show." Michelle closed her eyes for a moment to draw up a memory; apparently it didn't concern her that she was negotiating some fairly heavy airport traffic at the same time. "The station's on Boulwaire Avenue, I do believe."

"Think you can locate it?"

"Oh, I should be able to manage it before total senescence incapacitates me."

"Is a TV station the best place to meet with the guy? You know that we can't let a hint of this seep out to the news media," Montgomery said. He seemed to be conversing on automatic pilot while his eyes drank in the sights of an early Boulder afternoon.

"Russell, boobie, I've taken care of it. This is my turf. I can get us a private office for the interview and no one will know that it's anything other than a puff piece for Cavella's latest book." Michelle gunned the little car from an off-ramp into traffic with barely a glance and apparent deafness when the horns sounded behind her. "Actually, the station might be even more suitable than Cavella's hotel. That's where the convention is being held. Ever been to one?"

"No."

"You'd be surprised. Conventions are designed to allow normal, mousy bookworms the opportunity to go absolutely apeshit once or twice a year. Little bastards are all over the building once the festivities start, though I find the science fiction crowd to be rowdier than the mystery readers."

"Fascinating."

The interior of the car fell silent for almost a mile. Michelle Fallows' lighthearted assessment of literary conventions had been a facade, as Russell had realized, one adopted to insulate her from the chilling possibilities that she faced. She was a good operative, but she was human, too.

When she finally spoke again, the forced good humor remained, but her voice was a little more tense now. "I set up this meeting on the flight in. It was a last second, haphazard type of thing—'Hey, let's go talk to Peter Cavella *now*'—that I didn't have the time to design a proper scenario, so I had to take care of everything by phone on the plane."

Montgomery had been at her side while she made those calls, so he knew most of the relevant details, but he said nothing. Michelle needed to ease the pressure of her sudden re-introduction to this particular case, and talking was the most available method.

"It's just a good thing that records came up with Nora Newland's name as the organizer of the event," the woman continued. "You know, she's a damned good writer herself. I've read seven or eight of her novels. They're sort of mystery/sort of horror. I remember that *The Cheval Glass* really had an effect on me when it came out. Did you read it?"

"I don't think so," Montgomery said quietly.

Michelle smiled, a little too intensely. "You'd remember it if you had. It was about this cursed mirror that twisted time and displaced those people who looked into it. Some half-psychotic guy from Georgia or Tennessee or somewhere down there was so struck by it that he tried to force Nora to write a sequel setting everything right. The police caught him breaking into her house with a gun. Like something out of Stephen frigging King."

"I'll bet."

"Anyway, we'll be meeting her at the TV station. I'm looking forward to it."

The silence returned, though for a shorter period this time.

"Jesus Christ, Russ, do you really think it's Bryant?" There was no strained artifice in Michelle's voice now.

Montgomery took a long breath. "According to the signs, the bodies in British Columbia and the three in Washington, it's his work. Details that were never released to the public."

"Christ," she repeated, "but I thought he was dead. He's supposed to be."

"I shot him, Mitchie. I sure as hell never expected the sick monster to ever hurt anyone else."

The car stopped for a light, and Fallows lowered her forehead onto the top of the steering wheel.

"Mitchie?" Montgomery said softly.

"I'm okay. You know me, Russ: I don't break down."

"The light is green."

"Oh." The car began to move again. "It's just that I saw some . . . I was on-scene with a couple of his victims, the first time. A boy and a girl."

"He likes to do multiples."

"What a wry observation," she sighed. "Why didn't you kill him? Why wasn't your aim just a little better?"

"Don't you know that I wanted to? I had to fight myself to keep from blowing his goddamned head to jelly and then cutting off his dick and force-feeding it down his esophagus. I saw the bodies, too. But my first shot had taken him down, and you know that we're in law enforcement, not summary execution."

Michelle gave a hoarse laugh. "Oh, great, the first time in his career that he follows the book and it has to be to let a homicidal maniac live."

Montgomery's only response was to stare at her.

She shook her head. "I'm sorry, Russ, that was a shitty thing to say. It's not your fault."

"I thought he would die," the man explained. "I've seen men hit half as badly choke to death on their own blood. But we knew beforehand that he wasn't like the rest of us. And then they turned him over to the W.P.P."

"Yeah, what genius came up with that idea?"

"Hell, you know what I know, Mitchie. Heywood had some cockle-headed idea about 'redesigning' an individual, physically and psychically."

"Better living through mad science."

"Those first buttheads in the CIA probably wanted to use him as a hitter, he was so damned good at his job. And then Heywood has to go and get himself flambéed in a plane crash without leaving behind any retrievable records."

"Sticking us with a living and thoroughly insane Calvin Bryant roaming the heartland," Michelle summed up.

"If it is him," added Montgomery.

"It's him. Man, I'm so certain of that. And to top it off, we don't even have an idea of what the greasetrap looks like now."

"That's our job, kid. That's why we're in the big leagues."

For an instant, Michelle removed both hands from the steering wheel without slowing the car. "Okay, okay, let's just step back and focus. Let's get our shit together. We're the professionals in this situation."

"Isn't that a comforting thought?" Montgomery asked with grim humor.

"He's just a man, after all, right?" When Montgomery

failed to answer, Michelle went on in an equally despondent tone, "Well, maybe it isn't him." And that was all that was said for the rest of the trip.

KBCM, Boulder, was a small cable-delivered television station that served only the immediate market. It was located in a modest four-story building just outside the city limits opposite the airport. So low-key was the operation that the parking area was an unfenced lot on the south side of the building. Fallows eased the car into a space near the entrance.

As the two federal operatives stepped from the rental car and stretched in the warm Colorado sunshine—they'd done a lot of traveling during the morning hours—Michelle said, "You never did explain why you've chosen to spend your dotage here in Boulder."

Montgomery stood for a moment and allowed his reasons to coalesce about him. "The weather," he answered, with a brief wave of his hand, "the mountains, the clear air. I like the way the city is laid out." He paused. "But I think the most important thing is that this just doesn't look like a place where people die."

They met Nora Newland, the writer-cum-convention organizer, in the lobby of the building. Michelle recognized the woman from the back-cover photos of her books and handled the introductions with convincing enthusiasm. Newland was an attractive and intelligent woman who accepted Michelle's compliments with humor while being well grounded enough to talk about things other than her current manuscript.

Due to the fact that Cavella was still being interviewed in an upstairs studio, the three of them had a few minutes to engage in this polite conversation in one corner of the busy lobby. And not once did either of the federal operatives hint to their keen-witted mystery writing hostess that actually they were in Boulder to ask Peter Cavella if he'd had any contact with a mass murderer who officially had been declared dead more than two years ago.

The Prince of Darkness stood behind the assassin and contemplated the many options open to him.

Naturally, the only appropriate measure was death. What the policeman had dared to inflict upon the very body of the Prince demanded no less than prolonged and sweetly agonizing death. That would restore some of the proper balance to the profane world.

All things work toward the eternal equilibrium.

He could have done it at that moment, too. With the revolver he carried in his travel bag, he could have offered up the blood and flesh of the murderer and the two women with him before anyone in the crowded lobby could interfere. But that wouldn't be in the best interests of the overall design. For one thing, the addition of two females and only one male would tilt the scales even more to one side at the expense of stability.

So the Prince stood behind the man who had tried to kill him in the most cowardly of ways—from behind—and bathed in the vitality of his own hatred. Finally, the taller woman, who had come into the building with the assassin, took note of his presence and directed a somewhat suspicious gaze at him. She doubtless was another police officer, but her face gave no flicker of recognition when inspecting him.

The Prince smiled with his interior being.

The sacrileges that the puppet doctors had performed upon his body and mind were deserving of punishment, but even this mutilation had its advantages. His enemies no longer knew him by sight.

Still, he decided to move along. It wouldn't do to arouse suspicion of himself now. Their reckonings would come later in the design.

Though he'd arrived in Boulder only this morning, the Prince knew the building well enough for his purposes. As soon as he heard of Peter Cavella's scheduled appearance on the interview program over breakfast in Denver, he had left to scout out the most likely sites for the success of his plan.

The building's security was a joke. His preliminary surveillance, minus weapons, had convinced him of this, as well as allowed him to map out the most effective manner in which to achieve his stratagem. Leaving behind the treacherous government pawns, the Prince strolled into a waiting elevator without drawing a second glance from any of the dimwitted creatures who might someday find themselves dependent upon his mercy for their lives.

Peter Cavella owed much of what he was to the late, unlamented, and conscienceless psychopath who had called himself the Prince of Darkness.

Cavella had dreamed of being an author from the time that he had spent at his grandfather's knee, swapping tales that bridged the generations with the aging man. Through a combination of desire and moderate talent, the young man had managed to achieve the foundation of his aching ambition. But he had been stuck at something of a mid-level point of making a living without really prospering for more than a decade.

Then the Prince had begun to write to him.

Peter was never sure why the nation's most newsworthy serial killer had chosen him as a confidant. His best guess was that the coconut had been favorably impressed by one of the many paperback mysteries he turned out each year to keep himself and his wife and kids from starvation's door. Whatever the reason, it had been the moment that the Fates had looked down and tapped the shoulder of Peter Cavella.

Once the crazyass letters had been authenticated, Cavella had followed his instincts and released them to national periodicals and newspapers, even as the law had literally begged for his cooperation. He knew the extent—and limits—of his own talents; there was no question of turning down this once only, career-making opportunity.

The Prince had been brought to earth soon after in the guise of a thoroughly average-looking nobody named Calvin Peter Bryant (Cavella always felt that their sharing of this apostolic given name was the reason for his selection as the monster's "pen pal"), and much of the credit was due to the information that the authorities gleaned from the letters Cavella had supplied. Still, this brief voyage in the sun had been enough. Cavella's reputation was made, and he had taken the next step up into the rarefied air of celebrity, "Good Morning, America" interviews, and movie deals that actually went into production.

The writer's ego had responded apace with his long-denied success, but he felt that, hell, after a dozen years of struggle, he'd earned it.

And that was what brought him to Boulder, Colorado on this gorgeous May afternoon. Following his interview on the Mickey Mouse local cable show, he paused long enough to scribble his signature in six or eight of his books, including old paperbacks of his earlier material and hardcopy editions of his currently best-selling *Prince of Darkness, Prince of Fools*, though he really was in a hurry to get back to Nora Newland and his ride to the hotel. He enjoyed being the celebrity at the Boulder convention.

He didn't run into the slim guy with the beard until he had pressed the "down" button and stood waiting for the elevator.

"Mr. Cavella?" asked the man softly as he approached Peter from behind.

Cavella sighed, but it was mixed with a healthy portion of self-satisfaction. "Yes?" he responded, reaching for his pen.

"Hi, I'm Danny Murphy. The people from the convention sent me." He extended his hand in a friendly gesture. He was slender and five-nine or thereabouts. The lengthy beard looked a trifle artificial, and its deep blackness contrasted starkly with the man's pale complexion. "There was a little bit of a problem, and the people who brought you to the studio had to leave. I'm here to give you a lift back to the hotel."

Cavella accepted the offered hand. "What sort of problem?"

Murphy shook his head. He was dressed quite casually in slacks, a pullover, and running shoes, with a canvas traveling bag across his right shoulder. "Your guess is as good as mine. I'm not even a member of the convention, just a neighbor of the organizer. I was drafted because I know my way around town and I have a car."

This was confusing to the writer, but nothing in it really alarmed him.

"I'm parked right outside," Murphy continued. "Ready anytime you are."

The elevator arrived with a ping. "That would be about now," Cavella said. "Can't sell many copies standing around here."

"I guess not," agreed the other with a grin, and they stepped onto the empty elevator car.

Murphy took it upon himself to select the floor button, and rather than pushing the lobby, where Cavella had entered the building, he opted for the basement level, one floor below it. There was an exit stairwell here that led to the parking lot. Cavella didn't notice this variation.

In fact, the pair had topped the stairs before a warning bell sounded in Peter's mind and he stopped. "Just a minute, that's Nora's car, isn't it?" He pointed to a shiny new Accord. "That's the one we came in."

Murphy took his arm. "Well, we're leaving in the one around the corner."

"Hey, hold on," Cavella told the man as he sharply jerked his arm free. "I don't want to seem ungrateful, but I'd like to see a little identification before we leave."

"How's this?" As cool as ice, Murphy reached into his traveling bag and withdrew a handgun.

"Jesus!" Cavella gasped.

"Uh uh, not a word." Murphy placed a forefinger on the writer's lips. "This is a .38 caliber police service revolver, and I killed the man I took it from. It can put a hole through both of your lungs and your heart with a single shell. Are you going to be quiet now?" It was the calmest threat that Cavella could have imagined, as the man's voice retained that utterly controlled and ingratiatingly soft quality.

Cavella felt his stomach turning to a block of ice as his sphincter threatened to release the contents of his bowels. He'd never had a gun pointed at him before. "But what do you want? I don't understand—"

"Mr. Cavella, please." The pistol's barrel moved from a point on his chest to one nearer his eyes. "I know you've written plenty of material dealing with violent death, and I'm sure you don't want me to demonstrate another right here. Are you coming?"

Peter nodded with numb instinct. He couldn't have spoken now if he'd wanted.

They walked to Murphy's green Ford like a pair of old friends.

Part of Cavella's mind was bathed deeply in irony. He'd gone through thirty-six years of life without once having as much as a dime stolen from him, and for much of that time he wouldn't have had a lot more than a dime to lose. Now he'd made it, *finally* made it, he had more than three thousand dollars in his wallet and money belt, and damned if he weren't being robbed for the first time ever. It was almost too fitting to be believed.

He sat on the passenger's side of the front seat, lawfully buckled in, while Murphy drove expertly with his right hand and kept the .38 aimed at Peter's ribs with his left. They left the city limits of Boulder quickly and unnoticed, heading east.

Cavella was still frightened at this point, but a little less so. He would give up his money gladly, though he didn't like the fact that they were leaving all signs of the city behind. He knew that transportation of a victim of any kind heightened the chance of violence.

Murphy broke the silence in a very casual manner: "How do you like my car?"

Cavella licked his dry lips before replying, "It's quite nice. It drives smoothly." Form a bond, his instincts urged, make him think of you as another human being.

"Doesn't it, though? You know, I picked it up in Utah, a little place called Fremont Junction. It was just sitting in an open driveway, at night, with the keys dangling in the ignition." Murphy shook his head in wonder. "You'd never see anything like that in Old New York. Probably in very few places east of the Mississippi. I snatched the plates off of an import in Nevada, you know, planning ahead."

Cavella took a shallow breath and said carefully, "That was very prescient of you. It'll make it more difficult for any police investigators to make a connection on the list of stolen vehicles."

Murphy looked at him with an intentionally goofy smile. "*Duhhh.*"

Cavella decided to shut up.

They rode for nearly twenty minutes, as the surroundings became completely rural. No houses or even billboards disturbed the striking beauty of the land, as gently rolling meadows lapped at the foot of a mountain that burst upward on the northern side of the two-lane road. Countless buttercups crowded together to top the meadows with a layer of yellow icing.

How glorious it might have seemed to Cavella under other circumstances.

"This looks like a good spot," Murphy said as he swung the car off of the road, through a shallow ditch, and into the buttercup foam.

"A good place for what?" asked Cavella. God, this didn't seem like a robbery. What did he want? Christ, why were they out here in the middle of nowhere?

Murphy failed to reply. When they were several hundred yards off of the road, so close to the foot of the mountain that one could feel its presence like an immense psychic weight, he shifted into park and switched off the engine. Then he turned to Cavella, still smiling genially through the beard.

"Congratulations, Mr. Cavella," he said. "I was almost convinced that you would make a grab for my gun the way that most all of your 'heroes' do in your novels, and I really didn't want to shoot you. Not in the car, I mean."

Cavella's throat was so dry that he had to try twice before he could answer, "It's different when it's real. I didn't . . . I didn't want to cause any accidents. You're obviously an intelligent man, so I realized that we could get through this without hurting anyone." He reached into his open jacket with his right hand.

The gun sprang from Murphy's lap seemingly with a life of its own.

Cavella froze. "My wallet, I was only going to give it to you! That's what you want, isn't it? What do you

63

want?" His voice began to cycle upward and dangerously close to hysteria. He didn't want to die.

Murphy's own voice remained composed. "Get out of the car."

"Here? Why?"

"Get out of the car, Mr. Cavella."

The writer opened the door to his right. The focal point of the gun was a hot circle wandering about his back, but for a moment, there was hope. Cavella could run. He'd always been fast on his feet, and while the road was much too distant to reach without cover, the mountain was closer and covered with forest. Peter felt that with his fear driving his legs, he might be able to sprint into the woods in the time it would take Murphy to leave the car from the driver's side.

This faint dream died when Murphy quickly slipped across the seat behind him.

"Sit down," the gunman directed when both were out of the car. "Make yourself comfortable."

Cavella first squatted among the flowers and then followed Murphy's lead by sitting on the soft ground. *Don't let me die here.*

Murphy allowed his eyes to drift over their sun-drenched surroundings. "This is just about the most charming spot in the United States, don't you think?"

"Charming," Cavella whispered. *But I don't want to die here.*

"You've heard the term, 'the last place on Earth'? Well, I've been there. It looks kind of like this." For a moment, he seemed to be searching for something at the top of the mountain that loomed over them. "Why did you call me a faggot in your book?"

Understanding dropped out of the ozone onto Cavella like a piece of the mountain. This wasn't about money: this man was crazy. It was not a reassuring realization. "What?"

"Why did you call me a faggot—wait, we must be politically correct, mustn't we? Why did you say that I was a homosexual?"

"No, I didn't . . ."

Murphy's eyes locked on him. "Denial, Peter? I read the trash just yesterday. Do you want me to quote it?"

A madman, a goddamned lunatic! "You've got to believe me, Mr. Murphy, I never wrote any—"

"Oh, I lied about that," the madman interrupted. "My name's not Murphy, and even though I try to be steadfast in the truth, there are times when it's necessary to improvise. Actually, you and I share a name: Peter."

"Well, you see, I never use my own name for a character—"

"Calvin Peter Bryant."

Cavella shut up instantly. For a second, both men were quiet. Then the name exploded with full impact within the writer's brain, and he jerked backward a couple of feet without rising from his butt. "My God, you're crazy!"

"That seems to be the consensus," Murphy said, with no change in his bland, strangely beatific expression.

"Bryant is dead! The police killed him, he was the Prince—"

"The Prince of Darkness, the chosen and anointed one," Murphy/Bryant said. "The man who is charged to bring balance and morality back to our present age. The man who trusted you to spread the word to the ignorant population, only to see you use that trust to betray him and then pervert it to your own financial ends."

"I don't know who you are, but you're not Calvin Bryant! He's in his grave, and even if he weren't dead, I've seen photos of the man, and he doesn't resemble you, mister!"

The madman laughed. "Even without the beard? They tried to kill me, Judas, thanks to your cooperation, they shot me in the back. And then they took my body and performed obscene operations on it, even unto my mind." He touched one corner of the heavy beard, and Cavella saw it pull away from the face, stretching out the skin with thick wires of makeup glue. He patted it back into place. "They took away my natural growth. Because of these experiments, no one knows me by sight. But I survived. Even altered, the Prince lives."

Anger crowded out a portion of Cavella's fear. "Listen, take my money if you have to—I've got three grand on me—but don't try to convince me you're a dead psychopath! What the hell kind of robbery is this, anyway?"

The voice was low and soft, like the purring of a recently fed jungle cat, while the eyes were wide with insanity, " 'Work with me and we will rescue the race from its own lusts and weaknesses; betray me and I promise that you will taste your own testicles in your mouth as you die.' Remember that, Peter?"

"Oh, my lord."

"Ah, you do recall. The only words that I ever spoke to you in my first incarnation, on the telephone, eleven-fifty, Friday night, March 20th. You didn't include that little conversation in your book, did you? You didn't even tell the police, because you couldn't be certain the call was from me and you were so shit-in-the-pants terrified that it was embarrassing. Am I right?"

"It's you," Cavella whispered.

Bryant grinned. Then he released the hammer of the gun and slowly straightened up. "Glad to get that squared away."

"Calvin, how . . . ?"

"The machinations of the profane world, my friend, guided by the hand that placed me on this earth. Now, I've read your book, the one that purports to be about me, and in it you say that I have engaged in my mission because I have homosexual beliefs. Why would you print such lies?"

Cavella found himself cold and trembling, in spite of the sunshine.

"Peter?" There was a slight change in the level of Bryant's voice. "I need for you to answer."

The writer looked into the soul of his nightmare. He had made his career in the blood of others; his fiction used violent death as its foundation, and his connection with a real life murderer—the Prince of Darkness—had lit a rocket beneath that career. His best-selling nonfiction work about the same man was packed with explicit photographs of the pathetic victims of Bryant's madness, but Cavella himself had never seen a dead person.

And now he was alone and staring into the eyes of death.

"Peter?"

"I . . . I didn't say that about you, Calvin."

Bryant had an excellent memory. " 'The evidence of the latent homosexuality of the self-proclaimed "Prince

67

of Darkness" is most compelling in the hatred he displayed toward women, the particular pleasure taken in their capture, bondage, torture, and death.' You must recognize the blatant fabrication of those words. I have never 'chosen' anyone for punishment, man or woman; they choose themselves by their actions and in balance. Always in balance. Even today I have visited redemption upon only one more woman than man." He placed the cold barrel of the pistol against his own forehead and closed his eyes. The metal rubbed slowly against his flesh. "I've been very conscientious about that."

"Calvin, can't you see what the rest of the world understands?" Cavella heard his voice forming the words but could hardly believe that he was speaking. "You're a moral human being, aren't you, and to take the lives of others simply is immoral. You're not well—"

Bryant's eyes flew open, overflowing with his insanity. "You don't believe I'm still the Prince? Because of the mutilations done to me, the marring of my outer self, you think I've lost my calling and my manhood?"

Alarms were screaming within the writer's skull. "No, no, Calvin! I didn't say that! Those were the conclusions of the psychological community!"

"Ha! Psychiatrists? Those modern witch doctors? Show me one patient a psychiatrist ever cured."

Cavella said nothing. All of his attention was focused on the gun that was once more pointing at his face.

"Then I'll show you who's no longer a man." Deftly, Bryant pulled up the gun and ejected five of the six shells from its cylinder into his left hand. Then he closed the cylinder and gave it a spin across his forearm.

"You know this little game, don't you, Peter? Do you want to play it with me?"

"No, that's crazy!"

The madman's face seemed to glow with cold delight as he raised the weapon to his right temple.

"Calvin, don't be a fool!" Why had he said that?

Bryant squeezed the trigger.

Cavella's eyes were closed when he heard the dry click of the hammer on an empty chamber, but his body still jumped. He looked up.

"Your turn."

Yes, Cavella thought with sudden inspiration, it is my turn. He held out his hand to take the gun.

"Damn, Peter, what do you think I am?" Bryant asked with a smile. "I'm psychotic, not stupid." He rolled the cylinder again and aimed the barrel at Cavella's head.

"Mother of God, Calvin, no, please!" he screamed. "Please don't shoot me, please!"

"Same odds as I had."

Cavella fell face-forward into the flowers, crying. "Don't kill me, for Christ's sake, please don't kill me!"

Time slowed to a stop. Bryant held his aim through this timelessness. Cavella remained huddled on the ground, but he still felt the burning pressure on the back of his neck. There was not a sound to intrude upon the moment.

Slowly, reluctantly, the gun drifted to Bryant's side.

"Who's the man now, Peter?" he whispered.

Cavella resumed breathing, and this brought with it a sobbing that racked his entire body. His tears fell into the grass.

Bryant's tone became more incongruously soft and caring, almost feminine. "I think you should take some time to consider your sins, Peter. You've done yourself and the world a great injury by conspiring to interrupt my work before its conclusion. Dwell on this. Decide how you can make amends."

I might live, Cavella dared to think. This crazy bastard is so publicity hungry that he might spare me to write more about him. "I will," he added aloud.

"That's good."

Cavella flinched when Bryant's hand patted him on the shoulder, but he kept his face in the grass and forced himself to say, "I can see how wrong I was, and the truth is becoming clearer with every second."

"Take your time; we have plenty of it."

"Thank you, thank you."

"Be quiet now."

Time began to pass. Peter Cavella remained prostrated before the man who held his life in the action of one finger, and he thanked a god he'd never fully accepted for each additional second. These seconds began to multiply in the silence, becoming minutes. Then the minutes began to grow heavy on his back and neck.

"Prince?" he asked tentatively. "May I rise now?" Only the slight breeze answered.

He opened one eye, blinking away the tears caused by the glare of the sun, and glanced before him, where Bryant should have been standing.

No one was there.

Still wary, Cavella raised his head and scanned his surroundings. He seemed to be alone in the field, with only the car to mark Bryant's recent presence. Had the lunatic actually left him . . . or was he waiting in the car and calculating how many more heartbeats he would allow his repentant captive? In looking to the vehicle, Cavella's gaze flashed beyond it, to the distant road, and there he saw Calvin Bryant.

The Prince of Darkness was walking away from him with a slow and easy gait. One arm lay placidly over his shoulder bag.

"I'll be damned," whispered Cavella. He had excellent distance vision, and there was no mistaking that slender figure, even from the back. "I'm going to get out of this." He worked his heavy feet beneath him.

The forest was only a few yards behind him, and he knew that he could reach its protection before Bryant could draw down on him with that damned gun. But if by some miracle the keys were still in the car, he could be away and safe within moments. It didn't seem likely that the keys would have been left behind, but the insane are also unpredictable, and Bryant was walking away. Cavella crept to the driver's side door and peered through the window.

They dangled from the ignition, looking more beautiful than any woman he'd ever known. At that instant, he loved those keys as much as he loved his family.

"You crazy son of a bitch!" Cavella shouted at the retreating man. "You bastard! I beat you!"

Bryant heard and turned to look at him.

Cavella opened the door. "Yeah, look at the man who's going to watch you die! You're going to fry, asshole, and you can bet your black soul I'll be there to see it!"

Bryant made no reply.

71

"Damn, what a scene to open the sequel," Cavella laughed to himself, just this side of hysterics. "You may be crazy, but you're making me a rich man, Calvin!" He turned the key.

The car exploded in a dazzling eruption of orange fire.

"Balance," said the Prince with quiet contentment.

Chapter Four

Friday had been warm and sunny at first, but this didn't hold true for very long.

Bobby Preston was in the middle of his cross-country run when the sky opened up and dumped its contents on the land below. This wasn't the best weather for motorcyclists, but Preston kept with it for several hours. The drenching held down the interstate traffic, and his skill with the bike was more than equal to a little rough riding time.

But even in his leathers and helmet, the constant pounding from overhead wore at his resolve the way that a year and a half behind bars had worn at his self-image. By six P.M., he decided to give in, at least for the night.

He was just outside the city limits of some podunk town called Arco, Kansas (or maybe he'd crossed into Missouri; he wasn't sure), when he swung off of I-70 and spotted a huge supermarket abutting an equally

73

large K-Mart store. According to the dozens of cars lined up in the combined parking lots, both places were pretty damned busy, despite the lousy weather and the encroaching night.

Bobby was something of an enigma, even to himself. Never the social type, he still held an almost childlike fascination with supermarkets. When he bothered to dwell on it, he decided that it had originated in his small-town youth, when *nothing* stayed open past seven in the evening, certainly not a warehouse-sized place that sold everything from Quaker Oats to forty-weight motor oil.

Of course, thoughts such as this led to intense efforts to bring up real recollections of his childhood from that shattered glass repository that had been his memory since the accident. Frustration generally kept him from engaging in these bouts of self-exploration.

Bobby pulled into the crowded lot with a strange but not really unpleasant sensation just beyond his grasp in the back of his mind.

There was a narrow alley between the grocery store and the K-Mart that was both dry and empty. He coasted into this dark passage and locked the front wheel of his bike to an exposed water pipe. Time to eat.

He'd noticed often before that a big store like this meant more to a small town than just an outlet for groceries. It was as much a place for herding, gathering to gossip, preening, complaining, and checking out the competition as were the malls in larger cities. This one was almost bursting with shoppers, including some who, no doubt, were just waiting out the long downpour.

The dry coolness of the air-conditioning sent a shiver through Preston's damp and weary body as he entered. Still, it felt good. Then he was inundated by the circus of humanity inside, especially the women.

Prison had been a tough stretch of road for Preston. There had been one continual struggle to keep from being forced into a sexual role he couldn't accept by men who were stronger, meaner, crazier, or more sly than he was. God, he had missed women, emotionally as well as physically. The first stop he'd made after being cut loose in Alberta had been in a whorehouse, but it had eased his needs only temporarily.

Just after that, there had been the matter of Leland Salter to settle. This had canceled out every other priority for its duration.

Now he was surrounded by women, young, old, wrapped like medieval virgins in their raincoats, and displaying long, slim, beautiful legs already glowing with rich tans before summer had even really begun. He wanted to be near them. He wanted to listen to their voices and breathe their scents, maybe to just talk for awhile before resuming his journey. He wanted to compare the free, bright smile of a schoolgirl with her mother's knowledgeable counterpart.

There was a problem, naturally. Bobby was not an oppressively large individual, which would have been an advantage in the jug, but he carried himself with a threatening grace by an instinct forced upon him by life. Forged painfully over the years, this instinct had achieved a graduate degree behind bars. Now it was so much a part of his character that he hardly noticed the hooded eyes when he passed a mirror or the don't-screw-with-me swagger in his walk.

Wherever he went, the crowded aisles parted before him and stares and whispers followed him.

Well, at least a portion of the whispers could have come from the fact that he was using his upturned motorcycle helmet as a food basket as he shopped.

Bobby wasn't surprised by the reception he received, and he didn't let it nag at him. He grinned a little to himself when he heard "Hell's Angels" muttered more than once as he passed. He'd never belonged to any group and wore no colors on his black jacket.

After some fifteen minutes of browsing, he brought his assembled, pre-packaged meal—a couple of cold sandwiches, potato chips, a microwaveable cup of chili, three fruit pies, and a quart of milk—to one of the long lines in the checkout row at the front of the store. Almost comically, the people ahead of him maneuvered their loaded grocery carts back into the crowded aisles as if they had forgotten some important loaf of bread or something, leaving Preston next up in the suddenly truncated line. Maybe looking intimidating wasn't all that bad.

"Will this be all today, sir?" asked the nervous cashier, a kid of no more than sixteen, who was just as intimidated as everyone else Bobby had encountered.

"Yeah," he grunted.

The boy gingerly plucked the items from the black helmet and passed them over the price scanner and then down the rolling belt to a very cute bagger no older than he.

"Paper or plastic?" this girl asked.

Preston had been out of circulation long enough for this ecological decision to confuse him. At first, he thought that she wanted to know if he would be paying cash or charging the five dollar tab to a credit card. Then he saw the sacks she held and made the connection. "Plastic," he said, glancing through the front windows at the still pouring rain.

He was going to take a cheap room someplace, but he didn't want to drag his dinner through the rain beforehand. There was a nice wooden bench covered with local advertising by the front door, and it looked a hell of a lot more inviting than the back of his bike. He camped on it and began tearing open the plastic packages.

It was a cold meal, but Bobby had had worse hot ones. The milk was chilled and went down sweet and smooth. He'd forgotten to pick up a plastic spoon during his shopping, but that was okay, too, since the chili in the microwave cup was thick with congealed grease. By bending the thin metal lid into a half-tube, he was able to scoop the chunky concoction into his mouth without spilling too much into his beard.

Like an invisible but noxious cloud, his spell over the people in the store remained strong. A long-haired, blackclad biker was as out of place in Arco, Kansas, as in Mr. Leland's neighborhood, it seemed.

They whispered about him while waiting in the checkout lines, and when he drank directly from the milk carton a number of offended locals reacted as haughtily as if he'd farted in church or something. Bobby ignored them.

The employees, mostly teenaged kids and middle-aged women, appeared to be a lot more nervous than offended, however. Their cheery greetings to the customers had died away around the time he sat on the bench, and the sidelong looks they continued to give him were responsible for more than a few wrong charges at the registers, he felt sure.

Look, he thought while tearing open a cherry pie with his teeth. Haven't seen anything like this since the geek at the sideshow, have you?

A lot of people passed him—quickly—on their way through the exit, but only one actually approached him. She was a little girl, no older than five. While her mother scribbled a check for the family's week's worth of groceries, she trotted up to the bench without so much as a hint of fear.

She was a gorgeous little thing, pale blond hair and crisp blue eyes, with a two-hundred-watt smile. But she wasn't attracted so much to this black-dressed hood who was eating his dinner with his hands. Instead, she began to run her tiny hands over the motorcycle helmet that was resting on the bench at his side.

"That's round," she said happily, "like a marble."

Bobby smiled back at her. He thought that a father probably felt the way that he did at that moment. "A big one," he said. "Maybe a bowling ball, huh?"

She nodded. With both hands, she tried to lift the helmet.

"You're not going to steal it, are you?" he asked.

"Uh uh."

"Want to try it on?"

Her eyes sparkled. "Yeah!"

Bobby carefully placed the helmet over her head. It

was so large that it completely covered her head and rested on both shoulders. The tinted faceplate dropped down to hide her face. The girl laughed at this, and so did Bobby.

That was probably what alerted the mother. The check-writing woman stopped searching for her two forms of ID in her voluminous purse and glanced about in alarm. "Tara?" she said, just a degree or so removed from panic. "Tara?"

Then she spotted the child standing close to this shaggy, dangerous-looking bum with milk and chili in his beard, and she very nearly screamed. Dropping her purse onto the checkout counter, she ran to the girl and grasped her arm fiercely.

"Tara Kimberly Dolan!" she said in a high-pitched hiss, "what on earth are you doing? Get away from him!" The woman slapped at the helmet and knocked it onto the floor before dragging her daughter back to the counter.

It didn't shock Bobby. In a way that he didn't care to admit, he even understood his own responsibility for the reaction. What works for you in one situation might kick you in the balls in another. He certainly hadn't gone out of his way to make himself more presentable to this woman, whose only point of reference to people who rode cycles had come from old Roger Corman movies.

Preston didn't need any trouble, so he made no response to her while coolly retrieving his helmet and returning to his pie.

At that point, a jittery young store manager (whose black necktie was the only indicator that distinguished him from the other bagboys and stockers) took a shallow breath and began to march toward a confrontation with Bobby. Clearly, he felt it his duty to protect the sensibilities of his customers.

Bobby didn't want trouble, but he didn't want to waste time with this idiot, either. He gave the boy the Look, that flat, hard, dead-eyed stare that had served him better than words in prison, and that was enough. The kid veered away to melt back into the safety of the crowd. Bobby went back to his meal.

Damned if the phones didn't work well in Arco, Kansas. It was no more than five minutes later that the cop car pulled up before the market and stopped in the loading zone. The arrival took place at Bobby's back, but his sixth sense warned him in time to turn and watch the three uniformed officers exiting it and skipping swiftly through the rain toward the market door.

Three? Shit, they overreacted to everything here in the heartland.

The pigs were there because of him, of course. He'd done nothing to warrant the attention of the police, unless eating indoors violated some Arco ordinance, but Bobby wasn't particularly surprised. He sipped his milk and waited.

The blue-clad group made straight for him, without so much as a nod toward the sweating manager, who was standing nervously in the door of his office. One cop was a woman, though she was so tall and wide-shouldered that Preston failed to notice her gender until she was within a dozen feet of him. He made a point of not letting them know he was wise to them. He'd gotten very good at locking his real emotions behind the Look.

"Good evening, sir," said the first cop to reach him, a big, rawboned guy with the unconscious air of superiority that even the most personable policeman eventually develops. There aren't any Andy Taylors out there. The cop's companions flanked him with almost military discipline.

Bobby continued to stare.

"We'd like for you to step outside with us for a moment," the first cop went on.

"What's the problem, officer? Wasn't speeding, was I?" Bobby added just the briefest of grins.

The cop's smile grew tighter. "Just come with us, sir."

Well, he hadn't done anything, so maybe if he cooperated he could smoke his way through this without inviting trouble. He began to gather the remainder of his meal.

"That can stay here, sir," the cop told him, hooking his fingers beneath Bobby's helmet and lifting it from the bench.

Won't be finishing this particular repast, Bobby thought wryly as he stood and led the three outside.

"Do you have any current identification, sir?" the spokesman continued once they stood beneath the overhang before the supermarket entrance.

The heavy cloud cover shut out most of the light of the dying day, so that it just as well could have been midnight. The parking lot lights glowed like yellowish stars.

Bobby said nothing as he dug out his wallet and handed his driver's license to the man.

The cop examined it. "This is you, Robert James Preston, of Alexandria, Virginia?"

"That's right," Bobby answered.

"Kind of far from home, aren't you?" The cop

focused a small flashlight on the photo of the clean-shaven man in the license and compared the image with the hairy figure standing before him.

"I'm on vacation," Bobby added.

"I see. And I guess that's the explanation for the long hair and beard."

"You got it."

"Where's your vehicle, Mr. Preston?"

"In the alley." Bobby led the way without being asked.

The lead cop flipped his flashlight over the bike's tag. "I think this may be a little out of date, Mr. Preston."

Bobby shrugged. "It's been a long vacation."

"You want to check this out, Mark?" He handed the driver's license to the second male officer, who swiftly jogged back to the police car.

Bobby knew that an expired Virginia vehicle license was of no interest to a city cop in Kansas (as well as being out of his jurisdiction), so he began to relax some. These jerks were out of shake him up a little, but that was all. He looked to the female officer, who really wasn't bad, close up, and grinned. "You know, I plan to get that tag up to date as soon as I get home."

The woman smiled back slightly, but the first cop wiped that out with a sharp, "You'll talk to me, mister."

Yeah, Bobby thought.

"Lean forward against the wall with your legs spread, please, Mr. Preston."

"Now wait just a minute, what the hell right do you have to do that?" Bobby demanded, knowing he should keep his mouth shut. "You haven't arrested me."

The pig patted the baton that rested against his left thigh. "Do it, please."

"Goddamn," he whispered to himself as he assumed the position.

The cop slipped his flashlight into his belt. "Got any needles on you, Mr. Preston, anything sharp? Now, don't you let me get stuck with anything, do you understand?"

"Nothing," Bobby muttered. And it was true: his knife was locked in the concealed compartment just in front of his bike's gas tank, along with a gun and most of the Canadian payoff money.

The cop went through a quick and expert pat down. "Well, that's fine. You can turn around, Mr. Preston. There used to be an actor named Robert Preston, wasn't there? 'Pool begins with P, and that rhymes with T, and that stands for Trouble right here in River City'?"

"My old man had no imagination." Bobby felt like saying something quite different.

The second cop trotted back into the alley. "No wants or warrants," he said.

Thank God Arco, Kansas, isn't computer-linked with Alberta, Canada, Bobby thought. He may have been cleared officially, but just knowing that he had done time for bank robbery up there would have provided these small town would-be hardasses with the trigger they were so hot to uncover.

The first cop took the driver's license back and then slipped Bobby's wallet from his jacket without asking for it. "Everything seems to be on the up and up, Mr. Preston." He pushed the laminated card into the wallet as he spoke. "Just passing through, are you?"

"That's right; I think I'll take a room for the night and get out of this wonderful weather."

The cop looked at the cash in the billfold. "Let's see . . . eighty . . . seven dollars. You're not a vagrant, anyway." With as smooth a motion as any professional pickpocket, he removed the money and sequestered it in his own jacket. "I guess you are now."

"Hey!" Bobby shouted. "What the hell do you think you're doing, man?"

The cop's anal smile twisted into a sneer. "Shut your slimy mouth, punk. We don't like your kind around Arco, so what you're going to do is get on this piece of junk," he paused to kick Bobby's motorcycle onto its side in the alley and smash one mirror, "and get your shit-stinking butt out of my town. Right?"

"You son of a bitch," Bobby whispered.

As if those were the secret words, the second male cop stepped behind Bobby, whipped his baton across the startled man's throat, and brought him to his knees, gasping. "What do you think, Jeff?" he asked.

The first cop grinned, his face looking like a skull in the faint light of the alley. "Is it clear?"

"Yep."

"Okay." He slipped his baton out, too.

"Just a minute!" Bobby tried to say, though he had little breath to employ. But it was too late by then, anyway.

They may have been small town, but they knew their stuff. "Jeff" started off the entertainment, with "Mark" maintaining the effective chokehold. For a fleeting moment, he thought that he might have a chance with the woman, chauvinistically hoping that her nature would be offended by this turkey shoot and force her to intervene. Wasn't that why Wambaugh claimed they made better cops? He looked to her.

The hope vanished when she whacked his side just below the ribs with her own nightstick.

He had picked up a few tricks of his own, naturally, tricks that would have allowed him to crush the nuts of the bastard holding him and then kick the nasal structure of the woman into sawdust. But that would still leave "Jeff" with time to draw his sidearm and leave another "perpetrator" shot dead while "resisting arrest." Finding no other options, Bobby turned off his raging anger and concentrated on minimizing the damage he was receiving.

They had stamina: it lasted nearly ten minutes, on and off, while they caught their breaths. No broken bones, nothing that would prevent him from riding out when it was over, but Christ, they knew exactly where to strike for optimal results and minimal evidence.

Finally, it ended. "Mark" allowed Bobby to collapse into the dirt of the alley. He had to fight to keep from vomiting everything he'd eaten in the supermarket onto their shoes. "Jeff" and the woman were breathing heavily and coated with perspiration, but a walk in the rain would take care of that.

"Now, I believe . . . we've made our point . . . Mr. Preston," the first cop said. "Are you ready to leave?"

"Yeah," Bobby gasped weakly, "yeah."

"Good. We'll see you back to 70."

On his hands and knees, Bobby crawled to his bike, unlocked it, and levered it upright. None of them bothered to help him, which was just as well, because he sure as hell didn't want this bunch in a position to spot his safety compartment and reward themselves with the nine-plus grand it held. With painful deliberateness, he worked one leg over the seat and then sat for a moment in an attempt to marshal his strength to kick off.

"We don't want to wait here all night, Mr. Preston," the first cop stated while the woman pulled the car around to the mouth of the alley.

"I'm going," Bobby gasped. "Gimme a minute."

The man's phony, preacher-plastic smile was back. "A couple of words of advice, buddy: have that side mirror repaired pretty soon. We could cite you for driving around with it in that condition, you know. Also, take time for a shave, a haircut, and a bath. Maybe if you looked a bit more . . . upstanding, this won't happen again."

Bobby had to say it, if only in a whisper, "Fuck you."

The smile remained. "Not me, friend. Not tonight."

Bobby managed to kick the bike to life and weave out of the alley and the parking lot. True to their word, the cops followed him all the way to the interstate.

As he shot through the rain and darkness, his own words came back to echo within his aching brain, no matter how hard he tried to shut them out. "Live by it, die by it: that's one dog with two sets of teeth."

"What goes around, comes around."

Chapter Five

Considering the circumstances of his last visit to Madison, Virginia, it might have come as a surprise to learn that Bobby Preston had pleasant memories of the city. Lying quietly to the south of its monolithic relative, Madison was D.C.'s direct opposite in civic personality, with little political activity, less street crime, and virtually no tourism. What it did offer were clean, tree-lined streets, two public libraries, a junior college, and, of course, the Madison Surgery Center.

The Center had secured Bobby's introduction to Madison. Following the catastrophic collision of his motorcycle with a down-shifting semi overloaded with unfinished machine parts (a form of encounter seldom won by the biker), Preston had been reassembled within its walls over six painful months. The results had been miraculous, though they also had been expensive.

Even as his sister Leslie had patiently walked him

back to health on those shady streets, teaching him to become accustomed to the chunks of metal that now resided permanently in his back, his skull, one leg, and various other portions of his body, Bobby realized that his medical bills would wipe out the modest savings she had accumulated through her writing. He'd promised himself that he would pay her back someday, in spite of his complete lack of prospects or marketable skills. Then, after just months of fruitless job-hunting, he'd become involved in that damned mess in Canada and paid for it with a year and a half of his life.

He cruised into Madison on the morning of May the tenth. His weekend had been spent in a hotel room in Sweet Springs, Missouri, recovering from the proficient workover that the Arco cops had carried out on him, but he felt pretty good on this bright Tuesday. Madison looked unchanged by the two years he'd been away. Simply rolling along its quiet avenues brought back those physically painful but otherwise welcome walks with his sister.

Part of Bobby's determination to find Leslie—a small but distinct part—was the chance he would have to give her the nine thousand dollars he carried in his cycle's secret pouch. Sort of a down payment on his debt.

He drove past the Center, three immaculate white buildings on half a dozen acres of softly rolling spring grass. Two of the buildings were large and multistoried; the actual medical procedures took place here. The third was much smaller and designed along the lines of a squat shoebox; it lay to the east of the others and was intended solely for records and administration. He paused at the corner light. He'd been literally reborn in that place. The light changed, and he drove on.

If Leslie were in Madison, Bobby had an idea where she might be staying: the same place she'd stayed while he recovered. It was a four-story apartment building called the Marian Rosewell Memorial or something, and it was only a couple of miles beyond the Center. His memory was right on target for a change.

The manager's office was on the ground floor, clearly marked as such both on an exterior window and on the first door inside the building. When Bobby left his bike unchained in the lot, it seemed odd to feel so unconcerned about its safety.

There was no Leslie Preston staying at the Marian Rosewell Apartments. The manager was cooperative enough when he asked her about this and when he switched the name to Leslie Salter—in case his sister had held onto the bastard's surname a little longer— even though she didn't have to reveal any information to him about the tenants. Still, there was a familiar nervousness in her expression and actions. She practically jumped out of her shoes when Bobby reached into his jacket for his wallet.

"She may be using some other name," he said, pulling out a snapshot, "but she looks like this. Have you seen her?"

The short, gray-haired manager glanced perfunctorily at the photo. "No, sorry. Don't know her." She walked toward the office door in a suggestive manner. "There's a Sheraton and a Howard Johnson's down by the interstate."

"You don't recall this woman at all?" Bobby asked. "She spent half a year here not long ago."

The woman responded with a fleeting grin. "Me, I just took this position last November. Maybe the police can help you."

Preston slipped the picture back into his wallet. "How much for an apartment?"

"What?"

"I need a place to stay. How much?"

"Well, I . . . I'll have to check . . ."

"You rent apartments here, right?"

"Oh, of course, I mean, we're in business . . ."

"You just won't rent one to me, is that it?"

The woman glanced to her desk and seemed to find something very interesting among the papers scattered there. "We're not discriminatory here, that's against the law. It's just that, well, what the Rosewell Apartments try to provide is a quiet, tranquil atmosphere for our tenants. The majority of our clientele are referred to us by the Surgery Center—you know it? Well, we're fully equipped to cope with all kinds of special needs: elevators, emergency alert devices in every room, a private ambulance on call at all times, things like that. To aid in their recovery, we strive to maintain calm and peaceful surroundings." She ended with a sort of pleasant, "I'm sure you understand" expression.

"Sounds relaxing."

The woman sighed. "No parties. No drinking or loud music or anything."

"Right." He thumbed a pair of hundred dollar bills half out of his wallet.

With that, the manager went against all of her instincts, and Bobby Preston got his apartment.

The shades were closed, but the lights were still up when Dr. Harrison Stafford began the Tuesday session at the Center later that afternoon. In addition to the doctor himself, Tracey Lund, Nonnie Bartlett, and the five session regulars, four new people were to be introduced to the recovery group that day, bringing the total number of people in the room to twelve. This was the largest gathering that Tracey had ever worked with at the Center. She wondered if it weren't time to form a separate group to meet on Mondays and Wednesdays.

"We're all friends here, and this is our little cubbyhole away from the world," Dr. Stafford began in his soothing way. "Before we lower the lights and start the open session, I'd like for our newest friends to say a few words to the group." He looked to the four, three men and a woman, who, though strangers to one another, were clustered together on one side of the circle. At least they shared one thing, a natural feeling of not belonging.

Four wide-eyed and perspiring faces stared back at Stafford.

"Anything, your names, where you come from, anything at all," Stafford continued with that practiced smile of his, the one that could charm a crocodile.

The woman broke the verbal blockage. "Hi. I'm Rowena, Rowena Carr. I'm . . ." she paused to cough, "I'm from Darby, Pennsylvania, and I was injured last year. Last spring. It was an electrical shock, actually. Dr.

91

Ansel Heywood performed my surgery—did any of you know Dr. Heywood?"

Most of the assembly responded to this, and Stafford added, "The good doctor touched the lives of many of us in one way or another. He was practically the patron saint of the Center."

"He was a good man," Rowena agreed. She was a rather tall young woman in her mid-twenties, with long, straight black hair parted in the middle. Though not heavy, her figure seemed to indicate an athletic past. "He recommended that I join your group last December. Just before he died. He hoped it . . . the group would help me in my social interaction. I kind of think I may be close to developing agoraphobia."

Stafford wasn't really ready to get into specific diagnoses. "Thank you, Rowena. That was just fine." He wasn't surprised that she had chosen to speak before any of the men. It had to do not so much with comparative courage as with women's generally greater verbal facility and readiness to open themselves before strangers. He looked to the man to her right.

This man noted the attention and immediately blushed deeply. "I'm Stanley Hollis," he said. Like the others, he had spent much time convalescing recently and looked a little thin and pale.

"It's nice to meet you, Stanley," Stafford said, guiding the conversation. "Would you like to tell us more about yourself? Your background?"

Hollis continued to redden; his eyes shone with fear or embarrassment. "No."

He reminded Tracey of Nonnie, the first few times

she'd met the young woman with the mind of a confused child. She'd been almost helplessly shy, too.

"Well, that's fine. Just say as much or as little as you wish." Stafford glanced to the next man.

He was slightly larger than his companions, somewhat more rugged or outdoorsman-like, and his voice was deeper than Tracey had expected when he said, "Dexter Stubbins. I'm from Maine. There was this boating accident. I still have some amnesia, and I get these blackouts sometimes." He fell silent.

"Everything takes time, Mr. Stubbins," Stafford assured him, "we'll all do our best to help you work through it. Have faith: *En Avant!* 'It's better farther on!' "

That left the fourth individual, a very thin and frail-appearing man who, like Wally Gaithers, was confined to a wheelchair. He knew that his turn had come and he felt the eyes upon him, but in some cases, effort alone isn't enough.

The fourth man tried desperately to speak, to give his name, but his lips could not respond to the directives of his mind. A stutter that was pronounced and agonizing in its severity was all that he could produce. He closed his eyes and concentrated, only to have it worsen. His breath became ragged while his thin, long-fingered hands clutched the arms of his chair fiercely.

Everyone in the room felt their hearts go out to the man. At his side, Wally Gaithers patted his arm with a knowing compassion.

"Perhaps I should do the honors, Mr. Lockridge," stated the doctor. "This is Michael Lockridge from, I believe, Ohio?"

The man nodded.

"Let's make them all feel welcome, shall we?"

With sincere sentiment, the regulars in the group clapped their greetings to the four. Each of them had been the wounded and nervous newcomer at one time or another, and they knew the benefits to be found in honest friendship and support during the long climb back to the simple victories of day-to-day living.

As with the end of every session, Tracey felt a little tired, a little relieved, and quite inspired. The courage she saw in these people focused a harsh light on the tiny troubles she faced in her own life. Such reassessment was good for the soul, and she knew that it would redefine her perspectives, at least until the next meeting.

Nonnie was as lively and eager as ever to get home to watch TV and do her lessons. The two of them had almost made it out to the parking lot before the hallway intercom began to call out her name. Would she please return to her office in the records and administration building? Technically, she still had some four minutes of time to put in, so, leading Nonnie, she headed for the enclosed corridor that connected the buildings.

David Julian was mopping only a few yards away from the meeting room. He certainly had gained no personal insight in the few days since their last encounter, and as the two women passed, he whispered, "Bitch," in a rather obvious tone.

Without slowing or looking in his direction, Tracey flipped him the finger.

The cause for her summons back to work was waiting just outside her office door. He didn't look very promising.

"Miss Lund?" he asked as she arrived.

"Yes?" she responded.

"Hi," said Nonnie brightly.

"Uh, hi," the slim, bearded man answered with some confusion. "Miss Lund?" he repeated.

"That's me, Tracey Lund," she said.

"Oh. My name's Bob Preston. They told me at the front desk that you could help me."

"Well, I'll try, Mr. Preston. What's your problem?" Tracey kept her keys in her purse; she wasn't in any hurry to open her office to this leather-wearing biker guy.

"I'm looking for someone, my sister, and I think she may have been a patient in the Center," he told her. "I'd like for you to check your records, if you would."

"Tracey, let's go," Nonnie whispered.

But this was her job. She produced the key and opened the door. "Won't you step inside, Mr. Preston?" The three entered the small office.

Placing Nonnie in a chair by the room's single window, Tracey slipped behind her desk and switched on her computer. She didn't offer a seat to the man, and he remained standing.

"Now, Mr. . . . Preston?" she began.

"Yes?"

"You believe your sister is a patient in the Center?"

He sighed. "The woman at the front desk checked the current files and couldn't find her, but she said that you could run through the records for the last year to see if Leslie was admitted during that time. Her full name's Leslie Jane Preston, though she might have registered as Leslie Salter."

Close family, Tracey thought. "Hmm. Through a

peculiarity of the law, Mr. Preston, anyone can check on a person who is presently a patient, but to have access to past admissions you must have proof that you're a relative or have some other legal relationship."

"She's my sister."

I believe we've established that much, anyway, Tracey noted to herself. "Do you have some identification?"

Preston pulled his wallet from his jacket and produced his driver's license. It contained a photo, and the picture might have been the same Robert James Preston standing before Tracey, though men with as much facial hair as he now sported tended to resemble one another in her estimation. He also drew a snapshot of an attractive, dark-haired young woman from the wallet and placed it on the desk before her. "This is Leslie."

Tracey studied the picture. In a strange, almost unsettling way, it seemed familiar . . . something about the wide blue eyes. But no name surfaced, and after a moment the sense of familiarity faded.

"Sorry, Mr. Preston, but I'm strictly a records worker: I seldom see any of the patients, and I'm afraid I don't recognize her." She handed the license and the picture back to him. "Let's see what the computer has to say."

"Tracey," Nonnie whispered from the window.

"Just a minute, hon." She scanned the screen. "Searching . . . searching . . . no Preston, Leslie. Closest entry is Mrs. Louise Preston, forty-nine, of Pensacola, Florida, facial reconstruction procedures following a house fire in February of last year."

"That's not her. Leslie is only twenty-nine." Preston stepped to the side of Tracey's desk and looked over her shoulder at the screen. This made her even more uncomfortable. "How about Salter?"

Tracey keyed in the second name. No one named Salter, male or female, had been a patient at Madison during the past year. "Sorry again. We could back it up another six months."

"No, thanks, anyway," he said, moving back to the front of the desk. "She couldn't have been here more than a year ago."

Tracey breathed a little easier. "Maybe it would help if we knew the nature of her injuries . . ."

"She wasn't injured," he said. "She would have been here for plastic surgery."

"Well, the Center does engage in some elective operations, but most of our work deals with cases of pressing need, either due to accident or birth defect. Would this be the case with your sister?"

"No." Preston's reply was rather startlingly abrupt, and he strode away from the desk toward the door in an aggressive fashion. Tracey saw Nonnie's eyes dart from the vast lawn beyond the window to the man. "She's trying to make a new start for herself, a new identity."

Tracey carefully switched off her terminal, stood, and walked to Nonnie's side. She placed a reassuring hand on the girl's shoulder. There was something very threatening about this man's presence, something more than his rough street looks. "This is a hospital, Mr. Preston, not some mad scientist factory. I feel sure that changing one's appearance surgically is illegal, anyway, if you're trying to escape debts or detection or—"

"How about a son of a bitch of a husband?" he

snapped. "A slimy bastard who gets his rocks off by punching you around?" He seemed to notice the transfixed Nonnie for the first time since they had entered the office. "Ah, I'm sorry about the language. But I was sure that she was here. This is where I got my 'new start' after the crack up, and I took it for granted that this is where she would come. Her husband is such a possessive . . . animal that he's sworn he'd kill her before he let her go, so she might be trying for a totally new beginning, even in her looks."

"Well, it's obvious that she didn't choose Madison," Tracey said, a little sharply herself.

"She could have used another name entirely, I guess . . ."

That was enough for Tracey. "I can't help you there. I don't have the time to go through the listings for every female patient we've had over the past year who might fit your sister's general description. Nonnie and I need to be leaving now, if there's nothing else we can do for you."

"Yeah," Preston said hoarsely. "Thanks." He left the office without another word.

Neither woman said anything for a long moment. Then Nonnie stood from the window chair and asked, "Can we go home now, Tracey?"

Tracey took a breath. "You bet. Just let me get my purse, and we're out of here."

She thought it was over, but actually it was just beginning.

No more than fifteen seconds after Tracey and Nonnie had left the Center parking lot and swung east toward the apartments, the big black motorcycle appeared in the rearview mirror. Of course, Tracey had no way of knowing for sure if the rider was the same strange man she'd just dealt with, but the dark riding leathers matched, and the fringes of a long beard and hair blew free in the wind from beneath the helmet.

Yeah, that was the same guy.

Nonnie failed to notice her increasingly pensive looks into the mirror, absorbed as she was in her newest reading workbook. According to her files, Nona Bartlett had been a very intelligent twenty-three-year-old college student before the car wreck that had nearly killed her. Now the external evidence of that awful trauma was virtually impossible to find, but her fresh good looks were a minor concession for what the accident had taken from her: her past, her maturity, in a real way, herself.

Still, she was regaining some of these attributes at a remarkable rate. In a few years, with some luck, Nonnie Bartlett just might be all the way back.

None of that was on Tracey's mind at the moment, however. The man on the motorcycle definitely was following them. He turned where they turned and was slowly gaining on the car, even though Tracey unconsciously had exceeded the speed limit by a good ten miles. She was glad that the apartment building was so close to the Center.

"What's this word, Tracey?" Nonnie asked. "S-u-r-p—"

"Not now, Nonnie!" she answered with rare brusqueness. Even in the corner of her eye, she could see the immediate deflation in the girl's attitude. "I'm sorry, sweetie. Wait until we get home." The Rosewell Apartments sprang up before them. "Which is just about now." She whipped into the driveway without slowing.

Okay, so she was paranoid. There were worse character flaws.

"Wow, that was fun," Nonnie said happily.

Tracey pulled into her assigned parking space feeling quite a bit better herself. She gathered her standard quota of personal and work material together and helped Nonnie with her books before awkwardly backing out of the car. "What was that word you were spelling for me?"

The girl furrowed her brow. "S-u-r-p-r—"

"What the hell took you little ladies so long?" asked a rough voice from behind Tracey.

She spun about, dropping files and picturing Robert Preston in her alarmed mind.

It was David Julian.

He was leaning against his own car, just four spaces away, and Tracey couldn't believe that she'd been too preoccupied to notice it while pulling into the lot. His thick forearms were crossed over his chest, a pose so obviously intended to project casual macho intimidation that it was ludicrous.

"I worked to the end of my shift, unlike some people," he said, "and I still beat you two here. Have a flat?"

"What do you want, Julian?"

He stood away from the car. "I didn't care much for that gesture you made to me."

Oh, great, a thin-skinned Neanderthal, Tracey thought. "Really? I don't appreciate being called a bitch, either."

He began walking toward her.

"Get inside, Nonnie," she said.

"I came for your apology." The clear fog of alcohol radiating from his breath billowed before him to reach Tracey's nostrils even while he was several feet from her. He couldn't have gotten so soaked in liquor in the fifteen minutes since quitting time; he must have begun drinking on the job.

"Go to Mrs. Bushnell, Nonnie," she repeated. "Tell her that Mr. Julian is here."

Nonnie understood more than she generally was given credit for, including what was happening here. "He better not hurt you, Tracey."

"No one's going to get hurt. Run along."

"Yeah, all I want is my apology," Julian added.

Tracey knew that there were several intelligent ways to react to the situation—among them, rush inside with Nonnie, call out for help, or apologize to the drunken goon—but none of them were representative of her first and most tempting impulse. She wanted to kick in his teeth. Barely governing rage like that had plagued her many times throughout her life. But she had to think of Nonnie.

"Okay, I'm sorry I upset you, David," she forced herself to say. "Now, will you just leave?" Nothing about the slobbering sot frightened her as much as Preston had without making a single threatening action.

As if responding to her psychic summons, Preston's motorcycle rolled into the parking lot.

Damn, it's turning into a convention.

"That didn't sound very sincere to me," Julian stated, not noticing Preston's arrival, or not caring. He stank of liquor, but his voice was clear, "Try again."

"Take a flying leap."

101

He reached out as if to grasp her arm.

"Hey! You leave us alone!" Nonnie shouted, running around the car.

"No, Nonnie!" Tracey called out to her.

Bobby Preston removed his helmet and swung one leg over his motorcycle. Without a word, he began to walk toward the entrance to the building.

"I don't take shit from bitches, whether they're tight-asses or retards." This was going much further than Julian had intended, but he couldn't back down before them.

Nonnie was scared and furious in equal measure, without really understanding why. "You go home! You don't live here, so go home!"

Tracey intercepted her. "Can't you see what you're doing, Julian? Just leave us alone!"

"We're not at work now. I don't have to listen to you, Lund."

"Then do it because I say so, asshole," added a quiet voice.

Julian looked around to find the biker standing behind him. "Who the hell are you, man? You'd better keep your nose out of things that don't concern you."

"You'd better leave these women alone," the biker countered.

Bolstered by the alcohol, Julian's nebulous anger focused itself on this new target. "According to who? You?"

"According to the guy who's going to knock your dick in the dirt if you don't."

The other man's voice never rose above a conversational level, but there was no questioning its power.

Suddenly, this was a different set of circumstances. "What's your problem, anyway?"

"Right now, you are."

"Yeah," whispered Nonnie.

Preston was forced to hide a smile behind his beard.

Julian stood for a moment and gauged his predicament. The guy wasn't very big, but he seemed imposing, nevertheless. He carried big. Julian shook his head. He wasn't looking to bust anybody's ass today. "Forget this," he spat, stalking around the biker and back to his car.

Nothing was said until Julian had left the lot, and then Nonnie stated in an admiring tone, "He was scared of you."

Preston allowed her a quick wink before walking toward the entrance.

Tracey knew she had to say something. "Mr. Preston?"

He stopped and looked back.

Tracey felt her face begin to glow in one of her more embarrassing moments. "Thank you . . . for your help."

"No problem."

"I don't think there's any reason to wait here, though; Julian's a blowhard, that's all. He won't be back. You can go home now."

"I intend to," he answered, turning back toward the apartments.

Tracey stooped to pick up her things. "You're staying here?"

"For now."

"Oh."

He walked into the building, followed quickly by an excited Nonnie.

What a day, Tracey thought wearily as she balanced

her files and purse and trailed after the two, all I need now is to find another rotting organ in the mail.

That night, the Prince moved through the streets of Madison.

The clouds rolled across the city like a high, thin sheet that caught the light of the moon and diffused it throughout the sky. Fluorescing it rather than blocking it out. There was a brisk and steady wind that was a little chilling after one had traveled through it for a few minutes.

Madison was unlike most of the places he had known. While it was of moderate size and laid out in the progressive fashion of the newer cities, its streets were still quiet and clean of the trash fouling most of those byways that he had visited. Both the real trash and its human equivalent. There was no night life to speak of in Madison, but it was neither unusual nor dangerous for a woman to be out after dark.

Naturally, he might not encounter very many souls deserving of salvation in such surroundings. But contrary to the world's perception, the rescue of soiled souls had always been tangential to his true purpose, never its driving focus. There was a greater reason for the Prince's presence in Madison. Perhaps the only greater reason.

He had seen the woman today. He had been in the same room with her, though this had been while he was trapped in his weakened, profanely manufactured other self.

He had been close enough to the creature to look into the deep brown eyes that had so enchanted the Doctor.

They were beautiful, just as the Doctor had described them, but the Prince could see beyond mere physical charm. He saw the evil that lay behind them. Tracey Lund had taken the Doctor from him, and she would pay for this and all of the moral decay that she carried within her.

But not yet. And not quickly.

The Prince strolled the shaded streets of Madison with a smile that was largely concealed by the artificial beard that he wore.

Chapter Six

Detective Ivan Perkins never ate lunch at the precinct house unless it was absolutely unavoidable. This intentional habit had nothing to do with his well-known aloofness or the fact that the Fifth Precinct building was about as healthy an atmosphere as a hospital pathology lab.

The truth was that Perkins enjoyed eating about as much as he enjoyed anything in his life. Had he taken lunch in his office, with his computer at hand and the trappings of his work all around, he never would have been able to fully appreciate the meal.

Returning from lunch on this overcast Wednesday afternoon, Perkins moved through the squad room without receiving welcome or giving it. Friendships, real or professional, meant little to him, so he didn't go out of his way to cultivate them, just as he refused to kiss the asses of those in positions to further his career. Detective Perkins sounded just fine to him.

He was back in his office and sorting through the newest wire reports before Lucas Bledsoe rapped once on the door and stepped inside. "How's the search for the missing body parts going, Sherlock? Found enough to assemble a complete person yet?"

Perkins didn't look up. "What can I do for you, Bledsoe?"

The white detective dropped an envelope on the desk. It was one of the large, flat manila types, but the way that it autumn-leafed through the air during its descent caused it to appear to be empty. "Your current damsel in distress came by while you were lunching and left this for you."

Perkins picked up the envelope and examined its face. It was addressed in a clear, almost machinelike print to "Ms. Brown Eyes, Apartment 2-E, Marian Rosewell Apartments," along with the rest of Tracey Lund's address. The postmark registered Boulder, Colorado.

"The lady's roommate found this in the morning mail and brought it personally to the surgical hospital," Bledsoe said. "The 'Brown Eyes' thing tipped her off. Lund ran it by here on her lunch break, but she didn't have the time to wait for you, and I'll be darned if your pager wasn't switched off again. Take a look inside."

Perkins turned the envelope over to find the sealed flap roughly torn open. Tracey obviously had been so eager to look at its contents—or so unnerved by the receipt of the material—that she hadn't bothered with her letter opener. Carefully, he looked inside.

All that the envelope contained was a single sheet of

precisely clipped newsprint. Perkins used the nails of his right thumb and forefinger to slide the page out onto his desk. The flag, included in the cutting, identified the page as coming from *The Boulder Citizen-Times* of the previous Saturday, the same date of the postmark. The mail system wasn't what it used to be.

"Some picture, huh?" observed Bledsoe.

Perkins stared at the color photo that dominated the upper portion of the sheet. It had been taken by a passing tourist and was of an automobile, make and model indeterminate, burning furiously and throwing great columns of sooty smoke into an otherwise clear sky. It once may have been a convertible: the hood and roof had been blown away by some terrific explosion.

The caption read *Author Dies in Auto Blast*.

"Impressive," Perkins admitted coolly. "Mob job?"

"Read the article," Bledsoe said. He was smiling as if this were a dirty postcard.

Perkins scanned the details. In brief, the article told of the mysterious death of one Peter Cavella, a well-known writer of both fiction and true-crime material, in the pictured vehicle outside of Boulder, mid-afternoon on Friday, May 6. The tragedy had taken place in a field well off of an isolated highway some twenty-five miles east of the city. The victim had been identified through a driver's license and credit card found partially intact in his wallet. Authorities couldn't yet determine if the explosion had resulted due to an accident, suicide, or murder, though they were sure that the device used had been extremely sophisticated.

"You know who that guy Cavella is, don't you?" Bledsoe asked.

"Yes, he's the—" began Perkins.

". . . the writer that that dickhead wacko serial killer wrote to a couple of years ago. Bryant, remember?"

Perkins nodded rather than attempting a reply.

"If you'll also recall, Bryant usually kept a souvenir from each killing to use when he jacked off later, an ear, a tongue, even an eye." Bledsoe's smile glowed with triumph, as if he'd just found Judge Crater trysting with Amelia Earhart.

"I wonder if this man's death could be connected with the eye that Ms. Lund received last week?" Perkins asked archly.

"Exactly!" Bledsoe missed the sarcasm in the comment altogether. "What you've got yourself here, buddy boy, is a copycat, a sick puppy who's selected Bryant as his model of deportment and your girl is his target for terrorizing. What do you think?"

"An entirely tenable theory, Lucas."

"You bet your ass it is. A case like this can make a guy's career, Ivan, and it won't be difficult to spread around a little of the glory, like to the man who first saw the light, right?"

So that was the source of his enthusiasm. "Of course, we have no real evidence that the events are connected at all, or that any of these mailings are anything more than an elaborate scheme for attention carried out by the supposed victim herself. We shouldn't make any wild leaps of logic until we have more data to work with."

Perkins' cold response and the labeling of his own theory as a "wild leap of logic" did sting Bledsoe. His ruddy complexion reddened a little more. "Okay,

Perkins," he said in a low voice that didn't carry beyond the office, "take it slow and safe, play with your computer, and, for God's sake, don't take a suggestion from one of the common people. Dig out all of the evidence you need at your own speed and keep all of the credit in your back pocket. Maybe this crazy jerk won't cut the Lund girl from ear to ear before you finally decide he's real, and then everything will work out fine, won't it, you prick?" He turned and left the room.

Perkins was used to such responses. An outside observer might have imagined traces of racism in the reaction, but actually the detective inspired much the same in his fellow African-Americans. It could be that Bledsoe's scenario was entirely correct, in which case Perkins' report would reflect the man's contribution. He just wasn't ready to focus all of his attention on a single hypothesis so early in the investigation.

And there was something naggingly off-key about Tracey Lund herself.

For all of his devotion to logic and hard work, Perkins had certain instincts that he also relied upon. Right now, these instincts were telling him that Tracey wasn't being completely forthcoming—if not about this particular series of events, then about the woman herself.

He examined the sheet of newspaper again, more thoroughly now that he was alone. Front and back. He would pass it along to the forensics lab soon enough, but he felt sure that this would turn up no fingerprints other than Tracey's and Bledsoe's.

The article touched upon Cavella's connection with Calvin Bryant, a.k.a. "the Prince of Darkness," which was probably where Bledsoe had received his revelation. Perkins punched up the name on his terminal to refresh his own memory with the available information.

It was depressingly familiar: Bryant had been raised in a dysfunctional household by abusive parents who were alternately stiflingly religious and roaringly carnal; he had been a child of no particular accomplishment in school or socially, growing into a desperate loner obsessed and terrified by sex; then followed the adult who realized that he would never create as much as a ripple in the ocean of life unless he could scream out his own proclamation of existence and worth by changing society's rejection of him into fear.

Among the atrocities visited upon Bryant in childhood was having a candle thrust into his rectum, which was then sutured shut. This had been done to the boy by his mother.

Sadly, little of this horror was new information to Perkins.

When would the adult world understand that it was creating its own demons by assaulting its young in this way? And when would the abused realize that victims' rights didn't include the permission to strike back by using the same or worse methods? Monsters like this one reinforced the glacial exterior that Ivan Perkins projected, even as his insides roiled with anger and revulsion.

Bryant had been the Fifteen-Minute Wonder of the crime world just a few years ago, until he was shot to death by a federal officer. There had been many before him, some yet uncaught, and the sickening part of it was that there would be many more to follow. Maybe Bledsoe was right and Bryant's psychic offspring already was marking out his territory.

Wishing he hadn't eaten so much at lunch, Perkins dialed the telephone number of the Madison Center to speak with Tracey Lund. If he were going to stand against the rising tide, he needed to forge his weapons out of all of the information that he possibly could uncover.

Bobby Preston didn't fully understand his real . . . impact on the world about him until he awoke late on Wednesday morning. He'd stayed up most of the night before, catching up on U.S. television following nearly two years' abstinence, trying to figure out what to do next with his life, and getting drunk.

When he awoke, still dressed in his road clothes, his mouth felt like it had been stuffed full of dust balls from underneath the world's oldest unmade bed, but his nose was functioning exceptionally well. He stank. The dirt, sweat, and alcohol of a couple of weeks and several thousand miles of road enveloped him so densely that he was surprised it wasn't visible.

In the jug, hygiene had been mandatory at regular intervals. Freedom had brought with it the right to get as funky and outwardly disgusting as he liked for as long as he wanted.

This was as long as he wanted.

The booze and a few residual effects from the Arco police department caused his stomach to spin frenziedly in a direction opposite his head as he staggered from bed, trying to remember where the bathroom was wherever he happened to be today. He barely made it to the bowl before his body began to throw up all of the toxins he'd shoved into it over the past fourteen days. It was the worst hangover he had lived through since the accident. For a while, all that he had the strength to do was shiver, curse, and puke some more.

Eventually, his body agreed that he'd suffered enough and allowed him to flush the toilet and wash out his burning mouth in the sink. He realized then that he didn't have a toothbrush.

Damn.

Bobby peeled off his clothing (in a literal sense at several points) and walked weakly into the shower. Here, a hot and hard rush of water began to wash away much of the detritus that he had allowed to build up. God, it felt good; the steam even seemed to scrape clean the insides of his lungs. He cleansed his mouth again and was surprised to feel his appetite returning.

Bobby Preston had been free of the prison system for the better portion of a month now, but the rage he'd felt toward his brother-in-law and the fear he'd held for his sister's safety had chained him within himself over that period. Now it was swirling down the drain, and he felt free for real.

With this newly clean thinking brought about by the shower came another wave of recrimination. He still didn't know where Leslie was. His crazyass comic book idea of her coming to the same medical institution that had put him back together to get a new face and a new chance at life had fallen apart like a sand castle once he had the opportunity to check it. She'd always possessed a soaring imagination, as her writing success proved, but she didn't need surgery to make another stab at happiness once she dumped that goddamned "husband" of hers.

That bastard. If he had only allowed her letter to go through, Bobby might have some real idea of where she was. Instead, he was stuck with a year-old riddle from Leland's memory.

Or maybe that was part of her plan. Bobby knew that he could only be a weight around his sister's neck. With his complete failure to approach life as an adult and equally complete lack of marketable skills, how could he have made her life any easier? Kicking Leland's ass had been fun but unnecessary once she had left the bum. Bobby had, at best, a fragile recall of his behavior before his head injury, but what there was of it didn't seem very much different than the present.

Maybe Leslie's new life was not intended to include a good-for-nothing brother. After all, after breaking away from Salter, she had stopped writing to him altogether, and for eighteen months his address sure as hell hadn't changed. It was a possibility that made him feel cold in spite of the steam.

So, what next?

He still wanted to find Leslie, if only to assure himself that she was all right. But where did he look? Alexandria, as close to a hometown as either of them had ever had? One of his clearest memories was of listening to her swear that she'd never go back there.

Did he put ads in the classifieds: "Leslie, all a mistake, I'm no con or shit-for-brains overage adolescent jerk. Bobby."?

And what did he do in the meantime? Nine thousand

was a good chunk of change, but it would last only so long in today's economy. Should he fill out job applications for all of the wonderful, high-paying positions for which he was qualified?

Suddenly, this shower didn't seem like such a good idea anymore.

Bobby left the shower when its regenerative effects began to give way to renewed self-doubt. Because the apartments were host to so many recovering patients from the Center, each unit was "user friendly," loaded with ramps, rails, and every reasonable form of mechanical assistance to make the facilities accessible. The mirrors in the bathrooms were full length right to the floor, as opposed to the silvered window panes found in most apartment buildings.

Bobby stood before his mirror and took inventory. He had never been overweight, and a year and a half of prison food topped by two weeks on the road had brought him to the point of gauntness. Only the muscle demanded by this type of living and traveling saved him from resembling a standing model in an osteology class.

And he was white . . . damn, his skin looked like soap. Couldn't a person develop rickets or something from lack of sunlight? Oh well, at this time of the year it wouldn't be difficult to bake in a touch of a tan, once he settled in one place long enough to hang up his riding gear.

Probably the most startling feature of the ghostly image in the mirror was created by his limp hair and beard. Both were midnight black and contrasted with his pale flesh like ink blotches. At first glance, an observer might have been reminded of some Jesus

Christ figure, rustic, elemental, holy, maybe a player in some cheaply produced religious training film. A closer scrutiny of the eyes ruined this impression, however.

The sullen threat that shown in them through the mass of hair had come to Bobby Preston over long and hard experience (not all white kids grew up in the suburbs). The quiet menace found in those eyes had served him well behind bars, where he was not the largest or strongest of the caged animals. But out here in the real world it just invited negative assessments from people who didn't know him and didn't want to.

No wonder the girl in the parking lot acted like she would rather have dealt with the drunk, he thought, I don't look so much like Jesus as I do Charlie Manson.

In the continuing duality of his life, there were few better examples of how his appearance worked both for and against him: spooking the moron and repelling the woman.

You're not locked up anymore, he reminded himself, not in a cell, anyhow. Maybe it's time to mow the lawn . . . and buy a toothbrush and some deodorant.

Bobby's reflection smiled, and this took him a little offguard. He felt pretty damned good, all things considered. He didn't know how he intended to find Leslie, what he would do when he found her, or how he would spend the rest of his life, but all of that could wait until later. Right now, he only wanted to kick back and take a few days off, maybe walk down a street without being gaped at.

Draping the towel over his shoulders, Bobby went in search of the least offensive clothing he owned and, after that, a barbershop prepared to handle an emergency case.

* * *

The Prince never slept. Not really.

Even when his raped brain slipped from his normal acuity into that totally artificial exterior forced upon him by his jailers, he was still there, still himself, still listening and learning and thinking. Perhaps he was hidden in the darker recesses of his own soul, but he wasn't asleep.

And every new dawn found him more powerful. Soon he would be able to storm forth into his true life whenever he chose, using this imposed second "self" as convenient camouflage.

He lived beneath the same roof as the object of his hatred now, though she had no inkling of this. Minutes passed like raindrops to flow into the river of time. Would he kill her tonight? Would he wait until a day had passed . . . or a week? Or a year?

Would he continue to send the clues to his presence that her cow-like mind would insist on overlooking? It might be pleasant to reveal himself to her, right now, in his new identity, and then to conduct her to the very brink of sweet death, only to give back her life at the final possible moment. Then he could return to the medical Bastille once overseen by the Doctor and have a fresh and different face built for himself before doing it all again. The pain would be worth it to continue the game.

Sometimes pain itself can be the sincerest friend.

(If he decided to do this, however, he would make certain that the blasphemous surgeons could not intrude upon his physical mind again and introduce yet another personality that he, at times, would actually believe to be his own. And he would make them restore the lost portion of his manhood.)

The Prince had no definite agenda, as yet. He had cause to remember something very important on that Wednesday afternoon, though. He had witnessed the grotesquerie that the woman had called "David" approaching her in the parking lot, reeking of the piss of Satan, and he had seen "David" threaten her. She was evil incarnate but it wasn't the place of someone so crude and carnal to bring her to her well-deserved reward.

There was only one Prince of Darkness.

It was no idle storyteller's cliché, hatred was very much like love. He hated Tracey Lund to the undreamed depths of his being, but he would not allow anyone else to usurp his duties of judgment upon her.

Love, too, required its price. At the age of eighteen, he had fallen in love with the physical beauty of an actress, a young woman who appeared on a television program in a secondary capacity. While she remained there in her under appreciated and often-mocked role, there had been balance to their relationship. He had loved her and she was his alone.

This balance was lost when she left the program to "expand" her career. By doing this, she had opened her life to the appraisal of countless other viewers, none worthy of her. She was no longer his private ideal. He couldn't stand the thought of the eyes of the sinful world contaminating a beauty of body and spirit that should have belonged only to him.

So he had gone to Canada, where she lived, and killed her. This had taken place long before he recognized his true vision on this Earth, but it had been acceptable to the overriding scheme because it had been done to preserve love.

Love is not far removed from hate.

"David" was ignoble in his desire to hurt Tracey Lund. His corruption was like a painful wailing in the sensitive ears of the Prince. David would have to account for his personal evil when the time was most advantageous.

Chapter Seven

By late afternoon, the overcast sky had become nearly black with rain clouds, and these split open as Tracey drove home from work. Two minutes more and she would have been indoors, safe and dry. Sometimes you just had to laugh to keep from crying.

Nonnie was laughing for another reason. As soon as Tracey shut off the engine in the parking lot, the girl ripped open her seatbelt and dashed into the driving rain like a seal pup that had just learned to swim. Her happy cries rang even louder than the pounding of the rain on the car's roof.

"Nona Bartlett! Get inside!" Tracey ordered as sternly as she could manage. Always a step behind, she had been trying to wrestle her umbrella from beneath the front seat of the car when Nonnie made her break.

"Why?" the girl called back. "It's warm, it's fun!" She

made an almost ballet-like pirouette with arms outspread to accept the sky's bounty.

"Because you'll catch pneumonia!" Finally winning the battle with the umbrella, Tracey reached across the seat to pull the passenger door shut and then nudged all of her stuff into a pile along with Nonnie's schoolbooks. She hoped to maneuver the enormous collection of odds and ends into her left arm while opening her door and the umbrella and then holding it above her head with the right.

Hey, you're a modern girl; you can do anything, she thought.

Somehow, it worked, if precariously. The rain soaked her from knees downward as she pursued a still giggling Nonnie and shepherded her into the apartment building. Getting the girl and all of the related freight inside without diving face-first into a puddle should have qualified Tracey for one Olympic event or other.

"Nonnie, get upstairs to your place and have Carla find you some dry clothes right this instant," she ordered as she shook out her umbrella in the foyer.

Instead, Nonnie laughed and spun again on one foot so that her long, wet hair whipped about and splashed Tracey. "Why?"

" 'Why, why, why?' Because you'll catch your death of cold, as soaked as you are." If Tracey had had a free hand, she would have swatted the girl's behind.

Nonnie abruptly stopped spinning and stared directly at her with a strange and sober expression. "People catch colds and flu by coming in contact with someone carrying those infections, not by getting wet or chilled. This is a common fallacy."

Tracey was startled by the complexity and scientific foundation of the statement, not to mention the confidence with which it was spoken. "When did you learn that?"

Nonnie instantly returned to her simple, beautiful innocence. "What?"

Tracey sighed.

"I'll race you!" With this, the girl darted up the staircase located next to the twin elevators.

This brief episode was not unique during Tracey's years of interaction with those who had suffered brain trauma, but it was rare enough to still amaze her. For a fraction of a second, Nonnie's previous life as a rising college intellectual had squeezed through a pinhole in her injury to reassert itself in her speech. A blip of knowledge from the past. Nonnie would never again be that specific person, but residue of the first Nonnie probably would bubble to the surface throughout her future.

Tracey's own apartment was dark and quiet when she entered it, still dripping. Delia had left town after dropping her mail by the Center that morning and would be gone at least until Friday. She had told Tracey that the reason was business-related. Of course, with Delia there was seldom any business that didn't involve a reciprocal amount of fun.

Delia was an adult, a woman in charge of her own life. But Tracey couldn't help worrying about her best friend, especially in these times.

Changing into dry clothes also reminded her that laundry day was at least half a week overdue. She watched an early news program while relaxing for a moment and nibbling a chicken salad sandwich to hold her until dinner.

Tracey had spent a lot of her childhood and youth alone, so normally being in her own company didn't bother her, but this evening was different. The newspaper article that she had received, its envelope alarmingly addressed to "Ms. Brown Eyes," was bothering her.

It wasn't the article itself, though reading about someone dying in a car explosion was hardly pleasant. She didn't know Peter Cavella and had never read any of his work. The fact that it had been sent to her—anonymously—in the first place was the disturbing element.

Was it connected with that damned eye that floated into her dreams every night now, and, if so, how? She had never received anonymous mail before in her life, so the chances of two pieces from separate parties arriving within days of each other were pretty slim.

Naturally, the descriptive address firmly cemented that argument.

What did it mean? Had she offended someone, or had she just been unlucky enough to become some nut's target for sick humor? None of the guys she'd ever dated seemed capable of going this far 'round the bend. Thinking about it made her feel even more alone.

Impulsively, she picked up the cordless telephone at her side and began to dial. It had been more than a year since she had used that sequence of numbers, but it still came easily to her memory. Within moments, another phone began to ring in Peekskill, New York.

"Hello, Mom?" Tracey said. "It's me. How's everything going up there?" She purposely made her voice bright and cheerful. "Oh, sorry, I didn't really think about the time . . . no, nothing special, I'm doing fine. It's just that I haven't heard from you or Daddy in awhile and . . . they are? Sure, I remember them. Nathan always loved your cooking, didn't he? How's Daddy—good, that's wonderful. Did you get my Christmas card and the gifts? Oh, of course, I under—no, don't let it burn. I'll talk to you soon . . . well, you don't ever call me . . . okay. Goodbye. I love you both."

The last four words had been spoken into a dead line.

Tracey sat for a moment in the empty apartment and collected herself. What are you going to do, cry? You tried that years ago, and it didn't help, remember? Soaking in self-pity may be exquisite, but it doesn't get the wash done, does it?

She switched off the TV and began to gather up her dirty clothing.

The laundry room was in the basement, and like most of the rest of the Rosewell Apartments, it was first class.

Eight large, side-loading washing machines designed for easy access lined either side of the room. Even when the building was crowded with tenants, as it was becoming now, there seldom was a long wait for the use of one of these. An equal number of dryers waited patiently on the opposite side. None of the sixteen machines were ever consistently out of service. The room was brightly lighted by banks of cool white fluorescent bulbs, and a television set was installed in one corner.

It still seemed cold and oppressive when Tracey carried her bundle of clothes down to it at six-thirty. For one thing, she was the only tenant there. This assured her of her choice of machines and complete control of the TV, of course, but it seemed small compensation, as she had no favorite washer and Wednesday was a lousy night for television.

She wished that there were at least one other woman down there to talk to while the clothes cycled through their cleaning processes. She wouldn't have minded helping Nonnie with her lessons or even listening to Mrs. de Groot's litany of physical complaints. Still, the building had adequate security, so she could have dumped in her things and retreated to her apartment until time to dry them.

And not talk to anyone there.

Get with it, Lund, she told herself. You've got that new Jackie Moore novel to keep you occupied down here, and she's always a great read. Unable to argue with this, Tracey began her wash.

Within ten minutes, Tracey had forgotten her nagging loneliness. Even those machines that were in best repair made a certain amount of noise, and this steady droning was almost hypnotic after a few moments. She remembered lying in the backseat of a car as a little girl and being sung to sleep by the hum of the wheels, even though she couldn't recall the date or destination of the trip. A smile danced at the corners of her mouth.

The book helped, too. She was engrossed in it when the man arrived. The washer noise masked his footsteps. Tracey jumped when he dropped his canvas bag filled with clothing onto a folding table at the far end of the room.

"Sorry," the man said, a little loudly to be heard over the washer.

Tracey said nothing in response. She was trying to

place him and having absolutely no success. He was kind of nice looking; about five-nine or ten, maybe a hundred and fifty rather thin pounds. He had shortish black hair and eyes that seemed somewhere between brown and gray at this distance separating them. His dress consisted of a casual pullover, jeans, and running shoes, but he looked young enough to carry it off.

He wasn't a tenant of the building, virtually all of whom she knew by sight, unless he had taken a room since yesterday like that hood Preston. The only other newcomers were Dr. Stafford's four group members who'd arrived on Tuesday, and he certainly wasn't one of them. Maybe he was a roomie to one.

The man was uneasy as the subject of her blatant appraisal. "Just going to rinse off some of the crud," he said while he poured wadded clothes from the bag.

Tracey turned her attention back to the book, a little embarrassed by her own curiosity, as well as disturbed by his unfamiliar appearance. In these times, it didn't hurt for her to be careful, either.

Out of the corner of her left eye, Tracey saw the man shove all of his large load into one washer, colors be damned. Then he read the instructions printed on the front of each machine and whispered something to himself. He didn't sound very pleased.

Detergent. That's what he needed.

He scanned the big room and quickly located the vending machine next to the sandwich, sweets, and coffee dispensers. To reach it, he strolled the length of the room and passed Tracey on the opposite side of the folding tables. She kept her face in her novel.

The next little drama developed at the detergent

machine. The man had a number of single dollar bills, but no change, which was what the machine required. Tracey smiled to herself as he took several moments more to zero in on the change maker; she knew what to expect here.

And that's the way it happened. This haughty money-changer refused his singles. The man carefully unfolded the dog-eared corners on each bill he tried, smoothed them briskly on the edge of a table, and then fed one after the other into the electric-eye slot in the correct fashion (Washington gazing implacably toward the horizon). One after the other, they were spat back at him. He shook his head and sighed.

Tracey wasn't bothered by the man's presence. He seemed perfectly ordinary—certainly no David Julian—and he'd already had plenty of time to make a threatening motion if he had intended to do so. She laid the novel open to her page on the table before her and walked up behind him.

"Need some help?" she asked.

It was his turn to start a little. "Oh, uh, hi. Yeah. I don't know if this stubborn machine takes U.S. currency or not." His voice sounded tenuously familiar, and up close his face seemed almost ready to trigger a name in her memory.

Tracey hated being this close to making a mental connection only to fall short. She stepped to his side. "Mind if I try?"

He handed her a dollar bill.

"The management keeps every piece of equipment in this building in tiptop order," she told him, lining up the bill, "except for this piece of junk. No matter how often we complain. There's a bit of a trick . . ." Just as the electric eye caught the edge of the dollar, she hit the metal face of the machine next to the slot with a solid thump from the heel of her right hand. The bill was sucked completely inside, and four quarters jangled into the catcher below. "There you go."

The man laughed. "You certainly know machines."

"First, you have to get their attention," she replied with the punch line to an old joke.

"So I see. My old man had just two things in his tool-box: a hammer and a bigger hammer." He scooped up the coins. "Will you need to do that routine with every bill?"

"Maybe not. Sometimes a swift shot will knock the obstinacy out of it for awhile. Give it a try."

He changed three more dollars without incident. "Well, again I thank you. You're nearly as handy with this monster as you are with a computer."

Tracey had been smiling until the instant that she heard this last comment. "How did you know I work with computers?" she asked. It was nearly a demand.

He appeared to be taken aback a little. "That's what you were doing when we met yesterday."

Yesterday? Her mind raced furiously. If she hated almost remembering someone's name, she hated having that same person know things about her even more. "When did we meet? Where?"

"Yesterday," he repeated. "At the Center."

She continued to stare at him.

The man suddenly understood her confusion. He rubbed his smooth jaw with his right hand, and his grin returned. "It makes that much of a difference, huh? Put a beard on this picture and lengthen the hair about a foot."

Tracey strained to do this. Then it flooded back to her. "The man looking for his sister—and in the parking lot! Preston . . ."

He nodded. "Robert; Bob or Bobby to my friends, both of them." He extended a hand.

Tracey took it by reflex. She wasn't sure how she felt about this man now. Both of those previous meetings had been less than engaging. Even when he was helping Nonnie and herself, he hadn't come across as someone she would be interested in knowing on a first name basis. "You certainly look different today."

"I'll take that as a compliment. Had myself cleaned up this afternoon because I was tired of frightening children and insecure cops."

"I'm sorry if I was short with you yesterday, Mr. Preston—"

"Bobby."

Not yet, you aren't. ". . . I was in something of a hurry both times. And there really was no mention of your sister in our files."

"It's not your fault that my harebrained idea didn't pan out," he said. "Do you have to drop kick this detergent machine to get some service out of it?"

She gave a slight smile. "No. The rest of them work fairly much the way they're supposed to."

"Any particular brand you'd recommend?"

"If you're washing in the hodgepodge style, one that works really well in cold water."

To Tracey's surprise, she quickly began to relax and the conversation continued. She showed him how to use the washer, though she felt sure he could have figured it out alone. They began to talk of other things. At first, he was friendly but a little guarded, but when Tracey carefully steered the topic toward the subject of his missing sister, he began to open up. No one entered the laundry room to disturb them.

By the time their clothes were fresh and dry, they seemed practically old friends. Tracey could hardly believe that this easygoing young man was the same person who had carried such a heavy aura of danger with him the day before. Now he seemed to be much more lonely than dangerous.

"I've been thanking you all evening, so I guess once more won't hurt," Bobby stated as he stacked his roughly folded clothing into one of the big plastic baskets that the building provided. (Tracey had talked him out of the grungy duffle bag.) "If it hadn't been for you, I suppose I would have lost two out of three falls to the change maker."

Tracey wasn't ready for the encounter to end. "Wow, it's almost nine. Have you had anything to eat, yet?" While she had difficulty in admitting it to herself, she was a lonely person, too.

"Not since about four," he admitted. "I saw a hamburger joint around the corner—"

"Would you like to have a bite with me?" Slow, cautious, remote Tracey Lund could hardly believe her own voice as she heard the words.

"I wouldn't want to put you to any trouble."

"No trouble," she assured him, "but nothing elaborate, either. Just a few things from cans. I have to make my own, anyway, and this will give me a chance to formally repay you for sending David Julian on his way."

The mention of the man's name seemed to light a

brief flare-up of the old, intimidating biker. "Hell, that shitheel wasn't going to hurt anybody. Sorry about that language. Old habits die hard. Besides, I'm sure you would have faced him down fast enough alone." Just as quickly, the new Bobby Preston was back. "But if I recall correctly, you weren't alone this afternoon, were you?"

"That's right," Tracey laughed. "Heaven help the man who incurs the wrath of Nonnie Bartlett."

"She seems like a great kid." He made a point of not asking about any details concerning Nonnie's mental age.

Tracey didn't offer any. "She's a sweetheart. So, are we on for a late meal, then?"

Bobby didn't answer immediately. Tracey saw a slight redness tingeing his unusually pale features. God, she thought, is he dumping me *before* the first date?

In another moment, he spoke, "Tracey, I'll be completely honest with you: I'd love to have dinner, but . . . you need to know something about me. I'm not the most ordinary guy in the world. For one thing, I've got a metal plate in my skull, and I still suffer the occasional 'lost hour' when time seems to escape me." He appeared to be stalling, looking for something. Courage?

"You've already told me about your accident, Bobby," she answered quietly. "I work with people who've been through the same type of problems, remember?"

"Yeah, of course. I still haven't told you everything, though. When I was out of the country for a couple of years, I wasn't just on vacation. I was in prison."

Tracey could almost hear the mean-spirited little angel of shattered possibilities laughing at her again, as it had throughout her life. Bobby had told her unflinchingly what he had so recently done to his brother-in-law; had that same sort of ugly violence sent him away?

Her silence seemed an answer to him. He grinned. "Okay, no long good-byes, eh?" He picked up his basket. "I'll see you around."

He had turned toward the door when Tracey said, "Mr. Preston?"

He stopped walking but didn't look back. "Yeah?"

"Do you like microwaved lasagna?"

It was a meal of odds and ends, mismatched vegetables and small portions of exotic meats. As a fairly accomplished cook under normal circumstances, Tracey should have been embarrassed by it.

Instead, it was the most enjoyable mealtime she'd spent in years.

Tracey had gone out with a number of men, but nothing of a serious nature had developed with any of them. She blamed herself. It was surprisingly different with Bobby. They seemed to attract one another like magnets. He was intelligent, funny, insightful regarding her thoughts and feelings, and warm, in spite of the veneer of menace that had surfaced only that once to be swiftly put down again.

He told Tracey the story behind his prison stay, how it had been basically a railroading carried out by angry and somewhat nationalistic officials, and the way that it had all ended up as a huge embarrassment for the provincial government. And cynical Tracey Lund believed him.

He had his statement of pardon in his apartment, but she'd refused to let him retrieve it as proof.

Something in Bobby drew similar disclosures from

Tracey. She told him things that she hadn't spoken of even to Delia, though he hadn't asked to hear them. When it became obviously painful for her, he had said that maybe it would be better to keep them secret. The truth was that it was the secrecy that was so agonizing.

So she had told him, and his quiet listening eased the hurt.

After the make-do dinner, she remembered the wine. "I know it's late, but would you like to have a glass of wine with me?" she asked. "If you drink, I mean."

He smiled, much more easily now. "There's a repressed and inhibited part of me that is dead certain that drinking alcoholic beverages is the toll paid onto the highway to Hell," he said, "but, fortunately, I'm much too strong to give in to that little voice."

It was a bottle that Delia had received from one of her many "friends." Tracey was sure that her apartment-mate wouldn't mind contributing it to the evening, providing that she ever noticed it to be gone. Bobby opened the bottle most elegantly (though, of course, he used an automatic corkscrew). The pair moved from the small kitchen/dining room into the den. Tracey put on some subdued mood music.

"I hope that elevator music doesn't have a nauseating effect on you," she said lightly. "I know that it does that to some people."

He sipped his wine. "You know, I believe there are too many laws in this world that we'll never be able to overturn: the law of gravity, the inevitability of politicians, the certainty that the line we choose will always turn into the slow one. To me, it's nothing but stupid to wrap even more restrictions about yourself.

"Some folks are conditioned to believe that they can enjoy only a certain type of music, film, food, whatever. Just because they're devoted to head banging heavy metal, the mere thought of 'elevator music' makes them scream with revulsion. Not me. Bob Seger rocks my ass off—you know what I mean. I'm a big fan of Seger's work, just about everything he's ever put out." He nodded toward the stereo and the easy-listening perennial that had just begun. "But I can't honestly say that I've ever heard a more beautiful song than 'Try to Remember.'"

Tracey smiled at him. "I'm partial to 'Autumn Leaves.' It's nice to discover that not all motorcycle riders belong to the 'Real Men Don't Eat Quiche' crowd."

It was Bobby's turn to smile. "Real Men can't spell quiche. Or maybe Real Men don't let anyone else tell them what Real Men do."

"I admire your honesty."

"Sure, I'm honest. Believe me, I didn't tell any guys that I enjoyed 'Some Like It Hot' when I was in prison."

She stiffened at the word. It wasn't a visible action, but Bobby could feel it even across the distance between them on the sofa. Jerk.

"This a family album?" he asked, indicating the book on the coffee table before them. This was his calm yet slightly desperate effort to obliterate his blunder.

She reached out and took the book in what seemed almost a defensive gesture. "Oh, it's just a few old pictures. Nothing interesting. Most of the photos are of Delia, the woman who shares the apartment with me, and her family."

"You don't live with the other girl, Nonnie?"

135

"No. She stays in another apartment with a nurse from the Center."

"Let's give it a look. I'd like to see if my mental portrait of you as a kid is accurate."

"Mental portraits already?" Tracey took another sip of her wine.

An ugly yet very basic part of Bobby Preston leered within himself as he watched her drink. *Suck it up, babe*, the dark side whispered, *want another glass?* Then still another facet of his personality gut-kicked the animal back into its lair. "It's a habit of mine. I don't have a family album. Don't even remember my parents very well now. I like to imagine people as they might have been while they grew up."

She set aside her glass and opened the book. "Prepare to be bored stiff."

As she had claimed, the first and largest portion of the album was devoted to her friend's pictures. This Delia McKenzie was a full-out fox, and Bobby could tell from her frozen Kodachrome expressions that she knew this fact quite well. Hardly any pictures of other family members disrupted the Delia Exposition. Tracey's photos took up a few pages at the book's end.

"Were your mental images close to the mark?" she asked.

Bobby saw the wallet-sized snapshots of a pretty little girl with all of the budding features that presaged the attractive woman at his side: fine, light brown hair, deeper brown eyes, a smooth symmetry in her face that might have led to a modeling career given the proper direction. Still, in every picture—and there were damned few of them—she seemed stiff and uncomfortable, perhaps even a little frightened.

Quite a lot like the adult Tracey.

In Bobby's experience, attractive women seldom gave off the mixed and uncertain signals that surrounded Tracey. She could have had as many attentive guys as she chose, with her obvious sparkling intelligence only complementing her looks. In a real way, she seemed to broadcast such a need for attention to the world. After all, she had a virtual stranger, fresh out of the jug, as a dinner guest in her apartment, didn't she? But there was a defensiveness woven into the sense of welcome.

An armchair psychiatrist now, are we, Preston? he asked himself. "Who's this?" He pointed to another pretty, brown-haired girl who was featured in roughly twice as many shots as Tracey.

She took a breath before answering. "That's Shannon, my sister. She was three years older than me."

"Was." You screwed it up again, big mouth, he observed silently.

"She died when I was four."

"Oh. Sorry." What else could he say? "Those are your parents, I suppose."

"That's right."

The man and woman looked about as sour as a pair of grapefruits to Bobby, though this time he was smart enough to keep his mouth shut. In appearance, they were only vaguely like Tracey, and in a way that nearly made him grin, they resembled the brother/sister team of the "American Gothic" painting.

He wanted to remark on the overall attractiveness of

her family, as civilized protocol directed. Instead, he heard himself saying, "You're lucky to have these things to look at."

"You don't have any pictures at all?"

"Tracey, I don't even have whole memories anymore." Jeez, did that sound like a sleazy sympathy line or what? Even though it was as honest as anything he'd said to her that night.

She didn't take it as a line. She laid the album on the table and looked directly into his face. "I really do understand, Bobby. I've met a lot of people who've suffered the way you have. Some have to start over completely, like Nonnie, and some will never recover. Why don't you come to the group therapy session tomorrow afternoon? It might surprise you."

He took a long swallow of his wine. "Thanks, but I'm not much good in groups."

"It never hurts to allow someone else to share your problems."

God, she was beautiful. Those brown eyes seemed to swell and fill his entire field of vision when he looked into them too deeply. Dressed in workout pants and a loose sweatshirt, she was more alluring than the naked Canadian whores who had lined up for him on his first night out of jail. Men know things that women can only imagine, and Bobby knew he was about to ruin her perception of him forever if he stayed so near her for much longer.

"I think I'd better go," he said through a tightening throat.

She was startled by this sudden decision. "Now? It's still early . . . I didn't mean to offend you, Bobby. About the therapy session, I mean."

He wanted to laugh again, this time at her misconception and mostly at himself in his weakness. He took her hand in both of his. "You didn't offend me, Tracey. You gave me a chance and made me feel like a human being again, instead of roadscum. Now . . . it may sound like a cliché that was outdated in the '50s, but it's been a long time since I was with a woman. I had a great night, and it's best for both of us if it ends right here. See you around?"

"Um, sure," she said in confusion as he stood. "I mean, we live in the same building, don't we?"

A moment later, she was alone again, with only her emptiness for company. Damn, she thought, even sex-starved ex-prisoners . . . She laughed a little.

And, as always, she blamed herself.

Chapter Eight

Detective Ivan Perkins saw the move that the boy was about to make at the exact instant that the idea seeped through the swamp of dead cells that encased his drug-scorched brain. The kid was going to snake his free left hand into Dieter Luffner's jacket and make a desperate grab for the revolver in the policeman's shoulder holster.

Then, according to the B-movie canons that had given birth to this highly unoriginal plan in the first place, the boy would take one officer or another hostage and brazenly storm out of the precinct building to resume his glamorous extended suicide of chemical abuse and crime. At least, that was the way it was supposed to go.

Perkins knew that a cat-quick Luffner, in all probability, would dislocate the boy's elbow and then inflict several other acceptable injuries upon him in the name of "subduing" the kid. Still, there was the chance that the boy would snatch the gun and thus precipitate his own death. Perkins was in no mood for that kind of commotion on this wet and unseasonably cold Thursday morning.

With deft economy, he stepped next to the strung-out kid and slammed the trembling hand down hard on Luffner's desk less than two seconds after the thought had made its ill-conceived appearance in the boy's mind. The boy gasped in pain and Dieter whirled about, holding the telephone receiver over his head like a club cocked for action.

"I believe the young man was on the brink of taking up a career as a pickpocket," Perkins explained, continuing toward his office.

"Didn't I tell you to sit still, asshole?" demanded Luffner. His rage originated more in embarrassment than in shock or fear. "Didn't I?"

"You goddamned nigger!" the kid hurled after Perkins. "You ever touch me again, and I'll cut off your balls, I swear I will, nigger!"

Luffner straight-armed the kid back into the heavy chair hard enough to draw a gasp of pain. "You shut your mouth, pissant!"

Perkins had to marvel at the policeman's indignation, since Luffner had called him much worse to his face.

Inside the office, his phone began to ring as if triggered by his presence in the room. He picked up the receiver and identified himself.

"Good morning, Detective Perkins," the caller said pleasantly, facilely. "This is Special Agent Russell Montgomery of the Federal Serial Incident Taskforce. How are you this fine day?"

Perkins understood that he was supposed to feel a little awed by the importance of the man's title, and, in truth, he was intrigued. Why was someone from the Serial Taskforce calling him? Madison hadn't had an unsolved homicide case in over four years. "I'm fine, Agent Montgomery. Thank you for asking."

"Please, call me Russ."

"What can I do for you, Russ?" The man's attempted tactic of familiarity amused Perkins.

"Correct me if I'm wrong, but I received a report that you contacted our Washington bureau yesterday."

"I called, yes."

There was a slight pause. "Might I ask why, Detective?"

Perkins' sense of intrigue rose a few degrees into real interest. "Probably nothing, Russ. I was just trying to find out if any copycat killings have taken place recently in the style that Calvin Bryant used. Do you know of him?"

Montgomery answered a bit too quickly, "Yes, I'm very conversant with the Bryant case. I took him down, you know."

"Oh, really? Congratulations."

"Does this pertain to an active investigation within your jurisdiction?"

Perkins would have liked to have mulled this over for awhile. Certainly, he was no fan of any federal agent he had ever had dealings with. In his opinion, the average male federal agent was a disillusioned would-be James Bond turned self-protecting glory hound ready to take all of the credit and shoulder none of the blame, and the average female agent aspired to becoming the average male agent. Perkins himself had always crusaded for interdepartmental cooperation, however, and, Bledsoe's beliefs aside, he had no driving ambition to solve every case alone.

"It may well do that, Russ," he replied. "Possibly not a murder, as such, but a strange form of contact harassment with strong overtones of the Bryant mode of operation. Would you like to have a copy of what we know so far faxed to you?"

The delight in the other man's voice practically sang through the telephone line, "That won't be necessary, Detective. Actually, my partner and I have some business in your neck of the woods, and we may arrange our schedule to meet with you this afternoon. Would that be convenient?"

Oh, brother, *convenient?* "Just fine for me."

"Good, good. We'll see how the airlines are going to treat us and give you a call when we hit town."

"I'll be waiting, Russ."

"Thanks, man." Perkins hung up the phone and took a moment to consider this. The Federal Serial Incident Taskforce was a heavyweight organization. Very low profile, very high priority. When they were interested in a series of murders, there was damned little that they couldn't swing anywhere in the nation by the weight of their badges, yet Perkins doubted that more than a quarter of his colleagues in the squad room had ever heard of them.

Why were they coming here?

Why had a few innocuous questions from a minor officer in a low-crime spot like Madison rung the warning bells in a couple of roving agents? Madison itself was really small potatoes as far as annual murder totals went. Even though the crazed inmates a few miles north in D.C. were on their usual record-breaking pace for mayhem, Perkins knew of nothing that indicated a serial killer was at work in that particular urban war zone. Turf, drugs, *machismo*, these were the "reasons" behind Washington's plague of deadly violence, and they had become almost heartbreakingly banal.

No, this was something else, something very hot and dangerous. Its seeds were in the odd gifts that a local woman had begun receiving, and the secret words seemed to be "Calvin Bryant."

But he was dead. Right?

The room was darker than normal as the therapy session progressed. The drumming of the rain on the roof and the cars in the parking lot next to the building added a depressing soundtrack. Tracey was tempted to switch on at least a lamp to make a tiny contact with the real world, but Dr. Stafford hadn't called for it, and this *was* his show. The darkness seemed to inundate the room.

The new members were speaking today. At least, a couple of them were.

All four had attended this second meeting of the week (an encouraging sign), but only two, Dexter Stubbins, the big man from Maine, and the woman, Rowena Carr, had responded to the doctor's urgings. Stanley Hollis was as mummified by his paralyzing shyness as he had seemed to be on Tuesday. Michael Lockridge, on the other hand, had real physical problems that might not allow him to participate in free discussion ever again.

Rowena Carr had spoken first. She appeared very

much at ease with the enveloping blackness, as if using it to hide herself (but wasn't that its function?). Her voice was clear and confident, leading Tracey to believe that she would be the first to leave the group and its purpose behind her. She hardly seemed like a typical agoraphobe.

There were minutely disturbing points in her story of how she sustained the injury that had brought her to the Center, however. On Tuesday, she had made a brief reference to some sort of electrical accident. Today, she changed that to a beating at the hands of an abusive boyfriend without a word of explanation.

It was almost as if the circumstances of her background were subject to her moods.

Truthfulness was not a prerequisite to membership in the group, but the truth as each individual came to recognize it was vital to the healing process. Tracey was proficient in blind shorthand (which, in large part, had won her this job to begin with), and she took note of every facet of Rowena's fluid story.

Dexter Stubbins was next. He began his first real address to the group a little uncertainly, but that changed in a rush.

"I really don't care to talk much about the accident," he told them in an almost unaccented voice. He certainly didn't sound as if he came from Maine (that is, he didn't sound like the television stereotypes they were all familiar with). "It was, well, my own fault, and there were other folks involved."

"There's no need to go into anything that you don't feel comfortable with at this time," Dr. Stafford told him. His voice came out of the same Stygian inkiness as the others, sort of the way God's voice must have come out of the preexistent emptiness of Chaos.

It was all a little too distancing, though, leaning toward creepy. Nonnie's right hand patted Tracey's left arm, to draw comfort rather than to impart it.

"Then what should I talk about?" Stubbins asked.

"Anything that comes to mind: your work, your family, any insights that you may have encountered during your recovery." Silence answered the doctor. "What do you think of the Center, or Madison in general?"

"It's a nice city," the man said. "Of course, I've only been here a few days. But I think it's a good influence on me. I've had only one blackout since coming here."

"Blackout?" Stafford repeated, to tug the conversation forward. Loss of conscious thought was not unusual around here.

"Yeah. They've come pretty often since my reconstructive surgery. Dr. Heywood did it himself. Anyway, I think the rain might have sparked it. The weather depresses me sometimes."

"Tell me about it," sighed Jessica Simpson, the most consistently upset member of the group. No one shushed her, but she said nothing more that might have interrupted Dexter's efforts to open up.

"I was in the apartment last night, and it was pretty late, so for awhile I might have been sleepwalking. Whatever it was, one second I'm watching an old John Wayne movie on the late show, and the next I'm dripping wet, soaked to the bone. I thought the roof had opened up or something.

"Then it hits me: I'm outside. It's dark, raining like hell, and here I am, out in the middle of it without so much as a coat on. But even weirder, I'm nowhere near the apartment building; I'm out in the countryside, somewhere that I don't recognize. I've never been there. Trees all around, a two-lane blacktop, no sign of any houses in any direction. It's like, how in the heck did I get here, you know? Only I do know, because it's happened before. Sometimes I just black out."

This is really developing into something, Tracey thought. Her right hand raced furiously over a legal notepad that she couldn't see in order to keep up with his words.

"So I start walking. What else am I going to do? I don't know the area and the clouds are as thick as mud overhead, so I've got no sense of direction. One way's as good as the other.

"I can't tell how long I've been outside, because my watch is laying on the dresser next to my wallet and most of my brains. It must be five minutes of walking before I see this house up ahead. Really, I see the porch light, like a smudge of white in the nighttime. And the rain's still pouring down, so this looks like salvation time, right? I'll just go up, knock on the door, ask the people to call Doug Slater, my sponsor at the Center, and hope that they don't shoot me instead, because I'm standing there in my robe and barefooted, looking like a drowned rat."

There were a few sympathetic chuckles at this point, and Stafford said softly, "It's a lucky thing that you came across the house, Dexter."

"It ain't over, yet, doc," the patient responded. "While I walk up the sidewalk toward the porch, I start to feel like maybe I'm blanking out again. It's like . . . it's crazy, like when you're real tired and your body goes to sleep before your brain, you know? You're awake, but nothing feels real."

"Disassociation," Stafford ventured.

"Yeah, I guess. Anyway, I can still see and think, but it's screwy: I kind of watch myself do things instead of make them happen. I don't go up to the front door the way I want to. I stop walking at the steps and just look.

"There're people still awake in the house—at least, the lights are on in the front room. But the shades are down, those white, pull-down kind of shade that spring back up if you don't catch them just right, not the venetian kind. I look at these shades . . . white eyes looking back at me. Like the house has a brain and a big face, watching me watching it."

Nonnie's hand stopped patting and lay still on Tracey's arm. I don't blame you, baby, Tracey thought, it's creeping me out, too.

"And there's this other Dexter . . . no, his name's not Dexter, but he's still inside me, a part of me. He says, 'Those people in there are living their lives without even thinking about you. They might be anybody, old folks, kids, your own family, and they're living there so that their souls seep into the walls and floors and ceilings. Leaving some of themselves in the wood. Making ghosts.' "

"You've got a terrific imagination, Dexter," Jessica said in an uneasy tone, not caring if she interrupted this free-association confession.

This time someone did shush her.

Stubbins continued, and his voice was lower, less emotive, and almost machinelike. He had achieved a form of self-hypnosis. "The other part of me said, 'They can leave some of themselves behind because they're alive; you're not. You're nothing. But if you could get in there and become a part of them, then you could be somebody, too.' So I walk close up to the house, staying off the porch. I look underneath one of the window shades, where there's just a crack of space.

"It's not like I'm a Peeping Tom or anything. This is the living room, not a bathroom or a bedroom. I can see inside. There's three people in there, a couple, maybe in their thirties, the man watching television—the same war movie I'd been watching—and the woman reading next to a lamp with wavy lines on the shade. She has curlers in her hair. On the couch is this kid, this boy, seven or eight, I guess, and he's sound asleep. They haven't put him to bed, yet."

Stubbins paused. "I feel like . . . I can *flow* through the solid window and under the shade and reform in the room with them, and they won't notice. I'll just be a member of the family. Years from now, when nobody lives in the house and it's being torn down, the wreckers will be able to hear my part in the walls and the framework. But I'm still awake, you know, to understand that this is crazy. People don't pass through solid stuff like ghosts. So I start to walk to the back of the house."

Stafford interrupted, "Dexter, perhaps it would be best if we talked of this in private."

Stubbins went ahead as if he hadn't heard the doctor, "When I get to the back door, there's another light on, in another room on the corner. I'm sort of a big guy, but something's telling me how to move so that I can walk across this old porch without making one board creak. I try to look into this room, too, but the shade's all the way down.

"I have to get into this room."

"Dexter—" Stafford began.

This time Jessica, or someone, whispered him quiet.

"I go to the back door. I know it's locked even without trying it. I got nothing in my pockets except an old ink pen, the cheap kind that you buy a dollar a dozen in Wal-Mart. What am I going to do with a pen? The other part of me knows what. I start to take the pen apart without knowing why.

"It takes no more than a minute. I've got this little plastic and metal barrel in my hands, and I'm poking it into the oldfashioned keyhole of the back door. I'm no locksmith, right? Not a cat burglar or anything. But my hands are smart. They feel the tumblers move. The door opens like magic."

God, Tracey thought, is Dr. Stafford going to let him go on? She didn't make the connection between Dexter's "magic hands" and the way that her own fingers were darting across the page to record every word he spoke without a conscious command from her brain.

"I'm inside the house. I can feel everybody who's ever lived there before. They spin around me like smoke, like the wind . . . like the breezes that kick up the dust into little funnels when it's dry in the summertime, you know. Even the people who are still alive are a part of it. I'm standing in the dark kitchen, smelling fish and potatoes, and all of these previous people are whispering around me. But I have to go to the other room.

"The rain drips off of my clothes and my hair, but I don't make any noise when I walk. It's like I know *how* . . . There's a short hall leading out of the kitchen and into that back part of the house. At the end is the room, with the light showing under the door."

This is self-incrimination, Tracey told herself. If it actually happened. Like the rest, she was too enthralled to make a comment.

"I stand in the door and listen. The house is real quiet, but I can hear the war movie real faint from the living room. Here, nothing. No TV, no pages turning or anything. Maybe it's empty; they left the light on by accident. I open the door.

"She's in there, in bed."

"Tracey," Nonnie whispered into her ear. Tracey took her hand and held it tightly, knowing that she should remove the girl from this accelerating strangeness but unable to tear her own attention away. Nonnie's small hand felt very cold.

"She's not a daughter, she's too old, but not a mother, either. She's asleep, so it's hard to tell how old . . . forty? Forty-five? She looks a little like the woman with the curlers, so I guess that she's a sister, an unmarried older sister living with relatives. She's not real pretty. There are some glasses on the nightstand with black rims and thick lenses. But I love this woman. Or part of me does. I walk over to the bed and look down at her, sleeping so sound, with a nightlight over her bedstead. She's afraid of the dark and she's grown up. It makes me smile.

"Just looking at her is enough, understand? I'm not trying to hurt anybody, but if I can, I want to stand over her all night and watch her sleep. It's enough. Then a drop of water falls out of my hair and onto her cheek."

Someone in the group, a woman, gasped.

"And he cuts out on me, the guy who got me into this mess, he runs like a dog and leaves me alone. I kind of realize what's happening all of a sudden. Good Lord, I'm in somebody's house!" Stubbins' voice began to rise from the mesmerized chant toward alarm. "The raindrop makes her wake up, but not all at once. I'm at the door, hauling ass, before she really comes around and starts to scream like I've tried to hurt her. The guy in the living room—he's pretty big—he yells back, and I'm lost in the dark. Somehow, I find the back door before he finds me, and I run like hell. 'Not to the road,' the other guy tells me, 'stay off the road!' So I run into the woods, into a fast stream.

"I don't know where I'm going, but it's away from that house, right? I hear police sirens after awhile. They're going away from me. I keep running for an hour, I know it's at least that long, and finally I come into the city. I recognize enough to find my way back to the apartment building. There's a window unlocked on the ground floor at the back, and I go inside that way."

So much for "adequate security," Tracey thought. This man's just confessed to a felony.

Stafford had heard enough. He switched on a small lamp. Though its bulb was only twenty-five watts strong, they all blinked like startled owls in its glow. "Nonnie, would you get the shades, please, dear?"

"Um-*hmm*!" the girl answered emphatically, bouncing to the window. That was quite enough of ghost stories for her taste.

"Dexter, I believe you've just recounted a vivid dream to us," Stafford went on, "nothing more than that."

"Then why was my robe wet and my feet muddy?" the man countered.

"He's giving you the chance to save your butt," Jessica Simpson hissed.

Stubbins looked shocked. "This is a patient/doctor confidentiality thing, isn't it?"

"Of course, it is, Dexter," Stafford assured him. "Nothing ever leaves this room."

"Not until now," whispered someone in a half-amused, half-alarmed tone.

"*Nothing*," Stafford repeated sternly. Sunlight flooded into the room.

"It's stopped raining!" Nonnie told them happily. No one had noticed while under Stubbins' spell.

"I think that's enough for today." No one disagreed with Stafford's declaration this time.

"This is serious, Doctor," Tracey said in a quiet but concerned tone. "I think we should take these notes to the police today."

The members of the group had left the room, and Nonnie was waiting for her in the hallway.

"I need not remind you of the issue of confidentiality, Ms. Lund," he replied.

"That doesn't apply in this case, not really. This is a *group* session, not a private one."

"Nevertheless, the basis for these sessions is founded on the fact that anyone can say anything without fear of repetition or reprisal."

"Under normal circumstances," Tracey stated with a touch of exasperation. "We're talking about criminal activity here."

"It may not have happened at all. Hallucinations aren't all that rare in cases of brain injury." Tracey started to respond, but the doctor pressed ahead before she could. "And even if it weren't a simple dream allied with a harmless sleepwalking episode, what harm was done? No one was hurt and nothing was taken."

Tracey could hardly believe her ears. "What harm? He broke into that home! My Lord, who knows what he—or that 'other self'—might have done to that poor woman had she not awakened? This has to be reported—"

"No! It does not have to be!" Stafford spun from his desk toward her. She'd never seen his face so livid or heard his voice so harsh. After a moment of holding this nearly enraged expression, he sighed and closed his eyes. When he opened them, full control obviously had returned to him. "Forgive me, Tracey. I'm deeply sorry for reacting that way. I understand your concern, but the authorities have no place in this matter."

She hadn't been spooked by his anger, and she wasn't assuaged by his apology. "Dr. Stafford, Mr. Stubbins is staying in the Rosewell Apartments. Most of the people in this group are also staying there. Nonnie lives there. I will not risk their safety simply to maintain the confidentiality of a man who may not be in total charge of his own actions." She meant this.

Stafford placed one hand on her shoulder. "Yes, you're quite right, naturally. But allow me to handle it, will you? I have colleagues here in Madison who will know exactly how to address the situation. I promise you, Stubbins will not threaten anyone, and he'll be removed from the Rosewell complex."

155

"You'll take care of it today?"

"He won't spend another night in the building."

Tracey could accept this, even though it didn't completely satisfy her. She had a wealth of feeling and sympathy for people who'd been through physical tragedies, but she wasn't blinded to danger even when it originated in one of those very people. Obviously, she viewed housebreaking much more solemnly than did Stafford.

"You will let me handle it?" he asked.

Tracey nodded and then left the room quickly. She collected Nonnie in the hall and marched to her car beneath damp but clearing skies.

Of the two, only Nonnie looked up when the jet drifted majestically over their heads in its landing pattern. Neither of them saw Russell Montgomery and Michelle Fallows aboard it.

Chapter Nine

Perhaps more to ease her own upset sensibilities than anything, Tracey adopted a calm and soothing exterior long enough to explain the matter to Nonnie as they drove home. Actually, she didn't explain so much as she tactfully lied.

Mr. Stubbins had been recalling a dream he had experienced, not something he really had done, she told the girl. There was no reason to be worried or frightened. This was all part of Mr. Stubbins' therapy, and some other doctors would be coming to the apartment building this afternoon to take him to another hospital so that he could receive even better treatment. There was no reason for *her* to have any nightmares over it.

Welcome to parenthood, Tracey Lund, she thought wryly. How does one handle a situation like this? I don't want Nonnie to develop a personality defined by fear and distrust, but she has to be made aware of people like Stubbins and David Julian.

(I don't believe I'll ever have kids.)

For her part, Nonnie seemed completely unfazed. It was all lost in that void that now represented the first twenty-one years of her life.

Tracey's thoughts turned to other matters, as well, when she parked her car just after Bobby Preston kicked his motorcycle stand into place and removed his black helmet only a few spaces away. Nonnie sprinted into the building with her usual energy, and Tracey was left alone to consider her conflicting emotions as she gathered her things.

Part of her was undeniably angry with Mr. Preston. So she had inadvertently stepped on his toes by mentioning his possible acceptance into the therapy sessions; was that a reason to turn into a jerk and walk out on her so abruptly? She had apologized for it.

Another part couldn't be ignored, however. Until that chilly departure, it had been the best evening Tracey had enjoyed in some time, maybe for years. He had taken all of her buried prejudices and preconceptions and turned them upside-down with his humor and intelligence. And he wasn't half-bad in the looks department, either. This part of Tracey desperately wanted to repeat that evening—tonight—but her pride wouldn't allow her to consider extending the first and second invitations.

Why were "relationships" so damned confusing? Why couldn't they be more like her work with computers? On second thought, maybe they were the same: "GI/GO," garbage in/garbage out.

Whether by chance or design, the two of them were

approaching the front door on convergent courses. Tracey made an effort not to engage in eye contact, but when she reached the door, arms full, and began shifting her amalgam of files, purse, raincoat, umbrella, and books (many of them Nonnie's), a meeting became unavoidable.

"Need a hand there, Miss Tracey?" he asked with a grin as he arrived just after her.

"Three or four more, actually," she replied pleasantly (there was no reason to be rude, as he had been last night), "but I think I'll manage."

"At least let me get the door." He opened it. "You'd think for the rent we pay, we could expect the services of a doorman."

They stepped inside. "In this part of the country, the rent that we pay would barely provide for doors at all in any other building."

He chuckled.

She was being entirely too congenial.

"Have an interesting day?" he asked.

Tracey didn't answer until she had reached the elevators and speared the call button with the protruding part of her umbrella. "Interesting doesn't really describe it. I think 'chaos' comes much closer." Okay, she lived only on the second floor and should have utilized the stairs every time she left or returned home, just as she should walk to work; right now, she didn't feel like concentrating on cardiovascular fitness. "How about you?"

Since he lived on the top floor, the fourth, he waited with her for the car. "Let me put it this way: if you ever decide to look for another job, don't wait until a day of record rainfall and then do your traveling on a motor-cycle."

"I can see how that could be a problem. You're look-ing for a job?" It was only then that she noticed his attire, not the expected leather jacket and jeans but dark slacks and a conservative front-buttoning shirt. In spite of the residual dampness from the rain, he looked sur-prisingly presentable.

"Well, I've got a fair little stash thanks to the largess of the Canadian embarrassment fund, but if I plan to continue a few bad habits like eating regularly, I figured that a paycheck might keep me ahead of the game."

"What kind of work are you interested in?"

"A better question might be what kind of work I can afford to turn down." He tapped his chest with his thumb. "N.M.S., No Marketable Skills."

The elevator arrived with a ping, and Tracey stepped inside. "Oh, I'm sure that you can fit in anywhere that you choose."

Bobby joined her. "Thanks for your confidence. Two, right?"

"Yep, hasn't changed since last night." She said this with a bit of veiled sarcasm. "If Nonnie wants her work-books tonight, it won't hurt her to walk down a floor."

When the doors eased shut, the two were alone in the car. As it began to rise, Bobby looked at her with an expression that differed somewhat from his former casualness. "Tracey, I really wanted to talk to you about something."

My, she thought with a touch of satisfaction, you've finally noticed that you hurt me. Is this where you drop to a knee and beg my forgiveness for being so boorish?

Instead, he asked, "You didn't have any more trouble with that loudmouth today, did you?"

That took her by surprise. "Who? Oh, you mean Julian? No, of course not. I haven't even seen him since yesterday."

He flushed a bit in embarrassment. "I don't mean to pry or anything, but I know people like him, and sometimes they don't give up so easily."

She laughed blithely. "Don't worry about me. He knows I can get him bounced right out of his job, and his prospects are a lot more limited than yours, believe me."

"I didn't mean that you couldn't take care of yourself," he told her, obviously struggling with the complexities of modern social interaction. "It's just that I'm so used to taking the . . . physical solution that I thought he might have tried to hassle you once you were alone. I mean, I might have aggravated the situation when I was trying to help—"

"Don't beat yourself up, Bobby. You were being chivalrous. Needed or not, it's a trait that's rare enough to be refreshing these days." The doors opened on the second floor. "See you around." Weren't those his last words to her the night before?

He caught the doors as they tried to close. "About that, why don't you let me repay you for that mouthwatering meal last night? I won't subject you to my infinitesimal cooking skills, but if you can recommend a decent restaurant, we can give it a shot."

Tracey smiled. This was working out nicely. "That sounds great."

"Tonight?"

She was as much a product of her background as he

of his, and she couldn't resist playing the game awhile longer. "No, thanks, my plans are pretty well set for tonight."

It didn't seem to dissuade him. "Soon, then?"

"Yes, I think so. See you."

He let the doors slide closed with a grin that appeared both honest and inviting.

Tracey walked to her apartment wearing the same sort of expression.

This is where the "game" gets you, she thought some time later, sitting alone, eating Oreos, and watching pap on the boob tube that would have sent Fred Flintstone in search of a library. As if to demonstrate to herself, she jabbed the remote control and switched the on-screen program from a twenty-year-old syndicated no-brain situation comedy to an eighteen-year-old one.

That clinches it, I either have to get a life or a VCR.

She jumped sharply when the telephone rang without warning—what type of pre-ring warning would a telephone have? she mused—and shook her from a rapidly developing alpha state. Zapping the situation comedy with the mute button, she answered after the second ring.

It was Ivan Perkins, the police detective. "I hope I'm not disturbing you, Ms. Lund," he said in that slightly excessive and annoying polite/reserved manner of his.

"Not at all," she replied. "Have you found out something about those things I've been receiving in the mail?"

"Perhaps. I was wondering if you would mind if a pair of colleagues and I dropped by to speak with you this evening?"

Colleagues? More cops? He sounded like Dr. Stafford. "I, um, don't mind, of course, but are you sure that it isn't something we could handle over the phone? You know as much about all of this as I do."

"I realize that this is an inconvenience, and for my part, I'd as soon have you come by the precinct at your time of choosing, but these . . . investigators may not be in town for very long. They would like to interview you tonight."

Like I haven't already spilled everything I know to you. "If it's necessary, then . . ."

"Good. You can expect us in twenty minutes or so."

"Okay." She hung up. "After all, this will be every bit as much fun as cruising around on the back of Bobby's hog and munching on burgers and fries."

Sarcasm, she decided, lost some of its punch when delivered to an empty room.

She spruced up a little and tried to dredge out some awesome revelation that she'd forgotten to relay to Perkins. A slight sense of foreboding began to develop as the minutes passed. Perkins had implied that these two newcomers were from out of town, and if this case were attracting attention from other districts, there was a good chance that it was more serious than she had let herself believe. God, what if it weren't some perverted joke? What if that human eye had been some sort of trophy carved out of a living body by the monster who sent it to her?

She stared at the bathroom mirror and showed her teeth. You were going to kick Julian's butt, remember? Will you allow some simple homicidal maniac to goose you into screaming terror? She growled to strengthen the image that faced her.

The security buzzer located next to her apartment door burped and caused her to start as badly as had the telephone. Laughing at herself, she hurried to answer it.

After six P.M., no one could go beyond the vestibule without a key or being rung in by a tenant or the night manager. Tracey was expecting visitors, of course.

She touched her speaker button first. "You're a few minutes early. Open the door when you hear the buzz."

"Ms. Lund?" The voice that responded was familiar, though it wasn't the one she'd expected to hear. "This is Dr. Stafford."

Her finger froze over the entrance button. She moved it to the speaker again. "I wasn't expecting you, Doctor. What can I do for you?"

His reply was touched with humor. "For starters, you could let us in. Then you could tell us what apartment Mr. Stubbins is renting. He's not yet listed on the call board."

"Yes, of course." The thoughts of the postal terrorist had preempted thoughts of an all too more immediate source of concern from her mind. Stafford had promised to get the nightwalker out of the building that day, and it seemed he was as good as his word. She buzzed open the vestibule door.

What apartment was he in? The manager would know.

Tracey took the stairs rather than wait on the elevator and met the four people in the lobby. Stafford was the only one of the group she knew by sight. Two men and a woman accompanied him, all very well dressed and distinguished-looking, with the men wearing beards that practically identified them either as psychology professors or low comedy facsimiles. They all seemed considerably older than the fifty-plus Stafford.

He introduced them to Tracey as Doctors Helen Abbott, a small, frail-appearing woman whom Tracey had seen from time to time at the Center, Brendan Makem, a tall, heavy man with brightly mischievous eyes and a glorious Irish accent, and Graham Ingram, a short and bald man with a Vandyke beard and the build of a former football linebacker. Each was pleasant enough, but it was obvious that they regarded meeting Tracey as a brief postponing of their real purpose at the Rosewell.

Which was fine with her. "It was nice to meet you all, and I wish you luck with Stubbins," she told them, "but I need to get back to my apartment. I have some visitors on the way."

Stafford placed a hand on her shoulder in that familiar way of his. "Surely you could spare us a few minutes more. We need to find out which apartment Dexter is staying in—"

"Mr. Dennison, the night manager, can give you that information," she said from behind a forced smile.

". . . and we'd appreciate your presence while we speak to the man."

That surprised Tracey and alarmed her a little, as well. "Why? I don't know him. You're much better acquainted with him than I am."

Stafford maintained his professionally acquired expression of friendly command. "We feel you would convey a sense of security while we explain the situation to Dexter. It may be true that you've just met him, but in a very real way he's known you for more than a year. Since his accident, in fact."

"What does that mean?"

"To put it briefly, you were recommended by Dr. Heywood. He personally supervised Dexter's reconstructive surgery and the earliest stages of his physical rehabilitation, and all the while he was preparing the man for an extended association with our therapy group. He spoke very highly of your empathy and skill as a stabilizing influence during the long months that Dexter's recovery will take. You know how persuasive Dr. Heywood was with his patients."

"He was a wonderful man as well as a great doctor," Tracey admitted. When Heywood died in the air crash, it had hurt her as terribly as if she'd lost a family member.

"Then you understand. Heywood was Dexter's only connection to his former self, and after the tragedy he naturally felt utterly alone. Knowing how thoroughly Heywood trusted your instincts, I'm sure that Dexter will accept you as a surrogate."

"But I really do have people coming to see me," she repeated. "They'll be here in minutes."

"And this won't take that long," Stafford continued. "Just long enough to introduce these new physicians to him and explain the importance of his coming with us to the private clinic, where he can be monitored more closely. We don't want a repeat of last night's sleepwalking foray, and I know that's uppermost in your mind, as well."

Snared by my own words, she thought. "All right, but I really can't stay very long."

Lloyd Dennison, the night manager, was not authorized to give out information concerning the tenants without their permission, but the weight of the medical titles marshaled against him, along with Tracey's assurances, bought his co-operation. Stubbins was staying on the ground floor, 1-G, along with Stanley Hollis, another newcomer to the group.

After a short stroll down the hallway, the five arrived at the apartment, and Stafford knocked at the door. It was answered by Hollis.

"Oh, Dr. Stafford, Ms. Lund," the slender man said with some mild surprise. As perhaps the most introverted of the therapy group, his natural reaction was to flash a weak smile and redden with embarrassment or discomfort. In the animal kingdom, his reactions would have indicated immediate submission to any aggressive challenge.

Tracey's heart went out to the man. She had seen his uncertainty and tentativeness in so many other cases such as his.

"Good evening, Stanley," responded Stafford. "How are you?"

Stanley swallowed before answering, "I'm fine, Doctor. Fine. Would you, uh, would you like to come in?" He stepped out of the doorway in invitation.

"Thank you, Stanley. Ladies." After Tracey and Dr. Abbott entered the first room of the apartment, Stafford and the other two men followed. Hollis remained by the open door, at a complete loss.

"Well, um, how nice to see you . . . all," he said. "What can I do for you?"

Stafford took his time in answering as he surveyed the neat room, and Tracey realized just how astutely he was employing the intimidating power he wielded as a doctor in order to silently proclaim his dominance of the immediate surroundings. This was something that Tracey had never noticed at the Center, in the dark.

"Is Dexter Stubbins in?" Stafford finally asked.

The relief was evident in the subtle change in Hollis' expression: perhaps he wouldn't be the subject of this visit. "Yes, sure, he's in his room. Would you like for me to get him?"

"That would be fine."

As Hollis passed on his way to the bedroom, Tracey glanced over the room. Quite orderly for the apartment of a pair of bachelors. The television set was playing a black and white movie (a Bob Hope comedy), its sound was soft, and even the kitchen seemed reasonably clean. It certainly didn't fit her idea of a potential rapist's lair.

Then she noticed the window. It was half-open and screenless. Probably the same window he'd used to leave and then reenter the building during his nocturnal wandering. Unconsciously, she took a step closer to the open apartment door.

Stubbins came out of his room a moment later. Tracey hadn't really noticed just how large the man was during the meetings at the Center. He was close to six feet tall and at least one hundred and seventy-five pounds in weight, larger than Stafford.

Don't let your imagination carry you away, she warned herself. He didn't hurt that woman, after all.

Stubbins' expression was every bit as confused as Hollis' had been, if a good deal less diffident. "Hi, Doc, Tracey. What's going on?"

"Dexter, we're sorry to disturb you this evening, but I have some people I believe you should meet." Stafford quickly repeated his introductions of Abbott, Makem, and Ingram.

"More pros to poke around and see if all of the pieces of my skull were glued back in the right places, huh?" Stubbins observed with a short bark of a laugh. "If you want X-rays to check it out, I've got an album full of them from all angles."

"May we sit down?"

Stanley Hollis rushed across the room to remove a couple of magazines from an end of the large sofa. "Sure, forgive me. Please sit down, um, on the couch here, and in the armchair, and . . . let me get some of the dining chairs." At equal speed, he hurried into the kitchen.

I don't want to sit down, Tracey complained silently. Then she recalled who her coming visitors were. What a choice. She sat in one of the dining chairs.

As the momentarily relieved host, Hollis sat next to her.

Stafford turned his benevolent god/schoolmaster gaze on the nervous man. "Stanley, we'd like to handle this in private, if you don't mind."

Another anxiety attack sprayed over him. "Well, of course you would. I'm sorry, I wasn't thinking, I . . . I'll wait in the hall?" He gestured toward the door.

Stafford nodded.

"Sure, take your time. I'll get the evening edition of the paper, catch up on the news."

Tracey watched him leave his own apartment, and she felt deeply sorry for the man. For all of their casualness, Stafford's tactics seemed heavy-handed to her, designed to jerk Stanley Hollis around like a puppet simply because it was so easy to do. Still, Stafford was here because of her own demands, so she had little enough room to criticize.

"Okay, let's don't waste any more time playing like nothing's wrong, Doc. What's on your mind?" Stubbins asked directly.

For a change, Stafford was equally direct: "It's about your sleepwalking, Dexter. When you entered the house the other night, that created a matter of strong concern for us."

Stubbins sighed. "Jesus H. Christ, Doc, why don't you just run an ad on TV? I thought I was supposed to be able to tell you anything without it making the rounds!"

"Don't get upset, Dexter. I've spoken to no one else about the episode, no one other than the people here tonight. I certainly don't intend for it to go beyond this circle. But I really don't think that we can risk a repeat of the occurrence."

"The break-in was reported to the police," Dr. Abbott added. "I checked into it, discreetly, and the people into whose home you entered believe that you were merely a burglar interrupted before you could take anything. As yet, there's been no formal complaint of sexual impropriety—"

"I didn't hurt that woman and I wasn't going to!" he snapped.

Stafford made placating motions with his hands. "No one has implied that you intended any harm, Dexter, but as you yourself have stated, there are times when you feel as if you're under the control of a 'different' Dexter,

170

a second personality. Surely, you can see the potential for serious repercussions—"

"I'm not a rapist, damn you!"

Stafford looked to Tracey, as if awaiting her sage intervention. Stubbins glanced her way, as well. *What in the hell do you people want from me?* she wanted to say. *I've never claimed to be Florence Nightingale.*

Instead, she said, "We know you wouldn't hurt anyone, Dexter; we're concerned about what might happen to you."

"At least somebody believes me," the man said so quietly that it was almost as if they had imagined his anger of a moment earlier.

No one in the room was more startled by this reversal than Tracey. *Thanks for the good buildup, Dr. Heywood.*

Dr. Makem picked up the train of the conversation and helped to mollify the atmosphere with his reassuring, pleasant brogue. "That's the heart of it, my boy. What if that homeowner had kept a gun at hand? What if the sleeping girl herself had cracked you across the apple with a water jug? What if those things and worse happen the next time you go wandering about in your dreams?"

Stubbins slumped visibly in his chair. He no longer seemed the least threatening to Tracey. "I don't want the spells to keep happening, honestly, but I don't want to be locked up either. I couldn't live that way." He rubbed one hand over his hair and massaged the back of his neck. "So what do we do, tie me to the bed at night?"

Stafford leaned forward with his elbows resting on his knees and his most earnest and comforting smile on his lips. "Nothing like that, Dexter, I assure you. Dr. Ingram has a private sanitarium just a few miles from here, outside of Prosser, and there you can rest and recover without having to worry about what might happen while you're asleep."

With sudden energy, Stubbins came to his feet. "You can't lock me up! I was in an accident, I didn't commit a crime, and you can't put me in jail. I know my rights!"

It was obvious that Stafford was losing control of the situation, and he looked for help to Tracey once more. She undertook a brief mental scramble. "You won't be locked away, Dexter, honestly," she said, improvising. "This is like a small private hospital. Isn't that right, Dr. Ingram?" This last was a desperately hopeful question.

"Exactly," the doctor agreed. "Not a single locked door if it distresses you, just trained personnel on duty twenty-four hours a day to make sure that there are no episodes such as that of last evening."

"You won't put me in a cell?"

"Not at all. In fact, at the risk of sounding immodest, I dare say that your accommodations will be more satisfying than those you have here."

Stubbins continued to stare at Tracey. "Well, if you think it's right, Tracey."

She felt like laughing out loud but resisted the impulse.

Stafford moved in. "Good, it's wonderful to have that settled. To stay in the sanitarium for the proper amount of time, Dexter, you'll have to sign a few papers, just voluntary consent documents, you understand, nothing very important."

From the hallway, the entrance buzzer sounded faintly, but Tracey took no notice of it.

"I suppose it would be for the best," Stubbins said slowly. "I can't go on having these spells . . ."

Never one to pass up an opportunity, Stafford already was on his feet and slipping some folded paperwork from the inner pocket of his jacket.

Wow, whoever said this psychiatry scam was tough? Tracey asked herself humorously. *I* whipped it in a single evening.

Then Stanley Hollis stepped into the doorway. "Excuse me, everyone. I really hate to interrupt, but Mr. Dennison asked me to tell you that those police officers you were expecting are in the vestibule, Ms. Lund."

Stubbins reacted as if splashed with scalding water. "Police? You bitch! You were just trying to trick me! I don't know why Dr. Heywood ever trusted you, any of you!"

"Dexter, Dexter, it's not what you think!" Stafford said in a frantic tone.

"It's *exactly* what I should have expected!" The enraged man turned and stalked toward his bedroom, with three of the four doctors rushing after him. "I don't under—I'm sorry if I disturbed anything," Hollis said, obviously distressed.

"Dexter, what's wrong? What did I—"

"Hollis! Will you please shut your mouth?" Stafford practically shouted at the man.

"I-I'm sorry, I . . ."

"Just get out of here."

Tracey shook off her stunned paralysis. "Dr. Stafford,

please calm down. Dexter, those officers aren't here to take you anywhere; they want to talk to me."

He spun about at his door and fixed her with a withering stare. It was as if the four babbling psychiatrists weren't in the apartment with them any longer. "Don't lie to me anymore, you little pig. You'll get yours sometime, you can't fool everybody the way you fooled Dr. Heywood." Then, rather than entering the bedroom, he roughly shoved aside the heavier Makem and sprinted across the room to the half-open exterior window.

"Dexter, no!" she called to him.

With another murderous look, he jerked the window upward and hopped through it into the night beyond. Abbott, Ingram, and Makem clustered about the window like alarmed hens, but no one attempted to follow him.

"Oh, for Christ's sake," Stafford spat. He no longer seemed anything like the calm and benevolent professional of the Center.

They all heard Stubbins' car when he cranked it and burned rubber in the parking lot.

"I'm sorry," Hollis repeated almost silently from the hall, "I didn't know, I mean, I wasn't trying to . . ."

"Ms. Lund," called the night manager over the impassioned—if subdued—hubbub in the apartment, "these police officers are waiting. They don't have a warrant, but they say you are expecting them."

Stafford brushed by Tracey on his way to the building's door, and she realized that her assistance and her damage in this particular incident was at an end. "Thank you, Mr. Dennison. Let them in, please."

Stafford passed the three officers in the vestibule, and each of them regarded him closely. Their training led them to view any adult in a hurry with suspicion, especially an adult dressed in civilian clothing. Detective Perkins saw Tracey and extended his hand.

"Ms. Lund, good of you to see us so late." He glanced again at the door through which Stafford had disappeared. "I apologize if we've come at an inopportune time. Has there been some problem?"

Tracey immediately decided not to exacerbate the circumstances. "No, nothing really, Detective Perkins. Why don't we go up to my apartment? We can speak freely there."

Once the introductions were completed, Tracey offered the three investigators coffee. The federal agents ("Call us Russ and Michelle") accepted gladly, while Perkins politely refused. Normally, Tracey avoided caffeine after early evening, but tonight she joined with the majority.

The job titles applied to the new pair hadn't exactly put her at ease.

"Let me get this straight, you believe this kook who sent the article and the eye to me is a real serial killer?" she asked.

Russell Montgomery smiled above his steaming cup. "Let's not take such leaps of logic just yet, Tracey. Certainly, we have no evidence whatsoever to reach such a conclusion, but since the clipped article concerning the writer's death did mention Calvin Bryant, the self-proclaimed 'Prince of Darkness,' we thought it best to look at all of the possibilities. Copycat killings are a sad fact in our experience. Suppose you tell us everything you know about these occurrences, which have been directed toward you thus far?"

Tracey sighed. "Is that really necessary? I'm sure you've received Detective Perkins' material on the case, and he knows everything I know about it. He's very thorough."

Acknowledging her compliment, Perkins nodded slightly.

Montgomery's smile didn't waver, but Tracey saw a brief flash in his eyes. "That's true. Let's talk a bit more about your background, then."

"My background?" A disturbing thought struck Tracey. "You don't believe I've been sending this stuff to myself?"

Michelle Fallows answered her quietly, "Of course not, Tracey. How could you have? Detective Perkins has assured us of the veracity of the postmarks on the items, and there's absolutely no indication that you've left the Madison area in weeks. Even if you had, you'd have to be one heck of a makeup artist to disguise yourself as a bearded man to the Federal Express operator." She smiled at the ludicrous image this inspired.

Tracey failed to see the humor. "Then what does my background have to do with anything?"

"Because you're a private citizen and not a celebrity of any kind, the connection you've made with this unstable individual must have some personal basis, even though you can't recall it. If it isn't someone from this vicinity, then perhaps you've met him—or her—in your former residences or workplaces. You lived in New York before coming to Madison, didn't you?"

"Yes. Peekskill."

Montgomery sat his cup on a coaster. "You worked with Dr. Ansel Heywood, is that right?"

"Well, yes. Not directly, I have no formal medical training, but I had basically the same job in his surgery hospital there that I have at the Center, records, billing, general PR duties."

"Did you know him well personally?" the agent added.

"Why?"

"Just to fill in the background gaps. Were the two of you friends?"

It seemed a reasonable question. "Really, I believe that everyone who met the doctor became his friend. He was a very outgoing and likable person. As well as a medical genius."

Montgomery nodded his agreement. "He certainly was that. Did you socialize?"

"Yes, to an extent."

"Regularly?"

The man's tone hadn't changed, but the words seemed sour in Tracey's ears. "Are you asking if we ever slept together?"

"Oh, no, not at all," Fallows replied quickly.

"Because, if you are, the answer is no. He was more than thirty years older than me and more like an uncle than anything. He was a real friend to me, probably the best I'll ever have, and I don't know where I'd be now without his guidance through the dark times in my life. There was never a hint of anything physical like that between us."

"I didn't mean to imply that there was," Montgomery stated. "Heywood was a man of great personal warmth as well as talent. Dozens of people feel about him the way that you do."

"I can understand that," she responded, mostly to herself.

"We all experienced a terrible loss when he died. In New York, did he ever speak to you about his medical cases?"

This was a point that had mildly concerned Tracey herself. "Actually, he didn't. It seems kind of strange, I know, as close as we were and working in the same place and all, but he never discussed his work with me."

"Did you correspond with him after moving to Madison?"

"Only in the most casual way." Tracey smiled. "On the major holidays, and he always remembered my birthday."

Montgomery sipped his coffee with studied casualness. "Mind if we see the letters or cards?"

"That would be awfully hard, I'm afraid. He didn't send actual letters. The greetings and messages always came through the computer, and I didn't make any printouts."

Montgomery and Fallows each allowed their professional masks to slip for an instant. "You were in contact with him via computer systems?" the woman asked.

"That's right." Tracey was a little embarrassed, but she didn't show it. "I know it's not exactly responsible to use the equipment for personal correspondence, but, hey, he was the reason that the Center exists at all, so who's going to say anything about it?"

"Would it be much trouble for us to examine the Center's computer records?"

Always pressing, poking, questioning, just like regular cops, observed Tracey. "It wouldn't be difficult, but it would be illegal. Patient records are sealed by law in this state, and you'd have to have a court order to open them."

"And you'd need a hell of a lot more grounds than you have to secure that order," Perkins pointed out. He'd spoken very little since arriving, and it seemed to Tracey that he wasn't pleased to be sharing the investigation with the two.

"Surely, with your cooperation, we could persuade an agreeable judge to allow a brief scanning of—"

"Mr. Montgomery, it may sound ridiculous to you, but I take my position at the Center quite seriously," Tracey told him. "If you had a definite name to search for and you could prove your relationship, it wouldn't be difficult, but only under those circumstances. Besides, our records cover only the patients who are admitted here in Madison, and I'm sure that none of them could be responsible for this stupid campaign. I really have almost no contact with them."

Stymied, the federal agents said nothing for a moment, and they struggled rather visibly to maintain their personable facades.

Tracey went on, "I don't mean to sound inhospitable or uncooperative, but unless you have more questions, it's getting late—"

"Was Dr. Heywood a family friend?" Montgomery broke in.

"Naturally. I thought I'd indicated that." They are trying to help you, Tracey, she reminded herself. "Well, actually, he was not so much a family friend as he was my own. He got along with Mom and Dad, but his interest seemed to be directed more to me, I guess.

After the accident, he seemed to feel responsible in a way . . ."

"What accident, Tracey?" Michelle asked in a soft voice.

Feeling as if suddenly she were on the other side of one of Stafford's therapy sessions, she replied, "The death of my sister, Shannon. There was an ambulance rushing an injured person to the hospital, and she . . . was in the street . . . Dr. Heywood did the very best that he could, but that was just one time that genius wasn't enough."

"And out of guilt at losing the girl he transferred his attentions to you?"

Tracey shrugged. "I was in the hospital for a long time."

"You were involved in the accident? How?"

Tracey paused. "That was so long ago. I was only four. I can't remember it well at all."

"But it might establish how Dr. Heywood became so involved with your life—"

Tracey shut down. "No, it wouldn't. And this whole line of questioning is on the wrong track. I think you should leave now."

The agents looked surprised and more than a little upset. "Tracey, you have to help us here," began Montgomery.

"No, I don't."

He glanced to Perkins as if for help. "Detective, won't you explain how important all of this is?"

Perkins smiled without warmth. "First, you'll have to explain it to me."

Montgomery seemed to attempt to signal his local associate with his eyes.

"Ms. Lund, I'm going to violate an ordinance that is taught to every candidate in the police academy," Perkins said. He stood, as he had a habit of doing when he wanted to make a strong point. "You, members of the public, are the enemy. If not the 'enemy' in a real sense, then at the very least, you're the 'other,' the great masses from whom we must be separate in order to function effectively. Yes, we claim to serve and protect, but part of that has to do with exempting ourselves from any strong feelings of kinship with the civilian world. And one thing we're never supposed to do is side with a civilian against a fellow officer, no matter what agencies happen to be represented. That's the precept that I'm dropping for the moment."

Perkins looked at the silent, but angry pair of federal agents. "There's a lot more to this than either you or I have been told. I don't know what it is, yet, but I will. Until I do, I plan to offer only the minimum of professional courtesy to Ms. Fallows and Mr. Montgomery, and I wouldn't blame you at all if you didn't say another word to any of us."

"Detective Perkins, I would hope that you would consider your actions a bit more carefully," Montgomery said in an icy (and, Tracey felt, for the first time sincere) voice.

"Or what?" Perkins laughed. "You'll turn in a poor performance report to my superiors? You'll have to look a lot deeper to find someone I haven't offended, yet, Russ." He pronounced the man's name with obvious amusement.

Fellows stood, also. "Let's all calm down, shall we? This is getting us nowhere, and all of our intentions are focused on helping Tracey and catching this loony, whoever he is, just in case there's a chance he may prove to be dangerous."

"And we're supposed to cooperate by remaining docilely in the dark, is that the plan?" Perkins responded. "What's the real purpose behind your interest in this case, Montgomery? This is two-bit stuff. Some twisted little introvert stuck in an infantile emotional stage has fallen in love with Ms. Lund 'from afar,' and, just like the child he is, he tries to impress her by shoving a different sort of frog into her face; isn't that the official diagnosis? What does that have to do with a dead psychopath like Bryant, or, better yet, what does it have to do with Heywood?"

Montgomery joined his partner in standing, which left only Tracey in a chair. "Detective, this is neither the time nor the place for this discussion."

Perkins glanced about the quiet apartment. "Seems perfect to me."

"Well, it isn't."

"Then you tell me where and when, and be sure that Ms. Lund can attend. I'm not keeping her ignorant of the facts just to ease your paranoia. I don't work that way."

There was no intimation of actual physical violence, but Montgomery took a step that brought him very close to the taller local officer, and the entire tenor of the moment leaped in intensity. Tracey could almost smell the scent of aggressive male hormones permeating the air and sparking electrically between the two men.

"Whoa, guys, step back and take a breath, this is getting too serious," Fallows told them. "Come on, now."

Montgomery turned his burning gaze away from Perkins and refocused it on Tracey. "Please, excuse me, Ms. Lund. It's not often that I witness such an unprofessional display by an active police representative, and I fear that I've allowed myself to overreact. I don't believe anything substantive can be gained by further questioning tonight, so please excuse us. Thank you for your hospitality. Michelle." He left the apartment without awaiting any sort of response from any of them.

Fallows lingered just long enough to echo, "I'm sorry, Tracey, really. Thanks for the coffee." Then she left, too.

"Any time," Traccy whispered in bemusement.

Only Perkins was left behind, and he appeared to be as collected as the first time Tracey had met him. "Quite a scene, eh?" he asked. "Don't worry, they'll wait for me. I have the car keys. This all served a purpose, Ms. Lund. The two of them are trying to use us while keeping their real agenda to themselves, and that doesn't sit well with me."

Tracey found her voice, "Do you believe I have anything to be really concerned about, Detective Perkins?"

He considered this for a moment. "In all sincerity, I doubt it. These things seldom develop beyond the fetishistic stage. But, at least until I can find out what Dick and Jane are up to, I would be a little extra careful if I were you. And watch your mail. Goodnight."

Finally alone in her apartment, Tracey had to wonder how she had ever dreaded spending an evening by herself. A sleepwalker-cum-housebreaker had taken the high hurdles through a window before her eyes, and now the lines of battle had been drawn up between city and federal cops in her living room. Add to the mix a reformed Hell's Angel who seemed to run hot and cold with the flick of a switch and you had one beautiful mess.

Tracey shook her head as she closed the apartment door.

Chapter Ten

The man had had the gall to show his face in the very home of the Prince. The coward, who had displayed no more manhood than to shoot him in the back, had walked into the apartment building as if he still possessed the right to travel among decent human beings. It was almost beyond belief.

You breathed my patient grace into your lungs as you walked within feet of me, and your dull senses gave you no suggestion of my presence, the Prince thought. Some people seem to run to embrace their own deaths.

But not now, not this night. I will be told when your moment of reckoning arrives, and until that time you may exist in your animal ignorance, unable even to recognize the angel of your judgment while you look into his eyes.

The lobby of the building had been crowded by that time, of course, with tenants drawn from all floors by the nearly psychic network of gossip. Everyone knew of the sad comedy being performed in apartment 1-G, and they all needed to steal a look at it, so it wasn't as if Montgomery had had but one face to distinguish. After the excitement had ended and the Prince was alone once more, he had walked, unseen, in the woods to gather his thoughts.

The need was upon him.

The world was metamorphosing into an extension of the real Hell before his eyes. He saw the cancer that was consuming the race of Man everywhere now, and he was but one individual ordained to struggle against it. Why didn't the Word come down from on high to point out the next creature enwrapped in perversion that must be eliminated? Why was there silence amid the fever in his head?

My God, my God, why have you forsaken me?

Another voice—not the holy one—whispered with irritating persistence somewhere within his soul. It was not unlike the false voice that Dr. Heywood's traitorous subsidiaries had planted inside of him with their drugs and their surgery; but where that voice was nothing more than a cretinous mask behind which he found it expedient to hide from the unchosen of the world, this one originated from deeper, where his spirit resided. *Calvin*, it goaded him with its catlike tone, *are you eager to rid the world of its foul excrement or do you simply hunger to kill?*

"No!" he shouted aloud, frightening only the residents of the forest about him. "I am the Chosen, my duty is holy and consecrated."

You are a murderer.

He stopped walking and sat on the damp ground, with his legs folded before him. He dropped his redesigned face into his hands. I kill because death alone can vanquish the rising flood of evil. I take no pleasure in it.

A murderer and a liar.

No one calls the Prince by those false epithets.

An even worse liar than a murderer, because you lie to yourself.

"Shut up!"

Or what will you do, little fool?

The Prince took the gun from his pocket and placed it, full cylinder, against his right temple. "Or this."

You don't have the courage for that anymore.

"Cavella thought I had lost my manhood, but I took his balls, I dared the risk that he begged me to spare him. Who has courage?"

That was long ago, a week ago.

Then the truth glowed with a pristine light in his mind. Evil exists not only in actions but in thoughts, like the thoughts that had crept their cowardly way into his very person. They were trying to remove him from this level of existence before the natural end of his life's mission.

The Prince laughed aloud.

Laughter?

"Yes, because I see the reality that you try to shield from my eyes."

Bravery, reality, if you have all of these things, why does God refuse to speak to you now?

"He speaks in ways beyond your detection or comprehension. He tells me what I need to know, and he explains to me how to ignore those who would turn me away from my destiny as his servant." The Prince turned the muzzle of the gun away from his skull and toward the spotted white moon overhead. The shot rang out and drove more of the forest animals away from him, exuding a terror that he could feel.

The other voice made no reply to this, because none could have brought to face its cruel truth in beauty.

It was almost midnight before David Julian left the tavern and drove to his home outside of the city limits of Madison. He had a decent buzz going, and the road seemed especially cockeyed as he maneuvered along it. He was lucky, though, as it was still too early in the month for the goddamned cops to be worrying about filling their ticket quotas. They hadn't bothered to quit boffing one another or to put out their own joints to hassle him.

Lucky thing, too. One more DUI and his mug shot would make its debut on the back page of the newspaper with the notation that some tight-assed judge had sentenced him to do time, even though he'd never hurt anybody. David had been drinking for seventeen years, even longer than he had been driving, and in all of that time, he'd never been involved in a single accident that had been his fault.

Like most of the problems in the world, this drunk driving shit had been brought about by women, Mothers Against Drunk Driving, MADD.

What group had that television guy said he belonged to? Yeah, DAMM, Drunks Against Mad Mothers. David laughed out loud and scrubbed the curb with his right front tire. The irony of the timing made him laugh a little louder.

If women would just keep their noses out of things, it would be a better world by one hundred percent. He often wished that he had lived during the '50s, when rock was young and vital and real, instead of the hairstyle and earrings of the week asshole British band or race-baiting, no talent rap groups, and when women had stayed at home and raised their kids instead of taking jobs from men and making them mop floors for slave wages.

Back when divorce was something dirty and wives didn't jump into it at first imagined opportunity, to take away your kids and half of your piddling paycheck every week so that you have to move back in with your mother, for God's sake.

Jesus, now he was depressing himself. When he pulled into the driveway and shut off the car, he slammed the door and tromped inside without worrying about waking his old lady.

Small rebellions.

She was waiting up for him, anyway. "Davey, I have your dinner warming in the oven," she said as he entered.

"Thanks, Ma, but I ain't hungry," he answered, dropping heavily onto the couch. Wonder if Demi Moore was scheduled to be on Letterman tonight?

"You should eat something, son. It's not healthy to go so long without food."

He smiled to himself. There was at least one old-fashioned woman left in the world. "I had a burger in town. I'm fine, Ma, so go on to bed, huh?"

She took a step toward her son but stopped. "Oh, and there was a call for you about an hour ago."

He sighed. "Who was it?" *Margret giving me a ring just to crack my nuts for the fun of it on a slow night?*

"I'm not sure. He gave me his name, but he spoke so soft I couldn't make it out." She began to search for something in the pockets of her robe. "Really, I couldn't even be sure if it was a boy, the voice was so faint."

"Do you know what 'it' wanted?"

She came up with the slip of paper and handed it to him. "He left this number for you to call when you got in."

Julian glanced at the number. It rang no bells.

"Are you going to call back?"

David considered. Sounded like a hassle, and he felt like shit. "Not tonight. Maybe tomorrow."

"It sounded important."

Could be Eddie with some fresh stuff, he thought, but *Ma would have known Eddie's voice.* "Okay. You run along to bed. See you tomorrow."

"You just be ready for a big breakfast, young man."

"You're on!" *Good old Ma: feed it and any problem disappears.* He began to punch out the numbers on the telephone.

It rang only once before a faint voice on the other end said, "Julian?"

"Who's this?" he responded carefully. He wouldn't put it above some woman's group or other (and weren't there way too many of *them* around?) to try to entrap him in a fake drug deal, especially anyone that that bitch Lund belonged to.

"A friend of a friend," the voice answered, a little

stronger now. Sounded like a guy, maybe a young one. "This friend says you're a good man to take product overload on consignment."

The fancy language confused Julian. "Did Eddie give you my name?"

"Bingo, brother. You interested?"

"In what?"

The voice chuckled slightly. "In moving my shit. I'm doing a canvass of the Madison area, sort of like a scouting trip to see what the market is around here, and the only name I can drop is Eddie's. Eddie tells me you can sell the material in a discreet but profitable way, and you're not a man to let mold grow on your inventory."

I'm not a man to hang my ass over the telephone, either, assbite, Julian said to himself. You make the first statement of intent, "brother." "What kind of inventory are we talking about?"

"You name it: grass, smack, ecstasy, pretty much whatever the market demands. Do much crack in these parts?"

That description had effectively compromised any possible case against him, David felt, and he was interested. A man could always use a second income. "The niggers do some, but it's kind of quiet otherwise. The shitheel cops are all over your case if you show a joint in public, so most of the 'heads' move on to D.C. Hell, even the mayor does it up there."

"Tell me about it; I sell to him. So, you interested?"

"I don't know, man. I got a record already, and like I said, the vise squad's got their noses up everybody's asses because they don't want to let Madison become a little D.C. Except for their own stashes, naturally. I might be looking to buy some for my private use, though, if the price is right."

The man laughed again. "The price is always right for a new customer. Come along. We've got what you need."

"Tonight?"

"No, noon tomorrow on the courthouse steps. Of course tonight."

"I don't know, it's pretty late."

"Past your bedtime, I guess. Maybe you can score off of Eddie later at his markup."

"Hey, hold on there, partner," Julian said quickly. It was always cheaper to connect with the source rather than some middleman. "Where you located?"

"You know the first dirt road that cuts off of Plymouth Lane about a mile west of the city limits?"

"Sure."

"We're doing one hell of a thriving open trunk business in a little hollow right down there. That's why I'm using the car phone now."

"Damn, you're moving it way out in the sticks, aren't you?"

The sardonic note returned once more. "Afraid we're going to roll you, Julian? Like we need a couple of fresh mops, right?"

Anger flickered like static electricity in David's gut. But a score was a score. "Okay, man. You open all night?"

"Until about four."

"See you before then."

Julian hung up and checked his wallet. Twenty-three lousy bucks. That wouldn't buy powdered sugar up in

D.C., but since this was an admitted Mom and Pop out-of-the-trunk operation, maybe he could get enough grass to split with the guys tomorrow and build up the kitty. Besides, tomorrow was payday, and if this jackass was going to open shop tomorrow night, too, he could do a lot better then. Margret could miss a check for a week or so and let her boyfriend drink Schlitz instead of champagne.

"I'll be back in a few minutes, Ma," he called, slipping on a light coat.

"You going out now, Davey?" she asked from her bedroom.

"Just for a little while. Eddie needs some help with his pickup." It was a lie he knew she would see through, but it gave her something to hold onto. Ma always thought the best of him, and she stood behind him. She'd even testified at the divorce that he'd spent all of those nights at home with her, even though she had to know that he was screwing around on Margret. She was a good woman.

"Be careful, son," she reminded him.

"I will, Ma. Goodnight."

He went through her purse for loose cash before leaving.

The advisability of the trip lessened with every mile that Julian drove.

Friday night would have been better, anyhow: he would have his cashed check then, he could pick up Eddie or Malcolm or somebody to make the run with him. This was shit, driving out here in the middle of nowhere at one in the damned A.M. just because somebody he'd never even met suggested it over the telephone. There weren't even any houses out here.

So what? another part of him thought. What's going to happen? They going to zap you and rack you for forty-six bucks? Don't be ridiculous. Muggers don't invite victims out beforehand. You're going to pick up a certain amount of shit and maybe party with it and one of those truck stop hookers over the weekend.

Or maybe the trip would mean more than that to him. He liked that concept of "consignment" selling. If he was slick and smart, with a low profile, it might be possible to move the "product" well enough to provide for himself and Ma and drop that crappy job at the Center. He couldn't really get used to the deformed kids they kept operating on, anyway. And while that Bartlett girl was cute as a button, when he thought that she had the brains of an undercooked biscuit, a chill that was only partly enjoyable passed through him.

Shoot, if he could prove to the court that he had lost his job, he might even get to stop sending his blood to that bitch who used to be his wife. This might very well be the night that changed his life.

Still, he liked the feeling of the knife in his right boot. Just in case.

When he reached Plymouth, the sense of isolation was so complete that it felt as if somewhere along the line he'd driven totally off of the earth. Not only were there no houses out here, there weren't even streetlights, and the only illumination was provided by the cones of light that his headlights were cutting into a night that seemed to inundate him. His greed was having a rough time holding off his nerves again.

Shit, what a great spot for a murder. The thought came to him unbidden.

A mile of Plymouth paving passed quickly, and Julian caught a glimpse of the turnoff road just ahead. It was a narrow, rutted, dirt path into the woods. He winced as his front wheels sank into the mud that still retained a lot of the rain from Wednesday. His reaction didn't originate in any concern for the condition of his car wash; he just didn't want to get stuck out here.

"It's a good thing I didn't wait until tomorrow," he mumbled to keep himself company, "because that's Friday the thirteenth, and there's no way in hell I'm coming this far into nowhere on Friday the thirteenth." He happened to glance at the glowing dash clock, which told him that it was "12:43 A.M." It *was* Friday.

Then he saw a whitish smear in the darkness ahead and relaxed a bit. The joker was down there.

Following a sharp left turn in the road, the other car came into view. As promised, it was sitting to one side in a small vale that bulged into the forest like an aneurysm. The trunk was open. The source of the light, a brilliant storm lantern, sat within it. Julian eased off of the road and parked just behind the other car.

"You Davey-boy?" asked a slight, shadowy figure as Julian stepped into the night.

"I'm David Julian," he answered. "Who're you?"

The figure approached him. "Just call me Noble; real names aren't necessary." He extended a hand.

"Maybe not, but you already know mine." While David shook the gloved hand, he tried to get a good look at the man attached to it. White guy with a long beard, slim, vaguely familiar around the eyes, but the name wouldn't come. Julian couldn't decide if he'd ever seen him before or not.

"Noble" laughed. "That's right. You interested in a few flights of fantasy?"

There was no one else about, and Julian was damned certain he could take this slender jerk, so he allowed his stomach muscles to unclench. "That all depends on your stock and your prices, man."

"Well, then, let's check it out," Noble said, leading the way about the car to the open trunk.

"You're doing a booming trade out here, aren't you?" Julian observed archly as he followed.

The guy snorted. "The trick is to work by appointment, get the right names and spread them out over the night so that the goddamned cops don't notice the traffic, right? I've got folks who would shock and amaze you scheduled for later on: housewives, judges, preachers, doctors—"

"I thought doctors supplied their own."

"They get free samples from the pharmaceutical companies, all right, but even they can't provide what I offer."

Julian smiled in spite of himself. "That sounds promising."

"You bet your ass it is."

They reached the rear of the second car, and Julian squinted in the lamp's brightness at an old, frayed quilt that seemed to be covering something in the trunk. "This?" he asked.

"Yes, sir. Right under there." Noble stepped back as if inviting his customer's inspection of the goods.

Julian picked up the quilt. "You know, man, I've been

reconsidering your offer, the consignment one, and I think I might be able to make it work. I know some people who will pay big time if the shit is high grade, and—"

There was a body in the trunk. A girl trussed up hand and foot like a Christmas present, with heavy duct tape wrapped about her mouth. She opened her eyes and made a wordless pleading sound deep in her throat. "What the hell is this?" Julian demanded, turning.

"Say goodnight, Davey."

The fishing line loop dropped out of nowhere over Julian's head and cinched about his neck. He gasped, but the air was trapped before it could rush all of the way up his throat. It felt as if a circular saw were beginning to decapitate him. Now he tried to scream.

Still behind him, Noble jerked sharply at the fishing line noose and set the bigger man into a frantic reverse stagger. Noble's end of the line was tied to a foot-long stick of wood that resembled a portion of a marionette's control rod, and he was using it in much the same fashion as a puppet master would.

"Your mistake, David Julian, was in immodesty," Noble stated in a remarkably calm voice while he dragged the strangling man away from the car and toward the surrounding forest. "Your sins are black enough, of course: drug abuse, intimidation, disrespect, ignorance. But those are the failings of the masses, and we can't reform every sinner, can we? Of what use is an empty world? No, tonight is your reckoning because you chose to step out of the common slime and interfere with the duties of a holy attendant."

Swamped in pain and terror, Julian could barely hear the rantings coming from behind him, but his mind remained clear enough to focus on one other thing, the knife in his boot. First he would cut himself free, and then he would find out how long it took someone to die while being skinned like a rabbit. His hand fumbled with desperate strength at his right ankle.

The knife was free and flashing at the taut line projecting from the rear of his neck before the tree branch clubbed his forearm and knocked it spinning into the ground. This pain was terrible, but it couldn't compare with the agony at his throat.

Blackness was rushing into Julian's eyes when the two men reached the specified tree. Rational thought had deserted him, and he dug gashes in his own flesh while trying to slip his fingers under the godawful line. Then it got worse.

With deceptive strength, Noble wrenched David upward, into the sky, where he hooked the control rod between the forks of a branch in the tree. Julian's tongue protruded so far out of his gagging mouth that it began to bleed at its base. He went up on tiptoe in an effort to ease the searing pain, and an eerie, sheep-like bleating came from somewhere in his neck below the ring of nylon wire.

Noble moved swiftly and with complete self-confidence. Using both of his hands, he pried Julian's right fist from the line and slipped another loop around its wrist. This, too, was wedged into the branches of the tree. Despite the death that seemed to be enveloping him, David fought when the monster came for his left hand; he clawed and punched and tried with every ounce of strength to catch the maggot and rip his face from his skull with that free hand. But Noble was equal to this, as well. Several hard blows to his kidneys froze Julian in the midst of his struggles. The remainder of his energy drained from him in an instant. It required no effort at all from Noble to secure his left hand as thoroughly as he had captured the rest of the big man's body.

Then the bastard did something incredible: he performed an act of kindness.

"Step up onto the log," he directed when the large cut of wood rolled against the backs of David's heels.

David followed the command, as swiftly as his limp legs could respond. This eased the tension on the loop around his neck, and Noble then slipped the penetrating knot about an inch outward to allow the air passages to open within his throat.

"Oh God oh God, thank you!" Julian gasped. Blood sprayed through his teeth with every syllable. His fear and confusion replaced the gratitude immediately. "Why are you doing this? I don't have much money! Who are you? What do you want?"

Instead of answering, the other man casually walked into his line of vision, stooped to retrieve the knife that had stabbed half its blade into the soft ground, and then returned and stood before Julian. He wore a beatific smile that was only just visible in the backlighting from the storm lantern and the thick beard. "I'm the Prince of Darkness, David," he whispered. Then he removed the fake beard.

Even in shadow, Julian recognized the face. "I didn't hurt you, I never did anything to you! Please, please!"

"'Please'?" repeated the Prince. "You sound so different now, so repentant. We all see the truth eventually, don't we? Let me get the lamps set up, and we'll begin."

A hopeless wail burst from the trapped man and fled through the empty forest.

When both lamps were lit and positioned for optimum effect and the witness was arranged to fulfill her part in the ceremony, the Prince asked his single request of his captive: "When you die, David, try to tell me what Hell looks like. I'd really like to know." Than he began to cut away the man's clothing.

David Julian was very strong, and he took most of an hour to die.

The Prince sat on the ground before the hanging, empty body, and his breath ran raggedly from him with the combined effects of his exertion and the emotions that coursed through him. Sometimes his lot was difficult, but he knew that he never would have been chosen had he not been equal to any demands that might be made upon him. Right now, he only wanted to return to the Rosewell Apartments and sleep.

He couldn't, however, not yet.

The balance was disturbed. A man had departed this level of existence for judgment and atonement; the eternal scales swung to the opposite side, hungering for a woman to join him. Tracey Lund was a woman deserving of his attention, but not tonight. Her time would come. Soon.

That was why he had collected the witness, of course. She was not a glorious representative of womanhood. At their best women were but a step below the angels, and this creature had lost all traces of the angelic very early in her life. The truck stops and drug alleys swarmed with the sisters of this pathetic being like flies on the decaying carcass of a slaughtered cow. They tempted otherwise good men and attacked them at their innate weak points to reduce them to the women's own level of degradation. Even in these times of retribution in the form of disease, these harlots painted themselves and profaned the sacredness of their own bodies for mere money.

The witness was no better than this in the eyes of the Prince, and for a moment he was tempted to release her naked into the forest while he searched out someone more evolved to fulfill the second portion of the ceremony, but only for a moment. He needed to perform both halves of his obligation tonight, here in this vale, which would leave him precious little time for another search. Still, the thought of her corrupted blood made his stomach turn within him.

He had no quarrel with the inspired statement that the blood was the life, but in today's world it was all too often contaminated with the sickness of its host.

The Prince was nearly exhausted. His changed physical form seemed not to have retained the stamina of his original incarnation. But the thoughts of taking one more step along the path of his holy journey sustained and even invigorated him. He turned to the bound and gagged witness, holding David Julian's knife as his instrument of divine power.

Chapter Eleven

She was running late to begin with and Nonnie was proving to be uncharacteristically difficult to get into first gear this morning—forgetting her this and that, a book or her completed lessons or an article of clothing, necessitating repeated returns to her apartment—so the last thing that Tracey needed was a virtual conference in the lobby of the building. But that's what she got when Rowena Carr spotted her, waiting impatiently, while Nonnie made what was hopefully her last return to the home base of the third floor.

"Good morning, Miss Lund," the rather large woman said brightly while descending the stairs. Her long black hair was parted in the middle, and it billowed playfully behind her as she moved. Her healthy figure indicated that she regularly took the stairs rather than the elevators.

"Oh, hi, Rowena," she responded. "You're looking fresh and relaxed for so early in the morning."

Rowena laughed. "Early? I've been up for *hours*. Speaking of time, won't you be late for work?"

Tracey glanced to her watch. "I already am. Nonnie, will you please come on?"

Rowena rolled her eyes in sympathy. "Oh, I see. Children, huh?"

"Huh," Tracey agreed.

Rowena reached her side, and her voice fell to a lower, more personal register. "How about what happened last night? It's all over the building. Did Dexter really cut out to avoid arrest?"

"No, not actually—"

"He did do the hundred yard dash through his window into the parking lot, didn't he?"

"Yes, but the police weren't here to question him—"

"I'll bet they're after him now, right? I didn't see him take off or anything, but I was here in the lobby—with just about everybody else in the building—so I heard what he was yelling, what he said to you."

"He was distraught," Tracey said, reacting defensively despite how she felt personally about the man.

"He's kooky, if you ask me. You know who else comes off as a little strange around here? That Preston guy, riding that big motorcycle and looking like a sleazeball out of a bad '60s movie one day and a smooth-faced junior executive the next. He was down here while all of that was blowing up last night, too. Did you know that?"

Tracey recognized the veiled, yet desperate appeal for friendship that the young woman was making, but there was just something about her . . . besides, Tracey didn't have the time to engage in any rituals of female bonding at the moment. "No, I didn't see him while it was going on, but that's not too unusual considering the circumstances and all."

Rowena placed a large hand on her shoulder. "Do you think that Dexter is really perverted? I mean, is he like *dangerous* or anything?"

"That's not really for me to say, Rowena. I'm sorry I don't have more time to discuss it with you, but . . ." Like an answered prayer, the elevator doors opened to reveal Nonnie standing inside. ". . . here's my wayward passenger now, and we really have to be going."

"I understand. We'll hash this out later tonight."

Not if I have anything to say about it, Tracey thought. "Nonnie, let's go! It'll be lunchtime before we even get to the car!"

Rather than cooperating, Nonnie jabbed one of the floor buttons and waved at her, laughing. " 'Bye, Tracey!"

Tracey dashed across the lobby to catch the sliding doors before they could seal the girl within the car. "Nona Julianne Bartlett! If you're coming with me, you'd better get your behind out to the car right now!" She took the giggling girl's hand and pulled her from the elevator. "What were you planning to do, go back to bed and sleep the rest of your life away?"

"Nope, I was going to write my book some more," replied Nonnie.

"With as much time as you've taken this morning, I can believe it." She directed the girl toward the vestibule, always making sure that she was behind her.

"So long, Nonnie, Miss Lund," called Rowena. "And, Miss Lund? Be careful out there, especially today."

The odd emphasis on the day caused Tracey to look back at her.

Rowena smiled. "It's Friday the thirteenth."

Ivan Perkins regarded superstition as crippling a disease as religion or atheism or any other rigid and inhibiting system of thought. He was not inclined himself to pay the least attention to any of the silliness that superstition inspired in otherwise reasonable human beings. Still, he fully expected this Friday the thirteenth to hold a certain amount of bad news for him when he came to work that morning. His bluntness with Montgomery and Fallows the night before didn't bode well, he knew. Like all federal employees, they were used to kid glove handling by the "common" people.

So, it was something of a mild surprise when everything appeared quite normal upon his arrival. Even the pair of imported brats were their usual phony-friendly selves. Maybe he still had the ghost of a chance of hanging around until pension time, after all.

Not that he believed in ghosts, of course.

But he would find out what big secret the two federal agents were hiding from him concerning this Calvin Bryant thing and its true relationship to Tracey Lund. It was a slow business morning, as well as a tedious one, with Montgomery and Fallows chirpily pretending that nothing untoward had taken place the night before. They hung around his office, which was SOP, using his terminal and telephone, and their anything-to-be-cooperative attitudes were almost nauseating. Perkins wouldn't allow them the satisfaction of knowing this, naturally.

The few calls that did come into the precinct (a stolen car, a minor scuffle between intoxicated street people, a break-in at a hardware store) were handled by the catching teams out in the squad room. Perkins was using his computer during a rare respite from Frick and Frack's presence to check on the most recent tenants at the Rosewell Apartments when a telephone call did ring in for him, the woman asking to be transferred to his office specifically.

Perkins recognized her voice at once. It was Charlotte Julian, a widow who had had occasion to meet with him through the petty criminality of her only child, David. David Julian was a smalltime drug user and lay-about who had engaged in some marked vandalism during his term in high school, but Charlotte herself was a good woman. She had come to like Perkins due to his efforts with her son, and he, in turn, liked and respected her, even though he knew by learned instinct that she would lose David someday.

She seemed to think that this was the day. Her son had been gone since making a mysterious phone call the previous night, and Charlotte was on the verge of being frantic. David sometimes stayed out all night and the day after, but he seldom, if ever, had left for such an extended absence after first returning home from his after-work haunts. He hadn't shown up for work, either, and today was payday. Charlotte, who did love the boy, after all, was beginning to become seriously worried.

Though the forty-eight hour waiting period required to file a missing persons report on an adult hadn't passed yet, Perkins assured the woman that he would keep an eye on all incoming reports to see what he might turn up later in the afternoon. This seemed to ease her concern. For his part, Perkins believed that the boy was drunk somewhere and would return when he was sober and hungry again.

This was basically the sum of the morning's activity. Superstitions might be primordial mental garbage, but if they held down the crime rate among the savages, they might be viewed as possessing one positive attribute, after all.

At twelve-thirty, Perkins' standard lunch break time, he again found himself alone in his office *sans* Fallows and Montgomery. This pleasant development left him without the social pressure to invite the pair to eat with him. Sometimes, in small portions, life *was* good.

He was halfway into his coat when they hustled through the door bearing grease-blotched boxes of Chinese food. "Our treat," Montgomery said with a friendly grin. "It's the least we can do to make up for last night's unfortunate scene."

Perkins glanced through the still-open doorway to see Lucas Bledsoe beaming with satisfaction.

"We were told that Chinese is your favorite," added Fallows.

Tracey Lund had a visitor around that time, too. She was just gulping down the last of her iced tea—making inelegant sounds in the Styrofoam cup with her straw that Nonnie would have sternly admonished her for, had she been present—when a knock sounded at the door.

"Come in," she answered, dabbing her lips with a napkin.

The door opened and Bobby Preston entered, wearing

something close to a subdued business suit and a smile. "Good afternoon. I was just wondering when the world's greatest computer mind interrupts her work to have a bite to eat?"

Tracey was glad to see him, almost surprisingly so. "About thirty minutes ago," she replied. She held up the paper bag containing the few remains of the sandwich the deli across the street had delivered.

His happy expression faded a little. "The story of my life: late again. I was hoping you'd show me a nice place to eat in this burg."

It was an idea that appealed to Tracey; she was through playing games. "Maybe next time. My, don't you look upwardly mobile?"

Bobby did an awkward turn for her. Dressed this way and without the heavy beard, he looked like a college senior attending a debate tournament. "I may be slow on the uptake, but the news eventually settles into my brain pan," he told her. "After a couple of days of zero response in my job search, it occurred to me that your average employer might not have an abundance of confidence in a guy who arrives to apply carrying a crash helmet under one arm and wearing jeans and a riding jacket. Think this will make a better first impression?"

Tracey stood and sat on the edge of her desk. "Works for me. I don't see how any thinking businessman could turn you down . . . unless he sees you wearing that suit while scooting down the street on a motorcycle."

He winked at her. "I've got that licked, too. Come here." He circled her desk to the exterior window, with its scenic view of the parking lot. "See that pale blue Saturn parked just this side of the black van?"

She joined him at the window. "Um-hmm."

He plucked a ring of keys from his coat pocket. "That should create a more professional impression."

"Bobby, you bought a car?"

"Well, rented one. I'll need an 'employment position' before the finance companies will even recognize me as a potential customer, but I can handle the rental payments until I manage to hoodwink some fool into taking me on. It's American-made, too, which doesn't hurt in the brown-nosing department."

Tracey stepped back and regarded him again. "You're planning to settle here in Madison, then?"

He continued to gaze into the bright and clear afternoon sky. "For now, I guess. I still want to find my sister, but I don't have a clue as to where to look for her. I thought that if I hung in one spot for awhile, maybe she'd locate me. I'm going to get a permanent address, for a year or so, anyway, send it to my brother-in-law and the Canadian pen, and there's an outside chance that Leslie will get in touch with one or the other of them while looking for me. Shoot, if I was still inside, I'd be coming up for parole in about eight months, and she would want to be at the hearing." He laughed shortly. "At least, I like to think she would."

"In other words, you've decided to let the mountain come to Mohammed."

"Well put. That only leaves me with the problem of finding some job that I'm remotely qualified for."

With raised brows, Tracey said, "There may be a janitorial position open here at the Center; according to the time clock records, David Julian didn't show up this morning."

"Could you put in a good word for me?"

"If the bribe's large enough."

He chuckled. "I'd better be on my way and let a real working person go about her job. How about dinner tonight?"

The suddenness of the proposal reminded Tracey of just how little she knew of the man. But it didn't alarm her. "Bobby, really, I know you have obligations, financial obligations, and I wouldn't feel right about adding to them while you're looking for a job. How about eating at my place again so that I can prove that I can cook something that doesn't come in a can?"

"I believe I've misled you. At the moment, I'm financially comfortable. It won't last a year, but I'm not worried about next week's rent, yet. I owe you a meal, and since I can't cook instant potatoes, I insist that you let me take you for tacos, if nothing better."

She smiled at him. "Okay. But I reserve the right to fix you a real meal in the near future."

"Done. What time is good for you?"

"I get off at four, plus time to get home and fix myself up after the wars of the day . . . how's six?"

"Sounds right to me," he replied. "I'll even pick you up at your door."

"How gallant."

"See you at six."

" 'Bye."

After he'd left, closing the door behind him, Tracey sat before her terminal for almost a minute and mused over the short meeting. Was this really the same thuggish-appearing man who had stepped into her life only last Tuesday and who had scared away a big goon

like Julian without lifting a hand? Now he seemed like
barely more than a kid, a good-looking, friendly, and
bright kid, to be sure. It was as if she were witnessing a
literal transformation, the butterfly struggling from its
cocoon.

Not that he gave the impression of weakness. Tracey
still wouldn't want to meet him in an alley on a bad day.
But he no longer radiated that kind of invisible threat—
the evening she'd passed with him in her apartment had
been as comfortable as she had spent with anyone in
years—despite the fact that there was no doubt that the
Bobby Preston who had grown up hard was still around
and ready to be called up if needed.

In fact, he was still the same man who had ruined that
Wednesday evening by walking out so abruptly. She
wondered what tonight would be like. Actually, if one
cared to look at it in a certain light, Tracey had made
two dates with him on this afternoon.

Sometimes Friday the thirteenth was a lucky date, it
seemed.

The call came into the precinct house at a little past
three P.M. A retired oil field worker turned eco-warrior
named Charles Houser had been doing his bit for
Mother Nature by picking up beer cans on an unpaved
road off of Plymouth Lane when he discovered the bodies. Had he not chosen that afternoon for his cleanup
effort, if might have been days or weeks before anyone
else found them.

There was no guarantee that the people who had left
those beer cans out there before would have felt it to be
a part of their civic duty to notify the authorities the

next time they returned to their hangout and encountered the gruesome scene.

Technically, this case was out of the Madison P.D.'s jurisdiction, since the location was beyond the city limits; the sheriff's department took responsibility in such a situation. However, because Houser had phoned the city boys and the cooperation between city and county officials was admirably solid, it was not unusual for the lieutenant in charge to dispatch two of his own detectives to observe the circumstances and render assistance to the sheriff and his deputies.

Today, the lieutenant selected Perkins and Luffner. Naturally, Montgomery and Fallows would not be left behind.

Charlie Houser was standing in the front yard of the home on the corner of Melvane and Plymouth from which he'd called in the report when the unmarked city car containing the four officers arrived. The county department had been notified by then, but they were running a little behind. Houser, obviously a hale and hearty man in spite of his advancing age, was pale and sweating as he climbed into his own car to show them the way.

"There they are," he said hoarsely five minutes later. "You can see the man from here. The girl's down . . . behind a few yards. I, uh, didn't touch them, because, damn, it's pretty obvious they're dead, ain't it? But my tracks are in the ground around them. I wasn't thinking, when I walked close to them, I mean. I just couldn't believe what I was looking at. Maybe I didn't destroy any evidence."

Russell Montgomery patted the older man's shoulder.

"Thank you, Mr. Houser. I'm sure nothing's been disturbed. Would you like to wait in your car until the sheriff arrives?"

Houser swallowed and looked away. "Yeah. I believe I would."

"Okay, but don't leave, all right? There will be some more questions. And don't move your car. There may be other tire tracks in the mud up there that could prove to be valuable evidence."

"I understand." Houser started to walk to his car and then stopped. "You know, I've seen dead men outside of a funeral home before, in the fields, at sea. But I never saw a little girl that way. It's awful . . ." He left them without completing the thought.

Perkins knew that it was David Julian even without glancing at the mutilated corpse. The kid's car was sitting just off of the road, no more than seventy feet from the body. He had gone out early in life and bad, just as Perkins had predicted, but there had been no foreseeing something like this.

"Son of a bitch," Dieter Luffner whispered to Perkins as they walked together to inspect the first body, carefully avoiding all of the prints that the ground still held. "I never saw anything this bad before. You?"

Perkins didn't need to search his memory. "This is a first." He glanced at the two federal officers, who were rushing down the path before them, and added, "But it seems that they have."

"Huh?"

"Nothing."

Julian was naked and still standing. Thin, strong, fish-linelike wires knotted about his neck and wrists and affixed to the branches of a tree held him in a grotesque pose that resembled some Grand Guignol puppet. His head lolled forward with his blackened and swollen tongue vomiting from his mouth. Dried blood had pooled in an oval beneath his body, and the noise of hungry insects added to the gruesomeness of the scene.

"Oh, Lord," Luffner whispered.

Both men started a little when a burst of bluish-white light flashed through the shadows. Michelle Fallows was taking pictures with a small and powerful camera that neither of them had seen her carrying before.

Perkins didn't approach the body closely enough to compromise any possible clues, but the shading of the visible flesh and the already revolting stench told him that David had been dead for at least a dozen hours. The vast amount of blood testified to the fact that his heart had been allowed to continue beating for a long time during the murder by a diabolically skillful torturer. Death had been about as horrible as could have been imagined.

Luffner seemed to be reading his mind. "Satanists. They're the only people who would kill like this."

It was a term that was growing in popularity in the law enforcement community as well as in civilian circles. For his own part, Perkins had never encountered any evidence of Satanism beyond the occasional thrill-seeking teenager whose attention was occupied by the illicit rituality for roughly a month before moving on. He said nothing.

"Any idea who he might have been?" Luffner asked. His complexion had gone as pasty as unbaked bread, and there was a beaded row of sweat glistening across his upper lip.

"Yeah." Without elaboration, he turned away from Julian's corpse and walked deeper into the forest where the girl's body waited.

Her death had been no easier than David's, and, if anything, the mutilation of her sexual organs was more extensive. She was white, looked young (though it was difficult to be certain how young due to the damage that had been inflicted upon her by the murderer and the additional ravages the body had suffered from insects and animals), and she was no one whom he'd seen before.

Unlike Julian, she was sitting, with her back to a tree and her wrists tied behind it to hold her. Her head was thrown back so that her face was turned up to the sky and her staring eyes were fixed on the afternoon sun. They were green. Like Julian, however, she was nude.

"God, it just gets worse," Luffner muttered upon joining him.

Perkins knew from prior experience that Luffner was a competent officer, as well as a tough man. It was simply that he had never confronted death this starkly before.

Fallows and Montgomery continued to photograph and examine David Julian.

"What kind of monster could do this to a woman, Ivan?" whispered Luffner. His voice was still low and controlled, but there was a powerful current of rage rushing through it. "Damn, can a person like that even be called human? I mean, aren't we born with some . . . morality? Some kind of natural *code* that tells us that this is wrong?" Now his words were rising in pitch.

216

"Calm down, Dieter," Perkins said quietly. "Don't give the federals cause to lose respect for you."

"Be like you, huh? Cold and steady." The struggle within the younger man was a visible one. "I only know what I'd do if I caught that son of a bitch, and there wouldn't be any appeals or reprieves, man, I'd kill the mother with my own hands, Ivan. I swear before God I would."

"Why don't you go back to the road and wait for the sheriff and the ME? Make sure that the car tracks aren't disturbed?"

Luffner took a deep breath and immediately regretted it. "Good idea."

When Montgomery and Fallows moved from Julian to the girl, Perkins kept out of their way. He found the rough pile of shredded material that had been their clothing and began to examine it without disturbing the configuration it had assumed. But he kept his ears tuned to the conversation going on behind him.

"These are his, Russ," Fallows was whispering to her partner. She seemed to be much more affected by the awful sights and smells of the scene, much more human. The same way that Luffner's reactions could be compared to his own, he supposed. "You know that the autopsies will prove it. We never released that to the public, but it'll be there, in both of them, and when it shows up that will prove that this guy is no copycat."

"At least then we'll be sure," Montgomery replied.

Do I sound like that? Perkins asked himself. No one should remain so unaffected when faced with the likes of this.

"Get a full facial," Montgomery continued dispassionately. "See if you can shoot the dental work."

Fallows' voice was weak. "All right. Step over a little . . . okay. She was pretty—oh, Jesus God! She's alive!"

Perkins snapped about to stare at the second body. It seemed unchanged . . . no, the eyes were closed.

Fallows was nearly hysterical. "She's still alive, Russell! She blinked!" The woman lunged toward the body, as if to help it in some way.

Montgomery caught her by the shoulders and pulled her away. "No, Mitchie, no! It was some kind of reflex action—the light! *Look at her throat.*"

Both Fallows and Perkins focused on the girl's exposed neck. It was practically severed. "Oh God, oh God, oh God," Fallows began to chant in a harsh gasp. Montgomery took the camera from her and resumed the photo recording.

After a moment, the federal agent noticed Perkins' continuing observation, a stare that took in both Fallows' shivering retreat from this second corpse and his own emotionless efficiency. He was disturbed to discover the private functioning of a Taskforce team so exposed to the eyes of an outsider. "Detective, why don't you jog back to the cars and help your partner to make sure that the civilian doesn't accidentally ruin any of the tire tracks or footprints up there? They could be vital in helping us to find the monster who did this."

Perkins' contempt for the man swelled like bile in his throat. "Luffner knows what he's doing, Montgomery. We have handled other crime scenes."

"Of course." Rebuffed but unruffled, Montgomery turned his attention back to the dead girl.

Perkins left the clothing and walked deeper into the forest. Ostensibly, he was scouting for any evidence that might help with the investigation, even though he found it highly unlikely that the killer had left the area on foot. In reality, he wanted to get away from the worsening odor for the moment.

He looked at the remains of David Julian from this deeper perspective. The body appeared to be strangely . . . elated. With the uglier details hidden by distance and shadow, its arms seemed to be thrown up in a frozen instant of victory, its clawed hands almost drawn into fists, and the feet touched the earth below only at the balls of each. From back here, it seemed in the process of leaping rather than sagging by wires from the tree.

An athlete's moment of victory, or, with head bowed, a zealot giving raptured thanks for successfully overcoming evil.

Perkins knew what he would have to do in a short time. Certainly, the pathetic, tortured body of the girl should have elicited more of his pity. She might prove to be an innocent who had accepted a ride from the wrong person, while the detective was well aware of the downward spiral of Julian's life. Her assaulted femininity did tear painfully into his chauvinistic heart; these things weren't supposed to happen to women. But he was removed from the girl in a way that it was impossible to distance himself from Julian. He knew Julian.

And he knew Julian's mother.

Finally, Montgomery finished shooting his rolls of film of the two corpses and joined Perkins a little away from them, where the air was fresher. Fallows had wandered out of their sight, but if she were weeping for the dead rather than taking the time to coolly search for clues, Perkins wouldn't consider her any less a professional. In spite of his own composure, he hoped that he never turned into a clone of Russell Montgomery.

"Kids, huh?" grunted the agent, referring not to the dead pair but to Fallows and Luffner and their emotional reactions.

Perkins said nothing.

"Quite a job someone did on those two," he added. He took a pack of cigarettes from his jacket and offered it to Perkins. When the detective shook his head, he returned the pack to his pocket. Montgomery didn't smoke out of habit, either, but he carried them as another tool of his work. "I don't think that our boy did all of the damage to his victims, however. Looks like animals had a good time of it, too. What sort of wildlife do you have around here?"

"Raccoons," Perkins said distractedly, " 'possums, a few deer, and a fox or two."

"I thought all of those other than foxes were vegetarians."

"You believe too much of what you see on National Geographic, Montgomery. Nature's not what the animal rights fanatics paint it to be. In the wild, any animal will eat just about any form of protein that happens to be available. I've seen a deer with a dead mole in its mouth."

"Kind of like people."

A faint shout from Luffner drew their attention. The county boys and the Medical Examiner were arriving.

"I guess that takes it out of our hands," Montgomery said.

Perkins looked at him unblinkingly. "As soon as they go through this trash heap of clothing and find the ID that I know they will, I'll need to get back to the precinct. You and your friend should be ready to leave then."

Montgomery's response was somewhat cheerful, disarmingly so given their surroundings. "Righto, old chap."

Before he turned to hike back to the road to meet the arriving officers, Perkins added, "And then, mister, you and I are going to have a talk."

The little house was not much to consider as far as the reward for a lifetime of work went: two bedrooms, one bath, pealing white paint and curling shingles that should have been replaced five years ago. As he pulled into the driveway, Perkins noted half a dozen things that a non-renting adult son should have taken care of without being asked. Now it was all that Charlotte Julian had left in the world.

He was slow in switching off the car and opening the door. He hated this, every second of it, and he realized that drawing it out this way only made the experience worse, but he hated the thought of saying those words even more.

It was something he'd done only once before. That had been far too much.

Charlotte saw him as he walked up the steps to the

porch. She met him at the door before he could knock. Apparently, his expression spoke more eloquently than his voice ever would.

"Detective Perkins?" she asked, holding onto the last flicker of hope with a mother's desperation.

He sighed. "Mrs. Julian . . . I'm sorry . . ."

The first person he had said those words to had hit him, as if the agony came from knowing. Charlotte Julian merely began to cry against his chest. He walked her back into the house and closed the door.

Chapter Twelve

Tracey was surprised to find herself so excited over a simple dinner date. The rest of the afternoon seemed to drag by as she automatically performed her work and used most of her mind to try to decide where to recommend that they eat. After all, what did she know about Bobby?

Did he like basic meals, meat and potatoes and maybe a salad if it were served without any fancy dressing? That was the first image that she'd formed of him (back when she'd thought him to be little more than another motorcycle thug). So much about the man—both in reality and in her perception—had changed so quickly.

He might even be a youthful gourmet, at home in the finest restaurants that Madison had to offer; with the proximity of D.C., the city boasted several four-star establishments. He might feel at home while slipping the maitre d' an appropriate bribe to secure a good table and then ordering fluently in the language of the restaurant. Hey, what would she do if he decided to order her meal *for* her, the way that dashing gentlemen had once felt to be *chic?* No one else had done her ordering since childhood.

No, something like that was her uncertain fantasy, not Bobby's reality. He was extremely intelligent and wide ranging in his interests—that was a big part of the reason that she had begun to feel comfortable with him so soon; illogical though it may have been, Tracey found it hard to imagine an intelligent man as also being a dangerous one—but his intelligence and style of handling himself remained of an earthy sort. He might well be able to order in French, but she would bet that he would prefer ordinary steak to Chateaubriand.

So, a nice steak place like Bonanza or Western Sizzlin' would fit the bill. It would do much less damage to his wallet as well.

Tonight's dress would be casual, then, and this also matched well with his admittedly limited wardrobe.

Tracey actually caught herself humming aloud. She laughed and shook her head. You had a date for the prom, kid, remember?

There was just something about this guy.

The flight from St. Louis to Madison was smooth and uneventful. The business in Missouri had gone well (basically), and she would be in line for a nice bonus when the contracts were signed. There weren't even any crying babies or Jade East-drenched, open-shirted, pretend Lotharios in the seat next to her. In short, at least on the surface there was no reason for Delia McKenzie to feel depressed or upset.

That didn't stop her from rigging the first of the fabled three sheets into the wind during the flight, though.

The hard part was deciding whom to be angry with: her boss, the client, or herself. The client was a fifty-four-year-old man with iron-gray hair, a perfect tan even in winter, and a tall body that was kept slim and hard by rigorous, non-steroidal-assisted exercise. The first time that Delia had met Matthew Classen, she had been impressed by these factors, and after coming to know him even better during their dealings through the months, she had been more turned on by his keen mind, obvious sense of humor, and, yes, his aura of command.

She had known early in the association that she really wanted to sleep with this man.

Which brought her to that afternoon in Classen's private suite in the best hotel in St. Louis. The business matters had been concluded in an entirely professional fashion, at least in Delia's view, and the late lunch had developed along an almost preordained path. Delia had found all of the things that Matt Classen was on the outside to be intoxicatingly sexy. If the world condemned this as a mere surface attraction, then so be it. She wanted to lay the man, not to marry him.

The act itself had been wonderful, ninety minutes of passion both raw and skilled in the same context. Classen had the stamina of a man thirty years his junior allied with mature experience and the powerful magnetism of limitless self-confidence. These had proven to be the best ninety minutes that she had spent in years.

All of this had taken place *after* their business negotiations had ended. Not a hint of the coming afternoon had passed between them beforehand. This was an important fact to Delia, one that she continually repeated to herself now.

At the very end of this exquisite period that they had shared, Matt Classen had destroyed the entire event and cast a heavy pall over her professional life with a few words intended as a compliment: "Your boss was right, you're one hell of a woman."

Simple enough, ". . . one hell of a woman." Not, ". . . one hell of an executive," or, ". . . one hell of a woman under any circumstances." Alone, it might not sound too hurtful, but connected with the cordial, "Your boss was right . . ." it spoke volumes to Delia.

She'd never slept with her (female) boss, and even though she had had private relations with two other clients over the past four years, there was no mistaking what that phrase had meant to Classen.

Sign with Olsen and Ferrante and you get Delia McKenzie as dessert.

After the first nearly physical impact of the words, Delia had tried to redefine the sentence to herself. Perhaps what Aleah Ferrante had said involved her skill as a business negotiator alone, and any postscript was nothing more than her own paranoid imagination trying to punish her for having enjoyed the encounter. It seemed that there was always someone, somewhere, who was upset when someone else was experiencing a little joy, even if that someone was only a conscience.

Delia had handled the moment well (mustn't react in any purely natural way that would disturb the client), but she had been unable to convince herself of the innocence of the remark. She had been offered to Classen as a part of the deal, even if only for an afternoon. She was a perk.

Damn you, Aleah, and damn you, too, Matt, for that matter.

And what about Delia McKenzie? If she didn't enjoy these interludes of physical love so much, if she had been welded to another person in marriage like Patricia Onorato, who couldn't breathe out of rhythm with her husband, or if she had been a walking, ball-busting NOW-sponsored nightmare like Harlene Naughton . . . or if she had been a capped fountain of unrealized potential like Tracey, then she wouldn't be viewed by her own company as something to up the ante when negotiations got rough.

Jesus, why couldn't she be herself?

So she had begun drinking on the flight in and had layered over the emotional pain with a fuzzy coating by the time the jet landed in Madison. Maybe she would vent her anger on Aleah in person on Monday. Maybe she would just cry it through. For now, the most accessible plan of action was to douse the hurt with alcohol.

At the airport, she had phoned the apartment to ask Tracey to pick her up, but after a combined thirty-five rings in two calls had failed to bring an answer, she had been forced to conclude that no one was home. Where would Tracey be at seven P.M.? Well, it *was* a Friday: she might have a date.

Right.

A cab had solved her transportation problem, but it also had given her the time to consider the afternoon without the ameliorating benefits of liquor. She had begun to simmer again by the time they reached the Rosewell Building. The poor cabby undoubtedly wondered what he'd done to deserve such a lousy tip.

The apartment vestibule was empty, a perfect reception to what had become one thoroughly crappy day. "Your boss was right . . ."

Delia didn't bother to unpack. Instead, she kicked off her shoes, found her friendly bottle of Chianti, and flopped onto the sofa in the dark room to plan her revenge on Aleah Ferrante to the accompaniment of the clinking of bottle against glass.

A timid knock interrupted this satisfying wallow only four or five minutes into it. "Who is this?" she called, setting aside the bottle.

A hesitant voice answered from the hallway with what sounded like, "Messy forme Lund."

"She's not here," Delia responded.

There was a slight cough, and the voice repeated a little more forcefully, "Yes, ma'am, I know that, but I have a message for her. I think, um, I think it's kind of important. It's from a policeman."

"Oh God," Delia sighed as she struggled to her feet. "What cop would be leaving Tracey a message?" Then she recalled the odd things that her friend had been receiving in the mail, and the situation took on much darker shadings. "I'll be right there."

By habit, she switched on a lamp and glanced into the mirror above the mantle. Her hair was a bit frazzled and her face could have used a touchup, but if she were still sober enough to trust her own judgment, she would pass. It was only a messenger boy. Still in her stocking feet, she walked to the door and opened it.

The young man on the opposite side of the door jumped slightly as it opened and swept back into the apartment. Then he focused on Delia as she stood in a shaft of light from the hall, and for a moment he said nothing. Inwardly, Delia smiled.

"Yes?" she said to break the stasis.

He blinked. "Uh, I, um, I have a message for Ms. Lund." He wasn't dressed in a messenger's uniform, just sloppy civilian, but if he were an apartment building resident, he was a newer one: mid- to late twenties, she guessed, five-nine, about a hundred and forty pounds, dark brown hair and green eyes. She didn't recognize him.

He was kind of cute. "Come in," she said as she stepped aside.

The man touched his face with an absentminded, shy gesture and followed her inside. "Is she back?"

Delia shut the door. "No. I share the apartment with her. You can give me the message and I'll see that she gets it." She walked casually to the table that held the bottle of Chianti, and his eyes never left her. It felt good to Delia, reassuring in a superficial way, yes, but in a way that had been very important to her throughout her life.

He swallowed nervously. "I don't think I should do that, really—not that I mean to offend you. It's just that the detective said that Ms. Lund should get the information personally."

Delia paused before picking up the wine. "A police detective?"

"Yes. He was the real thing, not an impostor. I mean, he showed me his identification and everything. His name was Perkins, C. Ivan Perkins."

"And what's your name?"

"Oh, I'm sorry, I should have told you before I came in. I'm Stanley Hollis. I just moved in, the first floor. 1-G?"

"Like to sit down and wait for Tracey, Stanley? We could have a drink together." Normally, Delia was not a user of people, the way that she was using her attractiveness to manipulate the reactions of this obviously timid man. But right now, she needed his reaffirmation. It wasn't wrong.

"No, uh, no, thank you. I can't right now. But don't let me interrupt you, Ms. . . . ?"

"Call me Delia."

"Thank you. I'll just go back downstairs and wait for Ms. Lund to get back. I didn't mean to disturb you."

Without seeming to be hurried at all, Delia moved around Hollis and cut him off from the door. "There's no reason to go to so much trouble. I'll bet you've been coming up here every fifteen minutes and knocking on that door, haven't you?"

He blushed. It looked very deep in the dim light from the single lamp. "It was no trouble, really. I didn't know how to ring this phone from my apartment, inside the building, and I couldn't really be sure if Ms. Lund had returned without my being, you know, aware of it . . ." His voice trailed off.

"How did you happen to get the message?" she asked, redirecting the thrust of the conversation.

He shrugged and laughed shortly. "Luck of the draw, I guess. Ms. Lund left a little after six, and the detective arrived only seven or eight minutes later, and he couldn't get in because after six you have to have a private key or ring someone from the vestibule. But you know that already. Anyway, he rang the night manager, and Mr. Dennison knew that I knew Ms. Lund—"

"How do you know Tracey?"

"Well, I'm in her group at the Center. Dr. Stafford's group, actually, but she's a great part of it, a great help."

Great, Delia echoed within her mind, another of Tracey's lost lambs. The luster of the game dimmed a touch for her.

"So Mr. Dennison rang me to ask if I would talk to the policeman, and, naturally, I said I would." Hollis was speaking so quickly that he seemed to be trying to recite a speech before he could forget it. He was too preoccupied to notice when Delia deftly took his elbow and guided him toward the sofa. "He had this important message for her, and he had tried to call her about it, but you don't have an answering machine or a service." He sat at her wordless gesture, the auto-pilot of his mind following directions without alerting the rest of his consciousness.

Stanley Hollis evidently was used to following orders, and he actually was kind of attractive in a reticent, boyish sort of way. Plus, it was Friday night and she was pissed with the world, which was not the best of times for Delia to be alone.

Without asking again, she took a second glass from the cabinet on the mantel and poured him some wine. Then she handed it to the man with the same unspoken command that she had employed to get him relaxed on the sofa.

He took it, still talking, "I wouldn't be making such a pest of myself, but it is important."

"Sure you can't tell me what it concerns?"

He took a deep breath. "Honestly, I wish that I could. I'm certain that if Detective Perkins were here he would agree, but he's not, and I gave my word . . ." When Delia sipped her drink, Hollis unconsciously imitated the action. He blinked again—several times—but a tentative smile came to his lips. "That's pretty good," he admitted in a slightly husky tone.

She nodded. "You saw Tracey leaving?"

"Well, yes. I wasn't *spying* on her or anything. I don't do that. That was Dexter's job." He laughed just a bit at his own joke and then became embarrassed again when it was obvious that she didn't get it. "Well, I was in the lobby. I have a lot of time on my hands at night. Anyway, she said hello-goodbye to me, and I answered her and Mr. Preston."

"Mr. Preston? Our Miss Tracey has a real date tonight, hmm?"

He took another sip. "I suppose . . . well, they may have just been going out for a bite to eat or something."

"You know this Preston?"

"Only to speak to. Ms. Lund introduced us, but I do know that he moved into the building only this week. He seems like an okay guy, you know?"

"So do you." Delia set aside her glass and then took Stanley's from his unresisting hand. "It was really nice of you to go to so much trouble for her, Stanley. Did you know that you look kind of mysterious in a certain light, like, I don't know, like an agent of some sort, a spy? A man who has secrets that he can keep and who knows how to be dangerous when the situation requires it."

He was breathing both heavily and fast now, and his face was so darkly crimson that Delia had to wonder if she were inciting an attack of some kind within him. "That's . . . that's very kind of you to say, Ms.—Delia, but, really, I'm nothing like that."

She gracefully unbuttoned the top of his shirt and rubbed her fingers over his smooth chest. "I'll bet you're many things that the world doesn't know about, yet."

His nervousness seemed to boil inside him. Delia guessed that he'd never even kissed a girl he wasn't related to, but the obvious arousal that her touch was creating swept aside any questions of his being gay.

"Sometimes you can meet a person and realize, within minutes, that he's the right one," she said seductively. *The right one for tonight, anyway.* "Have you ever had that happen to you?"

He was almost gasping now. "Oh, God, you're beautiful. I can't—I couldn't . . . we really don't know one another or anything."

"There's only so much that we need to know."

His hands came to her upper arms, hesitantly but trembling with need. "Tell me if I go too far. I won't force myself on you. Honestly."

Delia smiled for a number of reasons as they leaned forward to kiss.

The door opened. Laughing lightly, Tracey stepped into the apartment and flipped on the overhead lights. Stanley pulled back from Delia as if he'd received an electrical shock.

"Shit!" Delia whispered.

"Oh! Delia!" Tracey said in surprise. "I wasn't expecting you back until the weekend." She saw Hollis. "Why, Stanley, I didn't know you were here, either."

He already appeared to be retreating into timidity overload. Springing to his feet, he said hurriedly, "Ms. Lund, um, good evening! You, too, Mr. Preston."

The good-looking man in the hall behind Tracey smiled with a wry shifting of his brows.

Stanley continued to apologize in a voice that was nearing a stutter, "I came up . . . I came up to see if you were here, to give you the message, I mean, and, uh, Delia was here, and we, uh, were talking."

Tracey was into the circumstances now, as well, so she responded with a perceptive wink. "Don't let us bother you two. We didn't expect anyone to be here—"

"And we'll be going," Preston interrupted, taking Tracey's hand. He repeated the eyebrow exercise in Stanley's direction and took a step toward the door.

For Hollis, it was overwhelming, almost enough to make him forget the purpose that he had given his word to fulfill. Almost. "But I do have this message, Ms. Lund." He took the folded sheet of notepaper from his shirt pocket.

"Message?" Tracey took it from him.

"Detective Perkins left it. He came by just after you'd left for your . . . with Mr. Preston. A few minutes. He said he'd tried to call you." He watched as she gazed at it silently. "I didn't read it."

Tracey sighed, and that finished the evening for all four people. "Bobby, gosh, I'm sorry, but this really is important. I have to meet with Detective Perkins in—

what time is it? Eight-fifteen?—in just about fifteen minutes at the precinct house."

"Precinct?" Bobby looked confused and concerned. "Are you having trouble with that Julian guy again?"

"Yeah, what about it?" Delia added.

Tracey shot her a wordless but extremely informative look. To Preston, she said, "It's nothing, really, just some crank mail I've been getting. I hate to end the evening this way, but . . . ?"

He grinned. "Down in flames again."

"We'll do it later?"

"Right. If you're not under arrest, maybe tomorrow."

She kissed his cheek. Then she turned to Hollis. "Thanks so much, Stanley. You're a lifesaver."

Outside of Delia's powerful spell now, he reverted completely to the inhibited mouse that she had met on Tuesday. "Don't mention it, please, I was glad to help. I hope that it's nothing serious." He glanced to Delia, and she saw in his frightened eyes that she had lost him, at least for now. Still, the clear sense of regret that glowed through the fear in his expression comforted her. "I'd better go now. Goodnight."

"Me, too," Preston said. "Nice meeting you, whoever you are."

"Oh, Delia, this is Bobby Preston; Bobby, Delia McKenzie," Tracey said quickly.

"Hi, Bobby, bye, Bobby," Delia laughed.

"I'll see you around," he promised. "And you tomorrow," he added, returning Tracey's kiss. Then he placed a hand on Stanley's shoulder and said as the two of them left together, "It's back to the TV and popcorn for the strike-out artists, I guess."

When they reached the elevators, they lazily rang the call button. Two cars arrived within a second of each other.

"Here's where we go our separate ways, old man," Bobby stated. "I'm up, you're down. See you later, stud."

When he was alone in the descending elevator, Stanley Hollis shook his head in wonder. He still wasn't absolutely clear about how his life had been before his accident, but he felt certain that he'd never been a lady-killer. "Stud," he whispered. "Stanley the Stud."

Lord, she was so beautiful.

In apartment 2-E, Delia said, "So what's the story, Trace? I've been out of town, remember?"

Tracey answered while dressing down a bit in her bedroom, "You know as much as I do, Delia. I haven't heard anything from that creep since the newspaper article you brought into work on Wednesday. If Perkins has anything to report that's more pertinent than the standard cop routine, you'll be the second to know, I promise."

"Who gives a fart about the cops? I meant what's the deal with this firm set of buns you called Bobby?"

Tracey chuckled. "I could ask you the same about Stanley Hollis!"

The laughter of the young women blended almost musically.

Naturally, the police station didn't close for the evening at six, as so much of Madison happened to, but Perkins was officially off-duty at the present time of eight-thirty

P.M. No one objected to his use of the office, however, and the desk sergeant had standing orders to rush Tracey through to him as soon as she arrived.

The detective wanted to hold this meeting on neutral ground. He had taken his work home with him enough years to realize how disrupting the practice could be, even now, when he lived alone.

As this was a Friday night, the station was a good deal more active than it had been the last time that Tracey had been there, late Wednesday morning. She reined in her own curiosity and ignored most of the comments tossed at her as she swiftly passed through the lobby and squad room into Perkins' office. Here, she found the detective and the two federal agents of the night before waiting for her.

"Hello, Ms. Lund," Perkins said. "Come in and have a seat, won't you? We were just about to call your place again."

This looked serious. All of the relaxation and pleasure that her dinner with Bobby had engendered in Tracey vanished in the time that it took her to sit. "I was out," she explained. "I just got in and read your message twenty minutes ago."

"Sorry to cut into your social schedule, but it couldn't be helped. You remember agents Fallows and Montgomery?"

The two, seated by the desk in folding chairs, nodded to her.

"Yes, of course. What's this about, Detective?"

He was blunt in response. "An employee of the Surgery Center, David Julian, was murdered last night."

Tracey gasped.

"You didn't read of it in the evening edition of the paper?" Michelle Fallows asked her.

Her head was still ringing with the shock. "No. I was busy."

"It's all over the front page," Perkins said. His opinion of the press and its self-regulated standards of restraint was clear enough in his tone.

"Did you know Julian, Tracey?" asked Montgomery.

"In a way. I knew him by sight and we'd spoken a couple of times, but that's all." At that moment, Tracey was still so stunned by David's death ("... murdered ...") that she sincerely didn't think of the ugly moments that had passed between them. "Do you know who did it? Did you catch him?"

Perkins began to answer, but Montgomery cut him off, "He was tortured to death, Tracey. He was strung up to a tree by fishing line and strategically cut open until either shock or loss of blood killed him. And an as yet unidentified young woman followed him."

With no attempt to coat the starkness of the truth, the words hit Tracey like punches. A stream of revulsion leaped into her throat, causing her to choke.

Fallows rushed to her side. "Are you okay? Are you going to be sick?"

Tracey shook her head and coughed. "No . . . I'm all right. I was just . . . taken by surprise. God, tortured to death? Here? Who's responsible, Detective Perkins?"

He turned to Montgomery. "That's why we're here. Who killed them, agent?"

This was not a concession that Russell Montgomery wanted to make at this point. He had been forced by the obstinate local investigator to reveal more than he felt was necessary or safe due to threats of exposure, and he had no doubt that Perkins would carry out those threats. As if in a final act of resistance, he walked to the office door and stood with his back to it.

Perkins understood. "No one will disturb us. This room is secure."

"Okay," Montgomery said slowly. "What I have to tell you goes no further. Do you understand?"

Perkins and Tracey stared at him, but neither said anything.

With no recourse, he plunged into the explanation. "Dr. Ansel Heywood, whom you knew so well, Tracey, was not only the most gifted surgeon in the world, he was also an employee of the intelligence community of the United States of America. For the last thirty-seven years, until his death this past December, he was the medical head of the National Board of Physical and Psychological Research and Implementation."

"I've never heard of that organization," said Perkins, without really meaning to speak.

"And you won't, not aside from tonight."

Fallows spoke up. "Even with Communism dead and buried, America and freedom generally have their enemies. We have to stay ahead of the tyrants and the real anarchists if we are to survive, and this includes utilizing the fields of medicine and science as applied to the human being physically."

"You mean things like germ warfare and artificial diseases," Tracey said in a faint, disbelieving voice.

Montgomery sighed as if weary already. "That's like saying that the most important product of harnessed fire is napalm. The Board is dedicated to solving all of the

mysteries of the human body. Dr. Heywood was responsible for advances that are to this day considered overt
science fiction by the public world."

"They've performed wonders, absolute wonders."
Fallows' tone was pregnant with awe.

"And these 'wonders' bring us two dead bodies in the
woods," Perkins interrupted flatly.

Montgomery nodded with unavoidable—if momentary—defeat. "Yes, Detective, in a real way they have.
The Board performs many services for our national gov-
ernmental structure, one of which happens to be in conjunction with the Federal Witness Protection Program.
If a witness is important enough for one reason or
another and the usual fabricated documentation and
relocation efforts are not sufficient to fully establish said
witness in a new life, the Board can be counted on to
give the person an entirely different face and body."

"Plastic surgery," Tracey said.

"Your terms are very weak for the subject again. The
Board can change appearances, certainly, but their work
goes much beyond that. They perform operations that
the most liberal of civilian physicians will swear are
impossible: they can permanently change an individual's
hair and eye color, totally erase catastrophic scarring
and birth defects, add inches to a subject's height—or
subtract them—alter the basic metabolic rate to make a
fat person thin or vice versa, and, in occasional
instances, reverse paralysis."

In a rare example of scatological phrasing, Perkins
muttered, "Mister, you're peddling pure, steaming
bullshit."

Montgomery smiled at him. "Detective, they could

change you into a white man your own mother wouldn't recognize."

"I'm not in the least interested in undergoing any substantial physical alterations."

Fallows responded with a rather wan grin. "Not all of the W.P.P. subjects are, either."

"They, the Board, have a private hospital where they do these things?" Tracey asked.

"Five of them, actually," Montgomery replied, "including the one at which you're employed."

"No." Shaking her head, Tracey set aside her purse and stood. "This is ridiculous. None of this . . . this intrigue takes place at the Center, if it goes on anywhere. I'm in the records department. I would *know*."

"You're in the records department that the facility maintains to appease the public," Fallows told her. "You must know that there are areas within the hospital where only selected staff and visitors are permitted."

"Of course, but it's that way in any hospital. There are research wings and isolation sectors and pathology departments—"

"And no one ever suspects the activities that take place in them," the other woman agreed. "It was the same at the Peekskill facility, wasn't it?"

The idea manifested itself in Tracey as a sickly emptiness in her stomach. "You mean that . . . ?"

"There, too. And three others in the Continental U.S. And each of them has more developed space below the ground level that none of the civilian employees are aware of."

"But I don't know anything about this sort of stuff."

"We believe that," Montgomery assured her. "When

your connection with this case was recognized, we checked you most thoroughly. You're not a part of the Board's activities, but your involvement with Dr. Heywood was very interesting."

"I don't know anything about all of this, either," Perkins pointed out, "and none of it is shedding any light on those corpses we found today."

"You have to understand, Detective Perkins," said Fallows, "when the tire tracks at the site matched those of the stolen car found this afternoon, Tracey became the only shred of a lead that we have to Bryant."

Montgomery shot her a cold look that warned against any further unilateral disclosures.

"Who's Bryant?" asked Tracey.

The cat was at least halfway out of the bag, so Montgomery conceded more of his hoarded information, "David Julian and the unidentified girl were murdered, we feel sure, by Calvin Peter Bryant, also known as 'the Prince of Darkness.'"

The name meant little to Tracey, who tried to connect it to "The Night Stalker," Richard Ramirez, and failed. Then, she didn't dwell on the sensational and psychotic as avidly as did much of the public.

It was a different story with Perkins. "That bastard is dead. One of your people killed him, a Taskforce man."

"I shot him," Montgomery admitted quietly. "And I did my dead level best to send him straight to Hell, but my aim was off a little. He was badly wounded, but it was clear that he would live only if extraordinary measures were enacted."

"All of the official reports said that he died."

"Reports say many things. His 'death' spared everyone the time and expense of a trial that would only have seen him escape real punishment through a verdict of insanity. There's no denying that he was as crazy as a March hare."

For all of his innate and acquired cynicism, Perkins was finding this nearly impossible to accept. "You're saying that the Serial Incident Taskforce, a federal law enforcement organization, fabricated evidence of a death just to avoid giving a suspect his Constitutional right to trial?"

"I'm not saying anything like that, Detective. The main purpose of the deception was to provide the Board with the . . . raw material for a program they'd undertaken in conjunction with a number of other agencies. It was Heywood's brainchild, in fact."

"Dr. Heywood wouldn't have anything to do with hiding a murderer and changing him," Tracey said, fully convinced of every word. "He was a good man."

"He was many things," Montgomery replied, paraphrasing himself, answering without answering. "Again, I have to warn both of you not to repeat a word of this. If you do, you'll incur federal penalties and the results that accompany them." He looked at the two with a strange expression that seemed to mix deep reluctance with the infantile joy of divulging secrets. "You wanted to know. Don't blame the messenger if the truth is not in keeping with some of your personal conceptions."

"Just go on with it," Perkins told him.

"Of course. The program that particularly interested Heywood and a number of other people in past and present administrations had to do with the recruiting, reeducating, and implementing of the perfect assassin.

Double Oh Seven isn't entirely a fantasy; there are people in this world who have the permission of their governments to kill at specific times, including people in our own nation. We call it 'wet duty.' "

"Oh God," Tracey sighed, as much in disgust as disbelief. She sat heavily in her chair once more.

Montgomery hardly noticed her reaction. "Even the most committed of patriots grows tired. The blood becomes sickening for us all. I've killed six people in the line of duty, none of them by assassination, and they're with me every night, when I close my eyes. Even the worst of them."

Perkins, who'd never shot anyone but who had to face that possibility, understood.

"I may be called upon to kill again, perhaps it will be to stop Calvin, for real this time. And while my psychological profile is among the most stable of active agents, I can see myself eating my gun someday. Excuse me, committing suicide. I couldn't imagine such a thing when I began in this work, but I can now."

Fallows looked distressed by the admission, but she said nothing.

He continued, "Heywood and his colleagues got the idea that this too-predictable burnout was due to the operatives' very rationality. It's wrong to kill people, and we—you, Mitchie, I, and the whole sane world—understand this almost from the crib. It's crazy."

"So why not recruit a crazy man to do a crazy job?" whispered Perkins.

"Exactly."

"And have a loony toon racing from victim to victim,

eager to spill blood because he believes God is telling him to do it?"

"That was the beauty of Heywood's plan, as he saw it. I'm going on supposition to a great extent, since inter-departmental cooperation is not in the ideal stage we all would wish. If we at the Taskforce had known about this plan, it never would have been undertaken, not with a subject we had bagged for them, anyway."

"Bully for you." Perkins' sarcasm was obvious by design.

"You do what's right for your world, my friend."

"I'm not your friend, 'friend.'"

"You asked, Perkins."

"Please, Mr. Perkins," Tracey found herself saying. Now it was she who had to know more, all of it.

After a moment, Montgomery went on, "No matter how we try to spread the guilt now, the program was carried out. There are between twenty-five and thirty serial killers roaming the nation in any given year, but Bryant was special; innately cunning, careful even at the height of his sick passions, capable of changing his methods from one attack to the next and willing to do so, practically instinctive in his variety of killing systems. The FBI caught him virtually by accident, and once we had him, Heywood knew that he would be the perfect subject. In addition to the Board's expertise in rearranging a person's external appearance, they have brainwashing techniques that almost defy belief, surgical, chemical, behavioral, and others beyond our ability to understand. With Bryant and his fellow subjects officially listed as dead and no longer possessed of human rights, they could do anything they wanted to with them, as they did."

"They brainwashed them?" Tracey felt as if she were in the middle of a nightmare, not reality. What did any of this have to do with her? With an eye she had received in a bottle?

"Tracey, they—or, more specifically, Dr. Heywood—changed every cell of Calvin Bryant, from the skin to the brain. He went into that hospital one person and came out another entirely."

In spite of himself, Perkins was fascinated. "Wouldn't this severe brainwashing remove the traits that made him so effective a killer in the first place?"

Montgomery smiled at his renewed interest. "You're taking the 'washing' part too literally. Through psychological and physical operations that would have driven a sane man crazy, they split Bryant into two people: one was the original, a conscienceless murderer; the second, the manufactured personality, was a 'normal' person, capable of living in the real world in a way that Calvin never could manage to copy for more than a few days at a time. The second personality was totally unaware of his true, bestial self. Heywood gave him a split personality.

"In addition, he took the man's belief in a divine voice that directed his actions and turned it to his own advantage. Ansel Heywood *became* Calvin Bryant's god, a god able to call him up from the prison of the artificial identity to enact his 'godly' will by a mere word or phrase spoken over a telephone line. Bryant was not only the perfect assassin, he was also the ultimate sleeper, an agent who had no idea he was anything out of the ordinary for ninety-nine percent of the time."

"Good lord," Perkins said.

"Isn't it amazing?" Fallows agreed. "The things that the Board is able to do are fifty or a hundred years in the future for the world at large." Obviously, she was more comfortable dealing with the abstract elements of her work rather than their bloody and too-real consequences.

"Then Heywood died, and Bryant and perhaps a dozen other sleeper agents of varying degrees of potential danger were left again without their god," Montgomery concluded.

"And Calvin Bryant is killing again, killing right here in Madison," said Tracey slowly.

"That twin bill last night has all of his signature traces."

"But, I don't understand . . . even with Dr. Heywood gone, there have to be other people who know about Bryant, who can control him when this 'governor personality' isn't strong enough."

Montgomery shook his head, clearly and honestly embarrassed. "It's an imperfect world, even in government affairs. *Especially* in government affairs. Tried to do your own taxes lately? Heywood was a multitalented genius and one of the most accomplished men that America had produced since Ben Franklin, but he was also a man of obsessions, not too far removed from the compulsive people he used in his work. Just as he presented this lovable and benevolent facade to the public—"

"It was no act," Tracey had to say. "He really was good."

"I guess, in some ways, he was. Well, he was different to everyone. We at the Taskforce didn't know what he was doing, the FBI didn't know, the President didn't know, hell, the goddamned IRS didn't, and they know if you keep dirty books under your bed. Heywood's obsessive secrecy led him to keep private records. He knew that if word of this bureau of designer killers ever escaped, all of his humanitarian efforts would be exposed the next day. I'm sorry to put it cruelly, Tracey, but practically everything in his life was an act. He kept all of the details of nine or ten of his programs in computer files that were accessible only by his encoded, private means.

"We don't know these 'special' entrance keys or the word or phrase that gave him instant control over Bryant and his brothers and sisters, just as we don't know where the maniac was set up in his new life or what false identity he was provided. Only Heywood knew how and where to contact his sleepers. We don't even know what Calvin Bryant looks like anymore."

"But he seems to have been drawn here," Fallows pointed out, "and the only connecting factor is you, Tracey."

Tracey didn't feel as if she were in a police station surrounded by trained and armed men and women. She felt desperately alone. "Because of the things he sent me, you mean."

"Yes." Montgomery left his post at the door and approached her. His demeanor seemed the essence of friendly concern. "They were each addressed to 'Brown

Eyes'; are you sure you don't remember anyone else who called you that?"

"Dr. Heywood," she answered in a barely audible voice.

"We thought so. Heywood was genuinely fond of you, and in some twisted fashion, Bryant sees you as a rival for the man's affection."

"A rival? But the doctor's *dead*."

"He had recreated himself into a god, and in the minds of people like Calvin, gods don't die."

Perkins finally appeared convinced. "All right, we'll say that we accept your scenario, that this madman is alive and here in Madison. What do we do to find him and protect Ms. Lund?"

"As to the second part, the best plan of action would be to place the young woman under continuous surveillance. Michelle can move in with you tonight, and I'm sure that Detective Perkins can provide the manpower to unobtrusively watch the apartment building for the next day or so, until we can have more members of the Taskforce flown in to take over those duties."

"Wouldn't it be better to get her safely out of town?" the policeman asked.

"In the short run, perhaps. But once she's removed, Bryant will simply resume his search."

"Then how will we find him?"

"Less simple, I'm afraid. I hate to sound cold-blooded, Tracey, but having you here as the object of his obsession will at the very least localize the danger, whereas before we had no idea where he would turn next. With that said, we can only wait for him to do something to give himself away."

"Wait for him to kill someone else, you mean," Tracey said.

Montgomery and Fallows glanced at one another, but neither attempted a reply.

"You don't have any inkling of what he looks like now?" asked Perkins. "I find that unbelievable, Montgomery. Certainly there must have been other doctors on the Board who at least helped with the surgeries. Heywood couldn't have done it all himself."

"He had all of the help he needed, some of the best medical minds in the world, but this was no democratic undertaking, Detective. Heywood had the final word in every case, and he did keep all of the secrets. None of the other physicians even knew who they were working on at any particular moment. The ultimate facial designs came from Heywood's brilliance through his own hands. He kept all of his records in computerized form, and these self-destructed when we attempted to tap them. The Witness Protection Program doesn't even have copies of the damned near perfect documentation that they provided for the first eight or twelve subjects. Bryant could be anyone in Madison tonight, black, white, or Asian, young or old, and when he's in his artificial 'normal' mode he wouldn't even know it himself."

"Fingerprints?" Perkins interjected with something of a futile tone.

"Would you have us printing the entire male population of the city, Detective? Besides, according to reliable reports, even his fingerprints were totally and permanently altered."

"That's impossible."

"Does that word continue to have any meaning now?"

A sudden rap on the office door broke the spell of shadowy illusion that had engulfed all four. Montgomery touched his lips in a meaningful manner.

"Yes?" Perkins called.

The door opened, and a heavyset young man with an already severely receding hairline stepped into the room. "Sorry to interrupt, Perkins, but you wanted to know if anything hinky came in."

Adrenaline was injected into the bloodstreams of the three officers. "Another murder?" Perkins asked.

"Nah, it's that Peeping Tom again. The fella who phoned it in was screaming blue murder, all right, but most likely it's the same sicko who broke into the Seger home a couple of nights ago. I thought it might be of interest to you, anyway."

All three visibly relaxed. "Who's catching?" Perkins responded.

"Knight and Walters."

"All right. Thank you, Nathan."

When the man had closed the door again, Tracey asked, "You don't think that could be him?"

Fallows shook her head. "Doesn't fit the profile. Bryant was a doer, not a peeper. Even in his earliest crimes, he never stopped at merely looking."

"While we have to suspect almost everyone, we also have to remember that there will continue to be the regular criminal elements operating," Montgomery said.

"It's probably Stubbins, anyway," she concluded to herself.

The words fell like bombs in the quiet room. Perkins spoke first, "Ms. Lund, do you have some information concerning this offender?"

Tracey wanted to bite her tongue, but it was too late for that. She'd violated a promise and didn't feel right about giving them anything more. "Not really."

"Ms. Lund, I understand how disoriented you must be feeling right now. It's knocked me for a loop, too. But if we're to accept what we've been told—and there are two very real and very dead bodies as evidence of it—we can't keep any potentially useful knowledge secret any longer. Did you say that someone named Stubbins was involved in some incident that might be connected to the case?" Though he wouldn't admit it, "Stubbins" was a familiar name to him: he had encountered it while investigating all of the new arrivals to the Rosewell Apartments.

She sighed. "I'm not ethically free to tell you anything more. I'm sorry."

Perkins' interest kindled a fire in the federal agents, as well. "Tracey, this is far from a normal situation," Michelle reminded her. "If you know anything . . ."

The professional side of Tracey Lund was convinced that she had revealed too much already and that Dexter Stubbins was in no way associated with the wild story she had heard tonight. The emotional side countered that even if Stubbins weren't a hidden killer, he needed to be taken out of daily human society anyway, before he had the opportunity to graduate from voyeurism to worse activities. All three of the officers stared at her, their eyes like weapons focused upon her face.

"Tracey?" Fallows asked softly.

"All right. Some mental health care professional I'd make, caving in like a paper house." She licked her lips. "I believe that the Peeping Tom is the same man who was causing all of the trouble in the apartment building when you arrived last night, Dexter Stubbins."

"What makes you think so?" Perkins asked.

One step over the line was as bad as a mile, she decided. She told them the entire story, just as Stubbins had recounted it in Thursday's session. Her account was much briefer, of course, but it seemed just as mesmerizing to them as it had been to her. And when she finished with an explanation of what had occurred in the man's apartment on Thursday evening, she was surprised to find how deadly serious they appeared to be taking the tale.

"Could it be him?" Fallows asked her partner in a voice that sounded more than a little hopeful.

Montgomery mulled it over. "Yes. It could. Bryant was not a voyeur, but he was an accomplished housebreaker when he wanted something—or someone—inside." He looked to Tracey. "Did you say that Stubbins was recommended to this therapy group by Heywood himself?"

"Yes, but I don't know how significant that might be. All four of the newcomers arrived with Dr. Heywood's endorsement."

"All of them?"

"It's common practice. As you said, the doctor had a number of hospitals around the country that he used to perform reconstructive surgery, and Madison received many of his recovering patients from the other facilities each year." Her voice fell. "We just didn't know what else he was doing to his patients in those hospitals."

"It makes sense," observed Montgomery, "it could be some deep programming that he hid in each of them: if they didn't receive specific instructions after a certain amount of time, they would automatically return to the base hospital."

"Jesus, that would help us out," said Fallows excitedly. "That fiasco earlier last night might have been a trial run for what he accomplished on Julian and the girl."

"What does Stubbins look like?" Montgomery asked.

"Does it matter?" Tracey answered. "If he's Bryant, he's had plastic surgery—"

"It will help us to recognize him *tonight!*"

"Oh, yes, um, he's white, about thirty or thirty-five, I suppose, and pretty large, around six feet and a hundred and seventy or eighty pounds. He says that he's from Maine, but his accent sounds more Midwestern."

"That doesn't fit very closely with Bryant's physical profile," Perkins stated. "He was average height and slim, wasn't he?"

"Meant nothing to Heywood," responded Montgomery. "With leg and spinal grafts, he could add half a foot to a subject. This might be him, Perkins! Can we get in on the search?"

Tracey had never seen the aloof detective so excited as he appeared to be at this moment. "You're damned right we can. Just let me find out where the report originated."

The office was suddenly alive with excitement, and Tracey felt like an intruder once more. She hoped to God that they caught Stubbins or Bryant or whoever he was before he could hurt anyone else, but she wasn't too sure she wanted to be here when they brought him in.

Perkins was sliding into his jacket when he noticed her. "Ms. Lund, your help has been invaluable. I can't ask you to accompany us, but if you wouldn't mind waiting here to make an identification—"

"Tonight?" she asked.

"Well, it doesn't have to be tonight."

"Then I'd like to go home. I'll come back in the morning."

"Certainly. I'd prefer that you didn't spend the night alone." He looked to Michelle Fallows. It was clear that there was no chance of the federal agent accompanying Tracey to the apartment when she might be in on the capture of Calvin Bryant.

"My roommate's back from her business trip."

Perkins worked his jaw slowly. "Shoot me for being a male chauvinist pig, but I'm not much more comfortable with the thought of two untrained women alone."

A thought came to Tracey. It was a thought that she had been suppressing for several days but one that seemed to be the perfect solution now. "I'll stay in another apartment, with a friend. Even if he gets by you, he won't know where to look for me."

He gave her a quick nod. "Good idea. Now, if you'll excuse us, we have about fifteen miles to drive in as short amount of time as possible."

Neither of the federal agents said a word to her as they left, but she wasn't thinking about them, anyway. Instead, she was hoping that tonight might prove to be a sort of liberation for her even as it put an end to the awful career of the Prince of Darkness.

Chapter Thirteen

Tracey spoke briefly to Delia when she arrived at the Rosewell building, and she made the other woman promise to check every door and window lock twice before she went to bed (though Delia's promises generally were about as reliable as tomorrow's weather report). She wasn't really very worried about her roommate's safety or her own, however. After the scene with Stubbins on Thursday night, the management had tightened the lax security in the building, including warning tenants on all floors to keep their windows closed and locked. Bryant wouldn't find it so easy to waltz inside this time, even if he possessed Stubbins' doorkey.

When she told Delia that she hoped to stay overnight with another friend, the opportunity to infer an identity hadn't been lost on Ms. McKenzie. She said goodnight with, "Don't do anything I wouldn't do."

As if I could, Tracey thought.

It was still early, a little after eleven, when she knocked on Bobby's door. He was awake, and he answered in his robe and underwear.

"Good evening, Mr. Preston," she said brightly. "Would you happen to be busy this evening?"

He grinned. "Right now I'm about ten minutes into my eighth viewing of 'The Poseidon Adventure.' Have you ever seen it?"

"No, but I've always wanted to."

He stepped aside and waved one arm before him. "Be my guest. The popcorn is on the house."

The scene of this night's attempted break-in was on the opposite side of the city from Wednesday's episode, but in terrain it was not much different than that one . . . or much different than the spot where David Julian and some poor unidentified girl had met with their terrible fates.

Montgomery was thinking about this as he sat in the front seat next to Perkins, who was rocketing the unmarked car along the empty, tree-lined highway. "If she'd told us what was going on when we arrived last night, those two people might be alive now," he said darkly.

Perkins' eyes never left the road ahead of them. "If she'd known just what in the shit was going on, she would have called us when the man made his confession at the hospital, Agent Montgomery. Let's not try to localize the blame when there's so much of it to spread around, all right?"

"*Touché.*"

"This is no game, man. It may be only another chapter in your memoirs, but to the people of Madison, this is very serious. When Bryant kills one of us, there is no Dr. Heywood Frankenstein or Board of Impossible Medicine waiting to restore life and provide us with brand new identities."

Montgomery's reply was cold. "I didn't mean to imply that I wasn't completely serious myself, Detective, or that Tracey bore any responsibility."

"We're not even sure that this guy is Bryant," Fallows added from the rear of the vehicle.

"Who else, Mitchie? A second of Heywood's pigeons returning home independently? Isn't that stretching coincidence a little thin?"

"Why should it be? We know that there are at least six sleepers out there, maybe twice or three times that, and only five safe hospitals. Hell, they may *all* be in Madison."

"Good point," Perkins noted.

"Let's just deal with the devil we know, shall we?" Montgomery suggested.

The call had come into the precinct from the home of Reese and Penny Satterfield approximately twenty-five minutes earlier. Though this house, too, was isolated in the midst of the deep, old-growth forest that rose in almost every direction from the heart of Madison, it did fall within the jurisdiction of the city police. The land in this sector had been appropriated by the city three months before in preparation for the construction of a large mall.

When Perkins and his passengers arrived, a patrol car already was sitting in the front drive with its lights casting blue circles into the quiet woods. A pair of officers were standing next to it taking the statements of two irate homeowners.

The patrolmen recognized Perkins immediately and gave him what they'd learned so far. "It looks like our boy," the first officer, Kendall, G., according to his uniform tag, said. "Description sounds the same, five-ten to six feet, one-eighty, dark hair, pale complexion. He apparently peeked at two or more front windows before jacking the back door lock and coming inside. One of the children was in the kitchen with the lights off, and the perp failed to notice him as he entered. The boy screamed, which brought Mr. Satterfield on the run. The perp broke for the door and took off across the back yard."

"He escaped?" Montgomery asked.

"Yes, sir, but we were just about to scout—"

"He got away, but he's marked!" Reese Satterfield told them with a sort of angry joy. "He ran smack into our satellite dish while I was going to get my gun."

His wife elbowed him. It was an unregistered gun.

"He hit it so hard that it was knocked off-line," the man continued swiftly. "I flashed it with my four-cell and saw what I'm pretty sure is blood."

"So he's probably hurt," Kendall said. "What would you like to do, Detective? Go after him?"

"That's right, Patrolman," replied Perkins. "You put in a call for backup, as much as they can get here as soon as they can roll, by my authorization, and when they arrive, you and your partner start a sweeping maneuver from the east; go out fifty yards."

The young policeman stared at him.

"Do you have a hearing defect, patrolman?"

"No, sir, but you want how much backup?" the officer asked.

"The fucking National Guard, if they're available," Fallows answered him brusquely. "We're going to get this bastard *tonight*."

"As many people as possible," said Perkins. "We have reason to believe that this man is extremely dangerous, so conduct yourselves accordingly. Dogs and helicopters might prove helpful if they are available. Is that clear?"

"Yes, sir!" Kendall snapped.

Mrs. Satterfield covered her mouth with her hands and then ran back into the house to find her children.

"Mr. Satterfield, I'll ask you to gather your family together and present all of those guns of yours to one of these good officers. Then we'll get you out of here and safely into town as soon as possible."

"Who is this guy, goddamned Rambo?" the man demanded.

"Worse: he's real." Perkins turned to the second patrolman. "This is Agent Fallows and her partner, Agent Montgomery. We're going into the forest where the suspect was last seen. Advise the backup team of our presence so that they won't put a few rounds into us."

"You got it, sir."

He glanced at the federal operatives. "Ready?"

"You bet your behind," Fallows answered. She seemed more eager to be after Stubbins than Montgomery did.

With the two heavy flashlights from Perkins' car, the trio circled the house and raced across the backyard, which was littered with toys and the other predictable debris of the prowling grounds of younger children.

The black, ten-foot diameter satellite dish was cemented into the earth some sixty feet from the rear porch, and a swath of treetops had been lopped off to prevent their interference along the satellite arc. The moonless night made the structure virtually invisible. The three stopped next to it and swept the lights over its steel mesh surface.

"There," said Michelle. "Yeah, oh yeah, that's blood. See it?"

The men looked at the dark and glistening splotch that was running down the solid rim of the dish from a point about six feet from the ground.

"He's hurt good," she observed.

"Let's go," Perkins told them.

Montgomery leaned close to his right ear. "You know, I wish we could have kept this operation smaller. With as much commotion as your orders are bound to create, there will be a lot of difficult questions asked about tonight."

Perkins snorted in surprise and a little disgust. "Damn it, man, do you really believe you can keep a lid on this? After all that this animal has done to this community?"

"That was the idea," Montgomery answered.

"Just don't shoot me in the back. Let's go."

Where the lot had been cleared for the house, a thick curtain of brambles had grown up along its edges. In pushing through this curtain during his escape, Stubbins had left a clear indentation, and the three swiftly followed through it. Beyond the relatively dense ring of growth, the vegetation was sharply reduced by the permanent canopy that the intertwining branches of the ancient trees created overhead.

Their freedom of movement was much greater here, as all that they had to avoid were the tree trunks themselves. Tracking Stubbins became more difficult, however, due to the fact that the rich layer of duff didn't take footprints too well. They decided to push forward in a straight line.

For a few yards, this proved to be the right move, because they were able to pick out drops of damp blood in the rotting carpet of leaves, but this disappeared too soon. Using the lights of the house as a rear locus, the three tried to keep their straight course on a southern angle, reasoning that a panicked Stubbins wouldn't have been thinking clearly enough to try any evasive action.

No one spoke. The night was quiet inside the trees, with the leaves and needles absorbing their footfalls. The starlight was shut out from above, and only the two flashlights kept them from becoming totally disoriented.

Each imagined what the night might become for Stubbins, who was frightened, hurt, and effectively blind. Rather than making them more secure with their chances of finding and taking him, however, thoughts of this particular man being reduced to sheer animal terror acted only to increase their own fears.

It was like being trapped in a black cage with a wounded panther.

Perkins stayed in the point position. He knew that Stubbins had a car, and he also figured that it had to be parked somewhere nearby. Was this the right direction?

Was there even a road this far back, or did the forest run all the way to Chesapeake Bay? The backups would be rolling in any minute, but would their presence increase the chances of catching the maniac or only the chances of the plainclothes officers being shot by their own reinforcements? Maybe Perkins had oversold the urgency of the circumstances a tad.

Ten minutes into the search, Perkins brought it to a stop. He realized that soon they would have to retrace their steps or risk becoming lost until daybreak.

Montgomery inadvertently made his decision for him. "Don't stop here, Detective. If he slips through our fingers again, not even the programming that Heywood tortured into him will keep this creature in the Madison vicinity."

"Will you shut up and listen?" It was not really a plan, but it was all that he could come up with to counter Montgomery's demands.

They stopped talking and held their breaths. For several heartbeats, not even the background music of insects disturbed the silence. Then, even while the sense of defeat was becoming too strong to ignore, the sound of a large body crushing ground debris came faintly to them from at least a hundred yards away. They all heard it, and in the glow of the flashlights, they all saw it in one another's eyes.

"Over there," whispered Perkins. He moved to his left.

The tree limb whipped from behind the first trunk he approached and crashed into the policeman's midsection with the speed and impact of a baseball bat. His breath burst from his body in a shrill groan, and he was thrown backwards into Fallows. The flashlight in his left hand and the gun in his right pitched forward into the night with equal impetus. Michelle cried out in pain and lost her gun when they slammed into the ground together.

"Son of a bitch!" Montgomery shouted. He managed to avoid the collision ahead by resorting to a wild backwards dance. "Mitchie! Perkins!" His training forced him to hold his position and swing the second flashlight about madly in search of the source of the attack.

Had the limb struck Perkins higher, it certainly would have broken some ribs and possibly fractured his sternum, a potentially deadly injury in itself. Had it connected lower—well, he didn't want to consider that kind of damage.

Striking him in the stomach had caused a tremendous amount of pain but not enough real injury to incapacitate him. He felt as if his body had been caught in a gigantic scissors, yet he was able to roll off of the woman behind him a second after knocking her to the ground and falling on top of her. He was going to vomit, but later, when he had the time.

"Perkins, where is he?" roared Montgomery.

With no air in his lungs, he couldn't answer. In the same way that Fitzsimmons' "solar plexus punch" had momentarily paralyzed Corbett and won him the title, Perkins was rendered dead from the waist down. His arms worked, though, so that when he saw the attacker looming above him, a dark cloud filling the already blotted sky, he managed to throw out one hand and catch the man's left leg.

The attacker dived to the ground between Perkins and Fallows.

"Russ! He's here!" Fallows screamed. "Get him, for God's sake!"

Montgomery tried, and, in doing so, he tripped over his partner and plunged face forward to the earth himself.

Of the four people in the forest, the attacker was the least hurt at that moment. Both flashlights were useless by then, still burning but lying several feet away and illuminating nothing other than strips of decaying duff and the bottoms of tree trunks. So Perkins felt as much as he saw the large body next to him when it struggled first to its knees and then to its feet. The long and heavy tree branch scraped painfully against the side of his neck as the attacker pulled it high into the air.

The three law enforcement officers had come into the woods with guns, but it seemed as if a simple wooden club would create an end to the confrontation.

Perkins tried to call out a warning, but his lungs were still too empty to allow his voice to function. Vaguely, he could see the federal agents entangled with one another. Then the heavy branch moved through the night to a point above them like the hammer of some forgotten Norse god. It wouldn't take much to kill the pair of them, perhaps no more than two strokes.

Perkins' right hand darted to his right leg and fought to work beneath his pants. As the club began its downward swing, he jerked free the four-inch knife that had been holstered to his calf and lurched to his side, blindly slashing it before him. It struck home and pulled loose from his grip.

The man standing over him screamed so piercingly

that it sounded as if his larynx had split in two. His left leg buckled in agony, so that the branch thudded to the ground wide of either of its targets. The attacker continued to shriek as he dropped the club altogether and clutched the butt of the knife with both hands.

Perkins rolled to his stomach and tried to drag his unresponsive lower body out of danger.

"Goddamn you, goddamn you!" screamed the man. "I'll cut your frigging eyes out! Jesus!" The ear-numbing wail shattered the night once more while he pulled the knife from his leg. "I'll kill you!"

Perkins cast his hands out desperately for one of the guns that had fallen to the ground.

"I'll kill you!" the man repeated in fury and agony. He fell towards Perkins with the knife thrust before him.

A gunshot thundered only a few feet from Perkins. On his stomach, he didn't see the shot itself, but the muzzle fire lit the ground around him like a July Fourth rocket exploding. He had just begun to breathe again when the large body of a man who was trying to kill him dropped out of the sky like a 747 and emptied his lungs again.

"Mitchie, are you all right?" Montgomery yelled.

Her reply came amid a series of gasps, "I'm okay . . . okay. You get . . . him? You kill him?"

"I think so! Where's the damned flashlight? Perkins? Where are you?"

Perkins didn't try to answer this time, because he was employing all of his depleted strength to rotate to his back and then shove the man's body off of his own. What if it weren't Stubbins? What if they'd stumbled on some moonshining redneck or a pot farmer?

The feeling began to return to his lower body like pulses of acid in his arteries.

Montgomery found a light. "Where the hell are you, Perkins?"

"Here," he whispered laboriously. "I think you killed him."

The flashlight stabbed through the blackness and collided with Perkins' wide pupils. He hissed and Montgomery pulled the beam down onto the body that he had just pushed from himself.

"He fits the description of Stubbins," the agent said. "I sure hope he has the right ID on him somewhere, because if we just blew away some poor local jackass who was defending his property against trespassers—"

"But is it him?" asked Fallows, climbing to her knees. "Is it Bryant? You've seen him in person, Russ!"

Montgomery ran the light down the limp form and then rolled the body over to study the face, which was soaked in blood. "He's big, bigger than I remember Bryant."

"You said Heywood could have made him taller," she reminded her partner.

"Yes, but—"

"And he could have gained weight. It could have been something like a posthypnotic suggestion."

For the first time, in spite of the darkness, Perkins could see the naked fear that each of these people held toward Calvin Bryant. They were desperate to have his lifeless corpse in their hands.

"It could be him," Montgomery admitted. "It probably is." He reached into the man's pants pocket, came out with a wallet, and shined the light on it. "Stubbins, Dexter Ryan, Jonesport, Maine," he read aloud. "Well, our asses are in the clear, in any case. This is the man we came out after, and he attacked us first."

Perkins asked the next logical question. "Is he dead?"

"Damn!" Montgomery whispered, angry with himself. He touched the man's carotid artery and then placed a finger beneath his nose. "By God, he is alive. My shot got him above the right ear, but it didn't penetrate, glanced off."

"Then I suggest we get him to a hospital." Crawling to a tree, Perkins used the trunk as a ladder to help him stand. His lower body felt as if his insides had been removed and the void filled with dead mud.

"Kill him," Fallows whispered.

"What?" Perkins asked, shocked.

"Kill him, Russ!" Her voice grew louder. "You have to make up for the first time: you could have stopped him then, but you didn't! Shoot the animal!"

Montgomery was still standing above the motionless body.

"Don't be a fool, Montgomery," Perkins warned him.

The other man's voice sounded strangely empty when he responded, "She's right. It's my fault that those people are dead. If I had done the job the first time, none of this would have happened." He was still holding his gun in his right hand.

Perkins couldn't believe what was about to happen. "That's ridiculous. *You* didn't put Bryant back on the street. And what if this isn't him? Are you ready to kill an innocent man to ease your conscience?"

That triggered Montgomery's ingrained responses. "No." He holstered his weapon.

Michelle closed her eyes.

"Let's get some help out here," Perkins said. "Maybe it's all over. Let's go home."

Chapter Fourteen

The night flowed through Tracey with all of the joy and tenderness that she could have dreamed of having. Bobby was not in the least upset by the interruption that Detective Perkins had caused in their evening together, an evening that both of them had known could develop into this. He understood the police, he assured her, and none of the disruptions that they were so fond of creating were either new or particularly aggravating to him.

Tracey and Bobby had talked at first, with the low murmur of the television as background. They easily picked up the threads of the evening that had begun, really, during that Wednesday night in the laundry room (how romantic a setting). They laughed. They shared some surprisingly similar stories from their pasts. They nibbled at bread and cheese that Bobby had bought in anticipation of such an evening, and they sipped wine.

It all seemed right.

When the time arrived, they moved into the bedroom with unspoken understanding. Bobby's arm was around Tracey's shoulders, and his hand was softly caressing her breast. She wondered if he ached for her the way that her body longed for his. She guided his fingers to the buttons of her blouse.

But he hesitated. "I probably should keep my mouth shut," he told her quietly, "but, damn, I know what this means today, Tracey. I realize there are things you need to hear from me."

At that moment, her needs were so powerful and her trust in him so great that the questions hadn't crossed her mind.

He continued, "They tested us inside, every six months, and they segregated the infected. Canada is proud of having a progressive society, but prison is prison, you know? Things happen in jail. That's one of the reasons for my bad-ass attitude and the beard: I needed them both in there.

"I didn't do any of the drugs, and I didn't sleep with other guys, Tracey. My tests came back clean every time, no signs of any of the usual venereal diseases or of AIDS. I'm clean, but I'm also prepared, so that you don't have to feel uncomfortable." He stepped to the dresser and opened the top drawer.

She took his shoulders from behind and turned him to face her. "You talk too much," she whispered.

Stanley Hollis couldn't sleep. It certainly wasn't the absence of Dexter in the other bedroom—he'd never met the man before the manager had arranged for the two of them to share this apartment to help to defray their expenses, and after what he had learned about Stubbins' sleepwalking activities, Stanley felt a lot better being on his own. What was bothering him and preventing him from sleeping was what he, Stanley Hollis, had done.

He had taken advantage of Tracey's best friend.

Oh, sure, Delia had invited him into the apartment and offered him the alcohol, but he could have refused. He was the man, and a man was always in charge. He also knew how important it was to be even more than just a man, to be a gentleman, as well. He owed her an apology.

The next time he saw her, in the hallway or in the parking lot as she left for work, he would do what he must, no matter how embarrassing it might prove to be . . . No, not "next time." He should do this right now. Tonight.

It was late, and Delia probably would be in bed, but this was more important than the hour. He couldn't allow her to spend even one night believing him to be a cad who had been prepared to use her and then abandon her without giving a thought to her feelings. That was not how he defined himself as a person, and he wanted to be certain that it would not be her interpretation of him, either.

(One of the points that Dr. Stafford had made quite strongly during their private sessions was that Stanley gave too much weight to the opinions of others when evaluating his own self-image. In order to return to full, confident functioning in society, he would have to forge his concept of a good life from within, while acknowledging but not becoming a slave to the assessments of the outside world. That made plenty of sense, but for tonight he chose to ignore it.)

Stanley got out of bed and slipped on his robe. Prepared to apologize and correct any misassumptions that Delia had formed about his character, he strode into the bathroom to comb his hair. There he caught sight of himself in the mirror.

Was this really the picture he wished to present to her, especially at this time of night?

With his robe over his pajamas, he resembled a . . . libertine readied for activity, a figure out of touch with the social times as a similarly clad Hugh Hefner appeared on some ancient TV rerun. By gosh, he would have to dress, if only to keep from reinforcing the false impression she had of him the instant she opened her door.

And if he were going to dress, shouldn't he shower, as well? The image he wanted to impart, his true image, was that Stanley Hollis was a clean and honorable individual, not some alley cat for whom a morning's bath was sufficient for the remainder of the day.

The shower, plus time spent drying and combing his hair, brushing his teeth, using mouthwash, applying deodorant, and dressing, took the better part of an hour. It was getting deeper and deeper into the night, but he couldn't turn back from his commitment now; Delia might never see him for the real person he was, if he allowed her to go to sleep thinking that he was someone entirely different.

Bracing himself—this was no easy task for the so recently injured man to do—he made a final check in the mirror before leaving his apartment. He was already rehearsing his apology as he closed the door.

To his surprise, the building was not quietly asleep, at least not entirely. He met Rowena Carr on the staircase.

"Stanley Hollis," she said with a pleased smile. "It's after midnight. What in the world are you doing up at this hour?"

"It is Friday night," he replied, unable to resist applying a rakish hint to his answer.

"You don't have insomnia, too, do you? God, I wouldn't wish this on my worst enemy. I'll bet I haven't slept more than three hours a night since my accident."

Stanley surely didn't want to talk about accidents right then. He politely waited on the landing and exchanged pleasantries with Rowena, though he was longing to be about his business (strange, it definitely seemed more like a "longing" than a duty). Rowena was a rather attractive young woman, if a bit large and . . . well, broader than someone like Delia McKenzie or Tracey Lund. The plastic surgery that had restored her face was still a bit in evidence in the tension of the skin around her eyes and jaw line, but Stanley knew how unrealistic it was to rely on surface appearances when forming impressions of others.

What came the closest in Rowena to annoying Stanley was her almost incessant chattering.

"It gets pretty lonely, you can believe me, wandering these halls and others like them by yourself," she was saying at the moment, without waiting for a response or even offering him the opportunity. "But I'm alive and relatively well, and it certainly could have turned out differently, couldn't it?"

"Anyone who has experienced a close call can understand—" he began.

"You know, it's not all bad, though, being the only one awake while everybody else sleeps. You find out things about people. I even heard Stubbins leaving and coming in by the window the other night, and I'll bet you didn't. Did you?"

"Actually, I didn't, but Dexter and I weren't really friends as much as acquaintances, so that we didn't keep up with one another's activities—"

"Wasn't that *something*?" Her face glowed with illicit delight. "It turns out he was a Peeping Tom! Can you imagine what might have happened right here, to one of us, if he hadn't decided to confess it all in a session? When you stop and think that you saw him here every day and sat with him in that dark room during session—"

As much as it went against his personal code of behavior, Stanley realized that he had to interrupt the woman if he were to get anything accomplished tonight. "Please excuse me, Rowena. I'm, uh, expected upstairs, and I'm late as it is."

Her smile didn't fade, but it did take on a shade of melancholy. "Sure, don't let me hold you up. I've got things to do, too, you know. After all, I've only been here less than a week, which means that there are places yet to be explored, secrets to ferret out."

That sounded comforting. "Well, goodnight," Stanley said, suddenly feeling even more the royal heel.

"Right. G'night." She moved to the staircase, but rather than climbing toward the second floor with him, she went down, where only the laundry room and the cellar awaited.

He watched her for a moment. So lonely and so cut off from human contact. He thought this without once realizing its appropriateness when applied to his own life.

There was little time for reflection, however, because it was getting very late now and he was being drawn to Delia's apartment by his desire to correct the wrong impression she'd formed of him. Or something.

It was at the door itself that he nearly lost his nerve. What was he doing here? So she believed him to be a cheap womanizer. Weren't there worse things in life, like being labeled a thief or a pervert? Wouldn't coming here at this hour present a false image in itself?

In the silence of the corridor, he faintly heard the sounds of a television from the other side of the door. It had to be tuned quite loudly, because the walls of these apartments were almost soundproof. This, in turn, meant that it was likely she was still awake. It was hard to believe that she could sleep to that racket. Taking a fortifying breath, he knocked.

She answered surprisingly quickly. Dressed now in an attractive negligee covered by a delicate, virtually diaphanous robe, she held a water glass in one hand, and the look in her heavy-lidded eyes told Stanley that she was well on her way to being drunk. Her hair was mussed, her bearing less than alert, and her smile was slow, somehow off-center.

And she was beautiful.

Stanley was practically assaulted by her beauty. As

277

was common in brain injury cases like his, much of his earlier life was more of a dream than a true memory to him—a television show he had once enjoyed—but he knew with a kind of inborn certainty that he'd never been this close to a more attractive woman. His own body began to react in embarrassing ways that he hoped she couldn't notice.

"There you are," she said in a tone of slowly realized pleasure. "Come in."

He coughed into one hand, smelling mouthwash. "Thank you, but I can't, Ms. McKenzie," he told her. "It's much too late. I only came to apologize for my behavior. Earlier this evening."

"Apologize?" she repeated. "For what? If everyone was as gentlemanly as you, ha, there might not be a human race. Come on in here." Before he could refuse again, she grasped his shirt in her free hand and pulled him inside, shoving the door shut with her left foot. It was a remarkable display of balance and coordination under the circumstances. "You're not getting away this time."

She led him to the sofa once more while he tried to remember why he should have protested. They sat.

"Did I ever thank you for going out of your way to deliver Tracey's message?" she asked.

"Yes, you did, before . . ."

"Well, thanks. It was above and beyond the call of duty. Tracey's not here now, either." She leaned close to him. "Don't let it get around, but my roommate has herself a boyfriend, and a good looker, too."

Stanley felt really warm. "That's not any of my business."

Delia set her glass aside, as she had done earlier in the evening. "Do you think I'm pretty, uh . . . ?"

"Stanley," he supplied.

"Well?"

"I think you're very pretty, Ms. McKenzie." He sighed to himself. "I think you're the most beautiful woman I know."

She patted his shoulder. His flesh tingled with the touch of hers, even through the material of his shirt. "Thanks, Stanley," she said. "I needed to hear that."

"I meant it," he added quietly.

She looked deeply into his eyes, and the haze of drunkenness that had compromised the striking definition of her features evaporated like fog before a brilliant sunrise. "You do mean it, don't you?" she whispered. Then, before he could react, she leaned forward even more and kissed him on the lips.

Stanley seemed paralyzed throughout the lingering touch of her mouth on his, but inside his soul was running wild. His heart raced, and blood pounded deafeningly in his ears. He kept his eyes open, as if to assure himself that this was really happening, while Delia closed hers. He tasted the wine on her lips.

This close, he could tell that she had removed her makeup since his visit of a couple of hours before. Even without it, she was more beautiful than any fantasy that had ever drifted through his mind.

An erection began to swell between his legs, and it brought with it the wonderful discomfort that normally came to him only in his dreams. This was wrong, they weren't married or even dating, they'd met only tonight. But it felt so powerful and natural that the reasons for its shamefulness faded from his immediate thoughts.

How could it be wrong, really, when it came from so deeply within his heart? Could such a marvelous sensation ever be wrong when its origins were in purely natural instinct? No one ever lectured or condemned animals for engaging in the same natural behavior, so why wasn't he as a human being accorded the same rights as an animal?

It was only when Delia pulled away from the moment that Stanley closed his own eyes. He wanted to hold on to the living memory with his imagination, and he couldn't accept the idea of actually facing her after what he had just allowed to occur. "I'm sorry," he whispered.

"What?" Her confusion seemed genuine.

"I'm . . . I came here to apologize, not to become involved again. I'm sorry that I took advantage of you."

She laughed, but it was sweet in his ears. "You darling little boy! You feel you've taken advantage of *me?*"

"I'm the man," he said, reciting statements that had been used to form his character, "it was up to me to stop the situation before it came to this. Since I didn't, it's my fault. Actually, I shouldn't be here now, at this time of night, but I lied to you and to myself. I told myself that I was coming up here to apologize when really all I wanted was to see you again and to be close to you. I'll leave before—"

Her laughter came again. Once more, it failed to hurt or anger him, as laughter had affected him so regularly since his accident. "Stanley, if you insist on walking out on me again, after all that I've been through today, I suppose I'll just have to go into the bathroom and slit my wrists."

He opened his eyes, and there was a look of panic in them.

"I was *joking*. Stanley, can't you tell that I've been chasing you all evening? I like you, and right now I honestly and totally *need* you. I'm a big girl, you don't have to protect me from anything. Just be with me, okay?"

His voice seemed to escape from his command and hide in the darker regions of his mind. "I-I don't . . ."

Delia slid closer to him on the sofa. She gently slipped one smooth white arm about his shoulders and felt his tensed muscles beneath her touch. She really did feel an attraction to this poor, neurotic kid, and it now became a sort of challenge, as well.

"You've never been with a woman, have you?" she asked softly.

"That's not really the, um, issue . . ."

"There's nothing wrong with being inexperienced. Aren't we all at one time? Hell, today it's an absolute advantage."

Stanley closed his eyes again and dropped his head. "I have beliefs . . . well, my family had beliefs, and I can't let them down because I'm too weak to resist . . . I'm not a homosexual."

She looked to the bulge in his loose trousers. "I never believed you were." Then she touched his erection lightly with the fingers of her left hand.

A moan escaped his lips as he drew his face up and back, toward the ceiling. "Please."

"It's not wrong, Stanley." Delia kept her voice low

and soothing. He was a child, and children must be guided. She undid the front of her negligee. "It's the most natural thing in the world. Here." She took his hand and brought it to her breasts, moving it in slow circles that encompassed each of them in her private joy. Through him, she began to masturbate.

His breath came fast through his clenched teeth, but he didn't open his eyes.

She wanted to take his other hand and welcome it between her own legs, but she was thinking of Stanley now, too. She moved her free hand to his stomach and from there to his thighs, always touching, clasping, massaging with the growing rhythm that she also was employing with his hand on her breasts. Then, bringing herself through stimulation and waking dreams to the beginnings of a climax, she squeezed him harshly.

He came with no warning, and his entire body shook with the intensity of his orgasm, an experience he couldn't recall ever undergoing while conscious. He clutched her to his chest and buried his face between her aroused breasts. His strength was startling.

When it was over, Stanley fell away from the woman as if totally drained of breath and energy.

"Baby, let's do it together, please," Delia gasped in her own need.

There was no indication that he heard her, however, for he turned away to the end of the sofa, drew up his legs in a near-fetal position, and began to cry.

Delia was stunned. "Baby?" she asked, unable to remember his name. "What's wrong, honey? Didn't mean to upset you."

"It's me," he mumbled through his tears. "I did it wrong—too soon, I don't know anything . . ."

She smiled and eased her aching body next to him. "Oh, my sweet baby, this is just the beginning. Don't . . . no, don't cry anymore. We have the whole night. Come with me now. There's so much to try, so much to enjoy."

Still shaken slightly by sobs, Stanley Hollis rose from the sofa at the beckoning of this living dream and followed her into her bedroom.

Tracey and Bobby made love in his bed with both urgency and gentleness. Passion infused them like fire, but they used it to the heightening of their own pleasure. Each of them needed someone desperately, and they filled this emptiness in one another, at least for tonight.

And maybe for even longer.

Bobby knew a woman's body, and he knew how to give pleasure as well as how to ask for it. Tracey had had boyfriends in the past, and from time to time, she had given herself to them; but she'd never felt anything like this with them. It was wonderful. It was like seeing the sun for the first time.

Especially important were the times that they spent simply holding one another. She had first been attracted to the man by the ease with which she was able to talk to him. Tonight, he proved that this was a basic facet of his personality rather than a selfish mask. They spoke in the darkness of their lives in the past and their dreams for the future.

And then they again made love like hormone-driven teenagers.

It was in one of the quieter moments that Bobby opened the callused shell that Tracey painstakingly had formed throughout the years. He asked about her family.

Once—even earlier in the night—she would have shut away her feelings from him, but now she felt as if she couldn't have denied this man any part of herself. "I'm not as close to them as I should be . . . as I would like to be."

Bobby didn't understand. He had no basis for comparison. How could anyone be estranged from living parents?

Maybe Stafford's concept of "the freedom of darkness" had some validity to it: Tracey found herself able to address this pain that she had refused to confront for most of her life. "It goes back to the accident, I guess, a long time ago. I was four years old."

"When your sister died?" he asked gently.

She nodded, forgetting that he could hardly see her. "Yes. Shannon was a few years older than me, in school already, and she was gorgeous, Bobby. You saw her pictures."

"Yes," he said.

"I can't remember very much about her because I was so young, but I know how beautiful and intelligent she was. Everyone knew that the world would be hers when she grew up. Whatever she chose to do, whatever she wanted . . . it was all waiting for her. God, how my mother and father loved her."

Bobby began to regret his curiosity. This was not going to be an easy story to tell or to hear.

"I guess, like any little sister would, I idolized her. I tagged after her everywhere, tried to act like her and talk like her." Tracey was quiet for a long moment. "I'm sure that I aggravated her beyond all human limits, but she loved me, too. Then that afternoon came.

"It was in fall. I can still see the red leaves blowing in the street. The days were shorter, but it was still warm. I remember how warm it was. We had a puppy, a little cocker spaniel, I think. He had a collar and a leash, and I was taking him for his walk along the sidewalk in front of our house, while Shannon watched me. I felt so grown up; I'd never been trusted with such responsibility before."

"Tracey, I didn't mean to bring up old memories."

She didn't seem to hear him. "As I said, the days were growing shorter, and it was just twilight. That's the most dangerous time for auto accidents, did you know that? Twilight and daybreak. Statistics prove it.

"Anyway, the puppy was an excitable little thing. I've forgotten his name. Suddenly there was this noise, this piercing noise, a siren. I dropped the leash and covered my ears with both hands. I was still a baby, really. There were flashing lights . . . that's what I can't forget now, the sounds and the dazzling lights. Like an explosion inside of my head. I dropped the leash, and the puppy ran into the street. I ran after him."

Oh Jesus, Bobby thought.

"It was an ambulance, of course, with someone who had been in a car wreck. It was coming right in front of our house on its way to Dr. Heywood's hospital, and the puppy ran directly into its path. What could I do? He was my *responsibility*."

"Shannon came after you?"

She was already crying, though he didn't know this.

"She was my sister. Mother saw it from the window, and she says that Shannon didn't hesitate. She ran as fast as she could after me, and even when we were both in the street, she didn't try to save herself. She threw herself in front of the ambulance and knocked me toward the far side of the street. It hit both of us. Without her, I would have died. Shannon did."

She found him in the darkness and pressed her face into his chest. "I killed her, Bobby, I killed her."

He let her cry for awhile, conveying his sympathy and support only through his arms about her. Sometimes silence is more healing than words.

A few minutes later, he said, "You're not to blame, Tracey. Your sister did what she did because she loved you. It was an accident, and there's no one to blame in that kind of situation."

"It's easy to say," she whispered. "My parents were able to blame me, even though they never said it in words. My whole life has been preempted by what might have been if Shannon had lived. I can't recall either of them ever saying that they loved me or ever giving me a real hug. God help me, there have been times when I felt like I could almost hate the girl who saved my life."

He didn't know what to say, but he knew he had to answer or risk building a permanent wall between them. "You know, I'm no deep-thinker, but I believe you're blaming yourself as much as your parents are. There are no time machines, Tracey. We'll never be able to buy back a second of what's behind us. Leave it. You're away from your parents now, so don't let them control you any more."

"But I love them, Bobby."

"I know you do, sweetheart, and you can always love them, always leave that door open, but don't beg for anything back from them. This is your life. You build on it every day."

"Like Nonnie's book."

"Hmm?"

"Nonnie says she's writing a book, a page a day, so that she can tell how smart she's getting. In a way, that's what we all have to do, isn't it?"

Bobby had touched on subjects he hadn't anticipated. He felt like the fraudulent philosopher tapped within a conundrum of his own construction. "A really heavy-duty catch phrase, huh? 'Let go of the past.' Maybe I should take that advice myself."

"How?"

"By not indulging in flights of fantasy like believing that Leslie could have come to Madison in order to get some surgically-based 'new start in life.' It was easier than accepting the fact that she couldn't include me in her world any longer—"

"Oh my God!" Tracey sat up in the bed as if about to leap from it.

"What? What's the matter?" he asked.

"It could have happened, Bobby, it really could have happened just like you thought!"

"What are you talking about?"

So she told him of what she had learned from Montgomery and Fallows that same night. Naturally, with all of the dire warnings that the federal agents had made concerning the absolute need for secrecy, there was an instant of uncertainty before she spoke, but it was only an instant. Tracey had no doubt that she could reveal anything to the man next to her without a second thought. She told him everything she knew of Dr. Heywood and the National Board of Physical and Psychological Research and Implementation.

"Don't you see?" she asked upon finishing. "If Leslie knew Dr. Heywood from when you were hospitalized or in some other way, she really could have come here for that second chance."

"I've seen plastic surgery, Tracey," he said, "damn, I've had it, and it's never that successful. The person's never completely unrecognizable. There's only so much that the best doctors can do."

"Conventional doctors using conventional methods," she answered. "But they claim that these results are *years* ahead of the accepted boundaries. They can change hair color, eye color, even skin tone, *permanently.*"

Bobby could only whistle in a low register.

"So you may find her, yet."

He responded with a short, grunting laugh. "Yeah, I'm a lot better off: now I don't even know what she looks like."

"I'll help you." When he made no reply, she went on, "I'm the queen of the computer, remember? There are records that I'm supposed to steer clear of, but I know that I can worm into them. If Leslie had some sort of medical procedure done at the Center, I'll find out."

"I don't want you to risk your job for me, Tracey."

She danced her fingers like angel breaths over his upper arm. "I can't get Shannon back, but if it's possible, I'll help you to find your sister. No one will catch me."

He sighed deeply and wrapped her more tightly in his arms.

Tracey slipped into sleep moments afterward, and Bobby was well along the same course when the answer struck him like a white-hot iron being jabbed into his brain. It was so abrupt and so amazingly clear that it was if it had come from an entirely different consciousness, and his entire body stiffened with its impact. Somehow, he kept from awakening Tracey.

He had to be sure, even if it were one o'clock or two or later. He had to do everything he could to know for sure right now. It seemed like the wildest fantasy, but would he have accepted the possibility of meeting someone like Tracey a week ago?

He had to find out.

Moving with exceptional care, he slipped away from her and cradled her head on both pillows. He didn't turn on a light for fear of awakening her, and this meant that he had to find what clothing he could by touch. But Bobby Preston knew how to move stealthily in the dark.

Tracey slept on unaware as he left the apartment.

To Stanley Hollis, Delia McKenzie was the incarnation of beauty and pleasure. To Delia, Stanley was an unschooled but very willing and adaptable lover who had served a purpose for her during one of the lowest times in her life. They each got what they desired out of that night.

As he lay in her bed, holding her, exhausted but also filled with a new kind of life, Stanley believed that the holy Heaven that had been preached to him for years could not be more wonderful than this. He had no memory of ever being this close to another person, physically or emotionally. The love making had been far beyond his most elaborate dreams, but this—holding, being with one another quietly—was as remarkable in its own way. He loved Delia.

The telephone rang shrilly to shatter his reverie, but though it caused Delia to curse softly, it didn't really disturb him. He released her so that she could answer it, but there was no real separation. He could feel a connection with her even when they weren't touching.

"Hello?" she said rather thickly into the receiver without switching on a light. "Tracey? Yes, this is her apartment, but she's not here. What? Oh. Well, she's still in the building, but I don't know the number of the apartment. Yeah, his name is, um." She covered the mouthpiece with her hand and whispered to Stanley, "What's that guy's name? Bobby? His last name?"

"Preston," he told her. Stanley was good with names.

"Bobby Preston," she relayed to the caller. "Yes, I'm sure. The switchboard can connect you with his room. Yeah, yeah, you're welcome and goodnight to you, too." She hung up and fell back into the warm bed with a languid groan. "Goddamned cops."

Stanley turned down the sheets on his side of the bed.

"Hey, where do you think you're going, Jose?" she asked.

"I thought that it was time I left," he replied. "It's awfully late."

"And tomorrow's Saturday. I don't have to work in the morning; do you?"

"No."

"Then get your luscious ass back in here with me.

There are hours and hours left until daylight. We have the rest of the night to fill."

Still sitting up, he took her chin in one hand and held it while he kissed her. This was the first time that Stanley had ever initiated a kiss. "I love you."

Delia was very careful about her use of that powerful word. "You're in lust with me."

"I want to go back to my apartment for a little while."

"Hungry?"

"Not for food. I want to . . . clean up. I don't feel right lying here with you after what happened. You know, what happened first."

She laughed. "Did I complain? Besides, I have a shower right here, remember? Want to wash my back again?"

He smiled at the image. "I would love to, Delia, but right now I need to go downstairs, clean myself, and get some fresh clothes. Mostly the clothes. I wouldn't want anyone to walk in on us in the morning with these filthy things all that I had to dress in."

He was even speaking with more authority and fluidness, she thought. Delia McKenzie, sexual healer. "You're not walking out on me, are you? Leaving me another discarded conquest in the dark?"

He took it seriously. "No. Lord, no. I'll be back, if you want me . . ."

"You'll be back is right, or I'll come down there and carry you up the stairs on my shoulder." She groped him and, to her happy surprise, found him excited again.

"I'll be back," he repeated. He walked by memory to the door on his way to the bathroom and his clothes. He stopped upon opening it and looked back at her in the light spilling in from the hall. "Delia?"

"What, babe?"

Some of his old hesitancy returned. "Have you ever . . . was tonight the first . . . ?"

"No, honey, you're not my first, but let me tell you something: you are by far the very best." She couldn't tell if he was blushing as he faced her in silhouette, but she would have bet heavy money on it.

"You're wonderful," he responded and then closed the door.

Delia rolled in the remaining warmth of the bed and stretched luxuriously. She felt pretty damned wonderful. She couldn't recall even why she had been so down this afternoon. It didn't matter, though.

In the bathroom, Stanley pulled on his pants, shirt, and shoes. He never wore a pair of socks twice without laundering them, and his underwear was still disgustingly tacky, so he rolled it up and stuffed it in a pocket. When he got back to his apartment, he would throw it away.

Catching a glimpse of himself in the wall mirror, he grinned to see how ridiculous his hair looked. He ran a hand over it, but the effort didn't help much. Oh well, who would see him on his way back to the apartment this late at night, anyway?

Rowena Carr, She Who Never Slept, that was who. She practically ran into him as he left Delia's apartment.

"Hi, Stanley," she said with just a touch of volume control in deference to the hour. "You certainly look like someone who's been busy."

He felt the embarrassment rising in his neck. "How are you, Rowena?" he managed to ask.

She shook her head. "My, my, my, it's very late to be visiting. This isn't your apartment, is it? If memory serves me, it's Tracey Lund's."

All of the old symptoms were there: the heat in his face, the tightness in his throat, the stutter that was born somewhere deep in his chest and rampaged into his lips and tongue. Then a strange thing happened to Stanley Hollis.

He dismissed the sensations.

"Sorry, old girl, but I don't really have time to talk now," he told her with new confidence and an oily smile that others had always employed in their dealings with him. "I'm sure you understand."

And he left her, slightly aghast, on the way to the stairs with a whistle playing about his lips.

The telephone intruded into Tracey's dreams. Memory came to her swiftly, and she kept her eyes shut, waiting for Bobby to answer it.

The phone continued to wail from the table next to the bed.

"Bobby?" she said sleepily. "Aren't you going to get that?" Her hand slid about the bed next to her, searching for him. The sheets weren't even warm. "Bobby?"

She roused herself enough to switch on the lamp. The room was empty.

"Bobby?" she called more loudly. She didn't like the things she was thinking. "Bobby, are you here?"

There was no answer.

Sighing, she picked up the incessant telephone. "Hello?"

"Ms. Lund, God," came the voice that was becoming so familiar to her. "This is Ivan Perkins. It's imperative that I see you as soon as possible."

She was still a little sleep-addled. "What? What's wrong?"

"I apologize for the lateness, Ms. Lund, but this is extremely important. Do you understand?"

"Yes, sure, but . . . has something happened? Did you catch Stubbins?"

"Yes, we did—"

"That's great!" Tracey came more fully awake. "Is he him? Bryant?"

"No, we don't believe so. He has undergone identity reassignment, but we don't think that his original personality was that of Calvin Bryant. He became partially conscious in the ambulance and said—"

"Ambulance? Were you hurt? Were the others?"

"I'm bruised but well otherwise, Ms. Lund. Stubbins was the only person seriously injured, and he will recover. Your concern is gratifying, but there's no time for it now. And time is of the essence. Can you meet with us tonight?"

"Right now? I don't understand. If Stubbins is in custody, what do you need from me at this hour?"

The policeman's voice was becoming exasperated. "I'll explain when you get here. Can you come down, right now?"

"Well, I suppose so. You're in your office?"

"No. We're at the Center. Stubbins is undergoing surgery as we speak, and it's essential that you let us into the records and billing department as quickly as possible. Can you do that or will we need to secure another hospital official?"

Now she really was confused. "I can do it. I have the clearance and the keys, and I know how to shut off the alarm system, but it'll be deserted now."

"Good. Come as quickly as you can. We'll be waiting on you at the front entrance." He hung up so abruptly that Tracey at first thought that they had been cut off.

"What in the hell is going on?" Tracey asked herself. "Bobby disappears from his own apartment, and now Perkins acts as if the Devil were nibbling at his butt. Am I the only person not in on the joke?"

Still, Perkins sounded legitimately agitated and he was not the type to jerk her around just because he carried that gaudy badge. Maybe it had something to do with Bobby. She bounced out of bed and began dressing.

Bobby wasn't in the bathroom, the den, or the kitchen. The front door was unlocked, which was an unsettling discovery. Tracey always locked the door, even in this secure building, even if Delia almost never did so.

Tracey wasn't exactly alarmed during the few minutes that it took her to dress, but there was a kind of excitement coursing through her. Whatever it turned out to be, Perkins surely had made it sound big. She rushed out of the apartment.

She didn't pause at the elevators, taking the stairs instead. Two floors down, it struck her that she hadn't left any word with either Bobby or Delia where she was going, and she stopped dead, half-convinced that she should return to one of the apartments and at least leave a note.

This momentary dilemma resolved itself when Stanley Hollis stepped into the stairwell from the second floor landing. "Stanley!" she called from just above him. "Just a minute, I need a favor!" He looked as if he'd recently gotten out of bed, but that hardly surprised her, since it seemed that Delia had set her sights on him. She caught up to the slender young man. "Do me a big favor, will you?"

"I'd be glad to, Ms. Lund," he said happily. Yep, Delia had landed her fish. "Name it."

"I have to go out. Detective Perkins just called, and Bobby seems to have vanished. Don't ask me where he went. But if by chance he should show up at your place to ask about me, tell him I had to go to the records building at the Center, where I work. Okay? Got it?"

He nodded. "No problem at all."

"Oh, I guess I should tell Delia, too . . ."

"Don't bother. I'll tell her. After I clean up a little."

"You're going back? Stanley." She patted his cheek. "Thanks a million." She darted down the stairs.

"My pleasure," he said to her disappearing back. He touched his cheek.

What a night.

Delia was sitting at her dressing table, combing out her long blond hair. If Stanley could spruce up for her, certainly she could do the same for him.

In his own, inexperienced way, he was a marvel. With time he would become a wonderful lover for any woman. His lack of macho self-importance and selfishness allowed his partner to flower in the warmth of his affection. He would never develop into a jet setter cow-boy legend, but he would retain a sweetness that those self-indulgent roosters wouldn't allow themselves to display.

So, in a way, Delia was performing a service for the public good tonight. She stuck out her tongue at the Delia in the mirror.

She didn't hear the bedroom door open, but she caught a glimpse of it just above and behind her own reflection. The person who appeared there surprised her but caused no sense of alarm. She continued to primp.

She was still stroking her silken hair when the hand shot out like a striking snake to clamp over her nose and mouth. Before she could struggle, the knife flashed like lightning in the radiance thrown at it by the mirror while it swept down and into her chest.

Chapter Fifteen

The three officers were waiting just outside the entrance to the records building as they had promised to be. A yellowish anti-crime light flooded over them from one of the brilliant compound lamps. A couple of patrolling security men had stopped to question them five minutes earlier, but Perkins' credentials had satisfied them and sent them on their way.

Tracey pulled into the parking space next to his car. Perkins himself opened her door, not out of courtesy but in an effort to hurry her into the building.

"Glad you could make it, Ms. Lund," he said brusquely as he practically dragged her to the front door. Despite his urgency, Tracey noticed how he walked, in a hunched forward, odd-looking fashion. "We'd like to get inside as soon as possible."

Tracey tripped in his rushing grasp but maintained

her feet. "What's this all about, Perkins? What did Stubbins tell you, anyway?"

"When we're inside," he replied.

Fallows and Montgomery were waiting at the door for her. "Good evening, Tracey," said Michelle. She had a swollen and discolored lump below her left eye, as if she'd just finished a bar fight. "It's wonderfully warm out tonight, isn't it?"

Holding her keys before the deadbolt locks in the Records department door, Tracey could do nothing more than stare for a long moment at the woman who had made the ludicrously inappropriate remark.

The way that his body was beginning to feel again wouldn't allow Stanley to complete his standard routine of bathing, drying, brushing, flossing, and rinsing. The steamy water beat down upon him in the shower, but its heat failed to dissipate the arousal that was building in him as he thought about Delia, with those full, soft breasts and long legs wrapped about him and squeezing, ever tighter, forcing his being from him and into her body.

The erection that came with these thoughts both surprised and delighted him. Once it would have been a source of shame.

No more of that self-recrimination, however. It wasn't wrong or dirty. When two people desired it, it was the most devastatingly enjoyable sensation one could imagine. He would never be ashamed of his dreams again.

His hair was still damp when he combed it. Slipping into clean clothing, he ran into the kitchen to look for something that he could take back with him, an offering of a sort. He didn't drink (much), so there was no wine or even beer. No snack foods, in case she was hungry. But there was a cake in the refrigerator.

It was white cake with rich, thick chocolate icing, and Stanley had bought it at the supermarket for no special reason. He bought it because he liked it. The occasional binge had been Stanley's greatest physical sin . . . before tonight!

Laughing to himself, he whipped the cake out of the refrigerator. He imagined Delia licking the icing from his fingers. It made a beautiful picture.

The elevators seemed to be far too slow to wait tonight, and he almost danced up the stairs. He'd never known any night like this one, and he was determined to etch every second of it into the part of his mind that contained his permanent memories.

For all of the luck he was experiencing, however, he couldn't seem to go from one floor to the next without running into someone. Before, it had been Rowena (twice) and then Tracey. Now it was Bob Preston. Rather than being a sedate apartment building in the middle of the night, this place seemed more like an airport or something.

Preston looked strange. He was in his bare feet and wore only jeans and a T-shirt, for one thing; for another, his expression looked like a combination of shock and resolution. His hair was wildly uncombed, as Stanley's had been not so long ago.

He spotted Stanley as the latter stepped out of the stairwell on the second floor. He snapped his fingers and pointed. "Hey . . . Hollis, right?"

"Right, Mr. Preston," Stanley replied.

The man didn't seem to notice that Stanley was carrying a huge cake. "What's that girl's name, the one you're—your girlfriend?"

"Delia McKenzie?" (My "girlfriend," he thought.)

"Yeah, that's her. I need to speak to her. I can't find Tracey."

That nudged Stanley's memory. "Oh, I know where she's gone. She left a message for you."

"So? What was it?" Preston's tone was nothing like it had been earlier in the evening.

"She's gone to the Center, to her office in the Records department. That policeman called."

"Jeez, I wonder what the hell he wanted?" Preston shook his head sharply, as if to shake it free of distractions. "Never mind. I've got to talk to her." He made a move toward the stairs but stopped just as suddenly. "I guess I'd better put on some clothes first."

Stanley grinned. "That's probably a good idea. Goodnight, Mr. Preston."

Preston, who was racing for the staircase, didn't bother to answer.

This didn't upset Stanley. Tonight was the start of his second life, and it would really take a lot to ruin it for him. He continued towards Delia's apartment with renewed spring in his step.

When he reached the door, he balanced the big cake in his left hand and rapped lightly. This was one unbreakable habit. When Delia didn't answer, he tried the knob and was somewhat surprised to find it turning. *Oh, gosh*, he thought. *I forgot to lock up after myself!* He hoped this wouldn't upset her too much.

"I come bearing gifts for the most beautiful girl in the

world," he called from the den. He bumped the door shut behind him. "That's you, Ms. McKenzie, in case you didn't know."

There was no response.

"Delia, if you've gone back to sleep, I'm afraid I'll just have to wake you. We have hours and hours, remember?" He strolled jauntily into the bedroom.

The door was ajar, and he nudged it open with his right foot.

"I really hope that you like sweets, because I've brought something that will require both of us to polish off. Lots of rich, sugary calories, but calories are stored energy, aren't they? We'll need something to—" His voice broke off with the suddenness and finality that might have come from a set of pliers clipping through his vocal cords. He stopped in the doorway, with his lungs frozen and his heart beating only faintly.

For Stanley Hollis, the world had just ended.

There was blood all over the bedroom. It had splashed the walls like paint and drenched the carpet and the bed clothing. It seemed to hang in the very air as a reddish cloud.

Delia, who had produced all of this blood, was dead. Her body lay on the bed, its wondrous beauty ruined forever by the terrible rage sickness that fomented in the depths of some . . . animalistic mind. Her eyes were still open, and she seemed to be staring directly at Stanley.

He dropped the cake to the floor and staggered a few feet back into the kitchen. There was no way that his brutalized mind could deny what he saw or transform it into a sick hallucination. She was dead.

Stanley fell to his knees and released a wail of pain

that was too primitive to allow words. He sustained the sound until his chest was totally emptied of air, and then he filled his lungs again and repeated it. There were no tears, no pleas, only this ancient and unclassifiable note of ineffable suffering.

I have to get help! his mind finally was able to get through to him. He closed his eyes so hard that he saw twin balls of blue fire on the insides of his lids. But when he opened them, she was still looking at him. *I have to get the police or Tracey or Mr. Preston—*

Bobby Preston.

He had met the man on this floor. Coming from this apartment?

"Tracey, oh God in Heaven, what do I do now?" cried a voice that he only vaguely realized was his own. "I think he did this, I think Bobby Preston killed her, oh dear Lord, he killed her, Tracey!"

Where was she? Stanley stared about himself, and for an instant his reeling brain was unable to tell him where he was. Then it clicked into focus: she was at the Center, in her office.

"Call the police," he whispered frantically while he searched for the telephone. "No, I'll call her—she's with the police! I'll . . . bring them here, I'll show them and they'll have to believe me and kill Bobby Preston. Shoot him! Jesus Christ, why did he do it?"

Stanley ran from the room and an awful sight that would burn like fire in his brain for the remainder of his life.

"He said it several times in the ambulance: 'Happy Birthday, Brown Eyes,' " Perkins told Tracey while she switched on the computer terminal in her office. "We're convinced it's a code designed to allow Stubbins access to the second set of records that Heywood entered into your computer system here in Madison."

"*You're* convinced," Montgomery corrected him. He was the only one of the three not to display evidence of the forest encounter with Dexter Stubbins, either externally or in his movements.

Perkins cut his eyes at the other man, but that was his only response. "We know that Stubbins is not Bryant because he had a full set of unbroken ribs on the right side of his chest. Agent Montgomery blew away two of Bryant's when he shot him three years ago. While Heywood could transplant and fuse bone material, he wasn't able to trigger entirely new bone growth within the body."

"At least, we don't think that he could," added Fallows in a near-whisper.

"But Stubbins was one of his experiments?" Tracey asked.

"X-rays prove he's had extensive cranial surgery, and he obviously knows certain code words tied to the project, if only in a subconscious manner," Perkins answered. "Most likely, he was a petty criminal selected by Heywood due to his dexterity—get it?—with locks and other talents needed in breaking into buildings. His innate voyeuristic tendencies have begun to surface, probably due to the months that he's been removed from Heywood's influence."

"But how do you know that Dr. Heywood logged a second set of records here in Madison?"

"We don't know for sure, but it makes sense." Perkins

peered over her shoulder at the activated but blank screen. "With his expertise, it would have been child's play for him to piggyback them here along with the little messages that he sent to you."

"They would come in like a virus," Michelle said. "He used a similar tactic to destroy his original computer logs when we tampered with them in New York, sort of like the Michelangelo virus that was so famous for five minutes years ago."

"So how do we get at them?"

Perkins looked to Montgomery, who shrugged. "We could wait for our team of experts to get here tomorrow and let them have a go at it."

"The way they 'had a go at it' in Peekskill," Perkins said with cool irony.

"It's your show," Montgomery replied.

Perkins wasn't ready to risk everything due to his own eagerness, however. "We won't dig deeply enough to set off any defensive measures, just see if we can get a foot in the door with what we have. Try . . . 'Happy Birthday, Brown Eyes,' "

Tracey followed his instructions, feeling a bit violated by the personal nature of the supposed code, but she was rewarded only with a "No Record" response. "Nothing," she said. "Maybe we should wait until Stubbins is able to talk."

"I'm not sure that we have the time," he told her.

"What does that mean?"

He bit his lower lip in a unique display of nerves. "Fallows hit upon it, I believe. She said that there was a chance that Stubbins came to Madison and the Center due to an artificially ingrained homing instinct provided by Heywood, should anything happen to him. Which, of course, it did.

"If it applied to Stubbins, there's a damned good chance that the other subjects have the same programming. We're already ninety percent certain that Bryant did the job on Julian and the girl, so he could be any of the recently arrived patients at the Center."

Cold fingers scampered down the back of Tracey's neck.

"There were four just this week, right?"

"Yes," she said, "but how did you know that?"

"I have my own computer system," he reminded her, "plus a badge to give it muscle. I've been checking up on Stafford's operations."

"We can eliminate Stubbins, at least for the moment," said Michelle. "That would leave three."

Tracey nodded. "Count out Rowena Carr for her gender, and Michael Lockridge is confined to a wheelchair." She looked to Montgomery. "Did your bullet paralyze Bryant?"

"Contrary to my favorite description of the event, I actually missed his spine," he said. "The lunatic was badly messed up, but he wasn't paralyzed."

"Whoever worked on Julian wasn't in a wheelchair," Perkins pointed out.

"Can we be sure that Lockridge is?" Montgomery asked. "Could be a clever ruse."

"That man isn't faking it," Tracey stated. "I don't think his legs have the strength to support a child, even if he could move them. That leaves . . . Stanley, Stanley Hollis." She shook her head. "I can't believe that. Not sweet little Stanley."

"Heywood was a genius," Fallows reminded them all. "Any 'auxiliary' personality he created would be as perfectly unlike Bryant as you might imagine."

"Still, it's too incredible. I know him. I can't believe that he could ever hurt anyone."

"Maybe he didn't," Perkins said. "There are no fast rules that the returning killer has to have been a patient in the Center, and I know of at least one other person who's new in town this week. He lives in the Rosewell Apartments, too."

"Who?" Tracey asked, honestly unaware of who he meant.

"Robert James Preston." The words fell like stones in the quiet office.

It took a moment for Tracey's mental reflexes to return. "You're crazy. Bobby's no killer. I'm definitely positive of that."

"Think about it," Perkins advised her. "Bryant's trail leads from Washington State through Colorado to right here. Where was Preston before arriving in town?"

"In Canada," she answered. "He rode down to California and then east to Madison; he was in a Canadian prison for a year and a half until only a few weeks ago!"

"I'm sure he believes he was, when he's Preston."

"But there are records—"

"Records created and maintained by the government. The paper trails and the false identities are the easiest part of this entire procedure." The detective looked at Tracey with real sympathy. "And his name: Robert Preston isn't the most original of aliases, is it?"

Tracey recalled something the policeman had said in her first meeting with him. "And what's your middle name, Detective Perkins?"

He smiled. "But I had nothing against David Julian. I spoke with the manager of the Rosewell, Lurleen Bushnell, this morning. She saw that confrontation in the parking lot on Tuesday."

"He didn't hit him," Tracey said a little weakly.

"He has to be considered a suspect, Ms. Lund. A stronger one than Michael Lockridge or Stanley Hollis."

She turned back to the computer. "If Heywood's records are in here, they'll tell us who's who, won't they?"

"They should," Fallows agreed.

"Then let's find out just who the bastard really is. What's next?"

"It's a guessing game," Perkins said. "I don't know . . . try something along the lines of, 'Heywood says hello, Brown Eyes,' or 'Birthday Greetings, Brown Eyes.'"

She typed in both with no luck. "Come on, you can do better than this, you're supposed to be the investigators."

"Maybe the 'Brown Eyes' comes first," Fallows suggested.

"I have an idea—" began Montgomery.

He was cut off by the startlingly loud noise of a car screeching to a halt in the parking lot. Then the outer door flew open, and a man ran into the building virtually screaming out Tracey's name.

"Damn," she whispered, swiveling her chair about and standing.

"Stay there!" barked Perkins. He drew his gun and

stepped next to the office door. Montgomery and Fallows followed his example by pulling their weapons.

Half a second later, this door also burst inward and Stanley Hollis staggered through it. His face was scarlet with panic and his cheeks ran with tears. "Tracey, Tracey, God, she's dead! He killed her!" Three guns immediately fixed on him.

"Who?" she cried.

"Delia! Oh Christ, he cut her to pieces!" Stanley saw the guns through his tears, and his red face instantly drained to pale white. "Not me, him! Preston killed her!"

Tracey's legs died beneath her. She slumped limply back into her chair. "Oh no . . ."

"But it's my fault!" Stanley continued to wail.

"What are you talking about?" Perkins demanded. All three guns remained trained on the man.

"I left her door unlocked, when I went back to my apartment, and he walked right in on her! It was my fault!" Stanley's eyes grew wild. "You've got to get him, Detective Perkins! I saw what he did to her! He killed her and I loved her! Come on!"

With the same piercing urgency of Hollis' arrival, Bobby Preston's rented car roared into the lot and slammed on the brakes. The people in the office heard his door open and shut in the span of a heartbeat.

"God help us, he's coming in here! He's going to kill us, too!" Hollis wailed.

"Shut up, shut the hell up!" ordered Perkins. He switched off the lights and plunged the office into almost total darkness. "Be quiet and stay where you are!" His free hand found Stanley's arm. "Don't you flinch, Hollis."

Bobby was calling Tracey's name as he hit the outer door and lunged into the building. She felt hot tears burning down her face. Delia, Bobby, for God's sake, what was happening?

"Tracey, where are you?" he yelled. "I've got to tell you!" His silhouette appeared in the open doorway. "Are you in here, Tracey?"

"Freeze, you murdering son of a bitch!" screamed Michelle.

Perkins hit the lights, and, as Bobby blinked in amazement and confusion, he dragged the younger man into the room by the neck and threw him face-first into the wall. All the while, three guns alternated their aim between the heads of Bobby and Stanley.

"What's going on?" Bobby gasped.

"Shut up and assume the position, asshole!" Perkins directed.

Almost by instinct, Bobby spread his arms and legs and pressed the side of his face into the wall. Perkins patted him down while Montgomery held his revolver glued to the man's head and Fallows kept hers aimed at Stanley. Tracey began to weep openly.

"What's wrong?" Preston asked in apparently complete befuddlement. It certainly sounded real. "Tracey, what's going on?"

"Why, Bobby, why? What did she do to you?" she asked pleadingly.

"Who?"

"You were told to shut up, pussbag!" Montgomery snapped as he whipped a punch into Bobby's side.

Bobby choked in pain.

"He's clean," Perkins said. He holstered his weapon

and withdrew his handcuffs. "Robert James Preston, you're under arrest for murder. You have the right to remain silent; if you give up this right, anything you say ca—"

"I know my damned rights," he hissed, still throbbing with pain. "Tell me what's going on? Who's dead?"

"You killed Delia!" Stanley cried. He seemed about to throw himself upon Preston until Fallows firmly—but with surprising compassion—clutched his arm and drew him aside.

"Delia? Your roommate?" Bobby asked.

"It's not true, it's not," she whispered.

"I know it's not: I haven't killed anybody!"

"You dirty animal," Stanley spat, crying again, too.

For his part, Russell Montgomery seemed to be filled with a different sort of emotion. Seeing that Perkins had the handcuffed suspect under control, he rushed across the room like a bull. "It could be him," he was repeating to himself as a sort of mantra, "by God, it really could be him." Grasping Tracey's shoulder he spun her about to face the idling terminal. "When's your birthday?"

"What?"

"When in the hell were you born?"

"What difference does that make? Oh, Bobby—"

Montgomery grabbed both of her arms and shook her fiercely. "It may tell us if your boyfriend is Bryant, so when were you born?"

"Get off of her, you stupid ape!" yelled Preston.

"Russ!" echoed Fallows.

"Uh, October twenty-second, nineteen eighty," she answered. "I don't know what you want . . ."

"Feed it in." He took her right hand and laid it on the terminal keyboard. "Try the words first and add 'Brown Eyes.' If that doesn't spark anything, use the numerals."

Automatically, she typed it in: nothing. She tried the numbers.

"Hello, Aaron," the screen read.

"Lord, we're in," Tracey gasped. "What now?"

"Try . . . try, Stubbins, Dexter Ryan," he told her.

She fed this below the greeting and its response. The immediate answer was, "#11378-204, Loesser, Aaron Thomas, 8/1/72, Newton, Illinois."

"That's his name, his *real* name," Montgomery said triumphantly, "Aaron Thomas Loesser, and he was born August first, 1972 in Newton, Illinois. This is it, Mitchie!"

His fellow agent's face lit with excitement. "That's great, Russ! Who's Bryant?"

"Type it in," he directed. "Calvin Peter Bryant."

Tracey did so. The reply was a brief search followed by, "Not found."

"Shit!" Montgomery grunted. "I know he's in there! He's the killer!"

"Maybe you have to have a separate entrance code for each subject and this one works only with Stubbins," Tracey ventured.

"That must be it." He glanced to the thoroughly baffled and handcuffed Preston. "Try 'Robert James Preston'."

She looked at the young man who had just become so much a part of her life. "Bobby?"

"I'll do it," muttered Montgomery, trying to push her aside.

"No!" She glared at him. "I'll do it." She entered the

name. There was no response. In a way, this was a victory.

But not to Montgomery. "Damn, damn, damn, we're so close. Try the menu."

She did, without luck.

"We'll have to have his individual code, I guess."

"Try 'keyword,'" suggested Perkins, "or 'keyphrase.'"
The others looked to him.

"You said that a certain word or phrase could cause them to revert," he said. "Find out what it is."

"Damn," Bobby whispered to himself.

Perkins heard. "Worried, son? Afraid you'll find out something ugly about yourself?"

"I'm not somebody's puppet," he answered, but they all knew of his brain surgery and his blackouts following a supposed traffic accident, and they could hear the uncertainty in his voice. "I'm Robert Preston. I know who I am."

"Let's find out."

With a last glance at him, Tracey typed in the one word message, "keyphrase." The answer came up immediately, and she and Montgomery read it together, silently.

"What is it?" Fallows whispered. "For Christ's sake, tell us." She no longer believed that Stanley Hollis was capable of also being an insane serial killer, but she didn't deny her professional training. She held her aim on his ribs.

"What's the word, Tracey?" asked Perkins.

Bobby stood next to the policeman. His hands were cuffed behind him, with the chain passed through the

314

metal handle of a locked file cabinet as insurance. For an instant that seemed endless to her, Tracey stared at him.

Could it be true? The metal plate in his skull, his admitted presence on the West Coast, the fact that David Julian had died in slow agony only hours after confronting him . . . did these things add up to his guilt? Could the man who had just made love to her so tenderly be but one face belonging to a psychotic murderer?

Tracey didn't want to say the words. She didn't want to know.

"Tracey?" Montgomery said softly.

"Say it, babe," Bobby told her.

"Oh," sighed Stanley Hollis. He knew he wasn't a maniac, but in this wild situation, there had to be room for a glimmer of doubt. Like Bobby, he closed his eyes.

Keeping her eyes fixed on the screen, she read, " 'The light of countless stars can show us only the colors that God has used to paint our world.' " Then she closed her eyes, too.

Perkins stared into Bobby Preston's face, while Fallows watched Stanley Hollis just as closely. Montgomery snapped his gaze from one to the other.

Not a hint of recognition rippled across the face of either man.

During the following pause, no one spoke. Even in the silence, the palpable tension began to drift away. It was as if they were surfacing slowly from a deep dive.

Tracey turned in her chair. "Bobby?"

He responded with a rather tentative grin. "That still sounds like my name to me."

She ran across the room to him, filled with relief.

"Am I okay, too?" Stanley asked.

Michelle flashed a quick grin. "Looks like."

Perkins wasn't convinced, though. "We can't be sure that was the right phrase. It could apply to only one individual, like Stubbins."

Montgomery shook his head. "This is the universal keyphrase. It says that on the computer. It should work with any of his sleepers."

"Does it have to be one of the people at the Rosewell Building?" asked Stanley. "Don't you think that a lot of men have come to Madison in the last week or even before that?"

"He's right," Fallows said. "We may have to walk down the streets reciting this dumb phrase to everyone we meet."

"Not now that we're inside," Montgomery stated as his eyes swept across the computer keyboard. "This will tell us everything we need to know." He reached out as if to touch a key.

Perkins, who had some practical experience with computers, took a quick step in his direction. "Be careful, Montgomery. One wrong choice and you could activate another of Heywood's protective viruses."

Bobby tugged lightly at his cuffed hands. "Think you could get me out of these now, officer?"

Fallows answered for him. "We still have a witness who saw you kill someone, Preston." Stanley dropped his head. "I didn't . . . I didn't really see him do it."

Michelle looked at him in surprise.

"I haven't hurt anyone," Bobby repeated. *Not since California, anyway.*

Regarding him with a peculiar look, Perkins said, "You'll be freed in good time, son. You just cool your jets for the moment."

"If reliable medical examination proves that Michael Lockridge is truly paraplegic, there's still someone we have to consider," Montgomery pointed out. No one understood immediately, so he answered himself, "Rowena Carr."

Michelle's voice conveyed her sense of shock at the very thought of the possibility that he was right, "Russ, but she's . . . you don't honestly believe that Heywood would do that to Bryant, do you?"

All of the men in the room felt as if their stomachs were dropping from their bodies.

"I do believe it. Heywood had the type of personality that drove him to explore everything that was remotely possible. Can you think of a more effective disguise? A more diametrically opposed personality to introduce to him? And castration certainly would have a dampening effect on the sexual rage that was the foundation of his psychosis. None of Bryant's victims ever displayed traces of semen or any other exclusively male elements because he was driven to masturbate over his mental pictures in private."

"Would you tell me what they're talking about?" Bobby asked without being sure that he wanted to know.

"Rowena, from the apartments," Tracey repeated in a wondering voice. "Lord, I guess that it could be her, her size, and she never sleeps, so that she always knows what's happening . . . oohh . . ."

Before anyone could speculate further along these

strange lines, Perkins broke the stillness of the room with a victorious outburst, "There it is, I knew it! Do you see? 'Do you wish to proceed?' "

Montgomery grinned savagely. "You bet your ass we do! This will give us everything, names, surgeries, locations." He glanced to Tracey. "Will this give us a printout?"

"See the print key in the lower right-hand corner?" she responded, taking a step toward the terminal.

"I just touched the 'next subject' key," Perkins said, primarily to himself.

Russell Montgomery continued to smile as he located the print key. He literally seemed to be tasting the sweetness of this moment of success. "We've got the bastard," he whispered, "we've got him or her or whatever he is now."

Stanley tapped the shoulder of Michelle Fallows, who, like Tracey, had moved in the direction of the computer desk. "Excuse me, Ms. Fallows?"

She turned to face him. "Yes, Stanley?"

"You're dead." With speed, power, and coordination none of them had suspected him to possess, Hollis backhanded Fallows across the face with his left fist while wrenching her gun from her grip with his right hand. She staggered back, and when he shot her in the stomach, she fell.

Montgomery was clawing for his own holstered weapon when the next bullet from Michelle's gun crashed into his chest and knocked him back across the table next to Tracey's terminal, scattering the contents of her purse into the floor.

Crying out in shock and fury, Perkins managed to

squeeze off two shots as he spun about to confront Hollis. Unfortunately, both missed when Stanley dropped expertly to one knee and returned the fire. Perkins' breath exploded from his lungs in a great moan, just as it had when Stubbins/Loesser had attacked him with the tree branch, and he fell, sitting, against the far wall of the room.

The computer printer chattered out all of Ansel Heywood's precious secrets in a continuous roll of paper without regard to the deadly proceedings taking place about it.

Tracey screamed and raced toward Hollis.

"Think about it!" Stanley shouted. He thrust the smoking barrel of Michelle's gun into her face.

"God, Tracey, no!" Bobby lunged forward only to drag the ponderous file cabinet off-balance and collapse to the floor as it dropped atop him. Shock insulated him from any pain. "Don't shoot her, Hollis, for the love of God, don't shoot her, please!"

The terrible image of the gun paralyzed Tracey in her tracks.

Stanley smiled. "I have no intentions of shooting her, Preston." His expressions, his voice, his entire being had changed in a second from the painfully shy man they had known as Stanley Hollis to someone cold and deadly. "I have other plans for Ms. Tracey Lund, believe me."

"You're him," she whispered, "the Prince of Darkness."

He nodded slightly. "Guilty." He moved next to Perkins' body and stooped to pick up the gun that had fallen from the policeman's hands.

"But you didn't change . . . when I said the words."

Standing again, Calvin Bryant laughed. "What did

you expect me to do? Foam at the mouth? Spit and scratch? I'm a human being, Tracey, not a werewolf. The things that Dr. Heywood's followers did to me were vicious and unholy, but I've overcome them. Even when imprisoned inside that pathetically impotent caricature, I was aware and listening and learning, so can't you see how simple it was for me to continue to play the fool when the spoken phrase liberated me? Sometimes, with the proper provocation, I can escape without it."

Tracey turned her eyes from the gun when Bryant shifted it into his left hand long enough to slip Perkins' weapon into his belt. Her gaze fell on the three bloody bodies. "Why?"

"These?" Bryant asked blithely. "Self-preservation, of course. I had nothing in particular against Michelle or Detective Perkins, and I certainly didn't want to take these measures at this time, but they were about to read Dr. Heywood's files and identify me. What choice did I have?" It sounded thoroughly logical when he said it.

"But Delia . . . she *liked* you . . ."

Bryant looked at his living captives, Bobby pinned to the floor by the heavy cabinet and Tracey imprisoned by the more powerful grip of the revolver aimed at her face. He had been so calm, matter-of-fact, and normal in appearance to this point that it was another chilling shock to see the real madness of the man spilling from his eyes. "She was a whore. Her body was as base—in her own estimation—as the floor of a stable, where farm animals copulate. She used that body to entrap me— Stanley Hollis, and after using him with no more regard than she would have given a toy, the whore had the unimaginable effrontery to tell him that there had been others before him. She chose her death, not I. The instrument never selects the subject."

Tears of rage blurred Tracey's vision and seared her eyes. "You goddamned monster," she whispered.

Bryant seemed offended. "'Goddamned'? God-blessed would be more fitting." He glanced to Russell Montgomery, whose body lay face up on the table. "This one died for a different but just as trenchant reason. Acting with a contemptible cowardice by shooting a chosen messenger in the back draws its own reward."

Still watching the two, Bryant knelt to retrieve the gun that the federal agent had wrestled from its holster before being struck down. At this level, he seemed to hear something that neither of them could detect, and his appearance brightened. "Ah, I have been presented with a gift." He clutched a fistful of Montgomery's hair in his left hand and lifted the man's head so that even Bobby could see the slack white face from where he lay in the floor.

Montgomery groaned.

Tracey knew immediately what was about to happen. "Calvin, don't do this, please, please, oh God, please don't!"

Bryant reprised his smile. He whispered into Montgomery's ear with the silken voice of a lover, "Are you ready to see the other side, Russell? Or can you already see what awaits you?"

Montgomery's lips trembled and then moved with a weak desperation, "Help me. Don't let me bleed to death."

Bryant raised Fallows' revolver and placed its muzzle

against Montgomery's right temple. "Do you know who I am, Russell?"

"He can't hurt you now, Calvin!" Tracey screamed.

Bryant whipped the gun directly at her. "Don't you press me, bitch! I have plans for the person who monopolized so much of the attention of Dr. Heywood, attention better allotted to important matters, but I will not be pushed. You took the doctor from me, and you'll stand in judgment for that, but don't be deluded into believing you have some special dispensation. I'll kill you where you stand."

"You can't just shoot him!" she cried.

"Tracey, shut up!" Bobby knew many ways that he could kill Bryant, and he could feel his hands hungering for those attacks, but he also realized that nothing could be done while he lay chained to this damned filing cabinet. Now was the time for brains. "Shut your mouth! He understands that Montgomery is much more useful to him alive."

Tracey fell silent, and the madman favored Bobby with the faintest expression of approval. Then he returned the gun to Montgomery's head.

"Listen to me, Calvin!" Bobby said desperately.

"Don't profane a sacred moment," came the answer.

At the last, Montgomery understood. "No, Calvin, don't do this, you don't have to kill . . ."

"Goodbye," Bryant whispered. The gun exploded once.

Tracey covered her eyes and stumbled back to the opposite wall of the office. Bobby unconsciously began to thump his head against the floor.

Bryant considered his work for a moment before

standing. "The balance has returned," he stated, apparently to himself. "Delia tilted the scales toward the female, and Michelle forced it deeper. But Russell and the policeman have reestablished the eternal stability." He focused upon Tracey and Bobby with the attitude of a businessman assessing his stock. "One man, one woman. Always in balance."

Bobby knew that unless a miracle occurred, he would never leave this room alive. And worse awaited Tracey.

The printer continued to rattle on industriously. In the relative silence, it attracted Bryant's attention for an instant. "This is interesting," he said, reading the printout. "This is very interesting. I'll have to take this copy before I destroy the program. If you ever saw it, you would be most surprised, Mr. Preston."

What Bobby did see was a tiny shudder that ran though the chest of Ivan Perkins. The man was still alive. He looked to where Michelle Fallows lay and was so shocked to see her eyes open and searching frantically for Bryant that he almost gave himself away. Somehow, this most deadly of psychotic murderers had failed to kill two of the three people he had assaulted.

Focusing on him, Fallows struggled to speak, but Preston shook his head sharply.

"Oh my, there are all sorts of intriguing tidbits in here," Bryant muttered. "I never would have guessed."

"That's enough, you crazy son of a bitch!" Tracey shouted from behind Bobby.

He desperately tried to signal her, but his position anchored to the floor, prevented eye contact at this moment.

Tracey had been driven to her breaking point and

beyond, and the fierce creature that had always lived within her was fighting to be free. "You think you're some kind of god, don't you, some god of death? You're not even animal." She began to walk toward the murderer.

"I'm only a man," Bryant answered her, still composed. "But I serve the only God."

Tracey's laughter sounded as harsh as tearing fabric. "You think you're a man? That's hilarious. A man by whose estimation? You pathetic worm, you don't even come close."

He looked up from the fascinating computer readout with a slight sneer. "These fools on the floor learned of my power. I almost gave myself away with laughter when they were speculating that Dr. Heywood had changed me into *Rowena Carr*. The Doctor would never have perpetrated such an atrocity upon me, and even if he had God would not have allowed it to happen. Spare me your fraudulent psychoanalysis, please."

"You won't even fight *me* without a weapon. What kind of man does that make you?"

A redness began to deepen in Bryant's face. "That's enough of your foul tongue, Tracey. I have to warn you."

"Or what, Calvin? You'll kill me? There's a surprise. How does killing so many people prove you're a man, or anything else, for that matter? You don't like psychoanalysis because it tells you the truth about yourself, like the fact that gun is really your dick. Isn't that it?"

"Jesus, Tracey!" whispered Bobby.

"No more, woman! Your voice sullies your very gender! It's not for you to question me or my actions, so you will do as you're told!"

"What I'm going to do, *Calvin,* is get the key to the handcuffs off of Perkins' body, and then I'm going to release Bobby and we're leaving together."

"I said shut up!" Bryant abruptly fired the revolver into the ceiling above her head. Tracey stopped walking and closed her eyes against the horror that was enveloping her. She ground her teeth in fear, frustration, and resolve.

Bobby could see her now, and he could tell that even though she had stopped moving with the shot, this was only temporary. She would continue to press, even if Bryant killed her, just to be done with the madness. He had to do something to stop her from making that useless sacrifice of her life.

"A man shoots unarmed women, does he, Calvin?" he asked with revulsion dripping from his words. "Anybody can do that. Let's see how much of a man you really are. Let me up from here, and you and I can settle it in about one fucking minute. You man enough to do that, Calvin?"

His heart sank as Bryant roared with laughter. "Fighting? That's your definition? I'm not afraid of you or your bitch or death or anything, because I am chosen. I am in a state of grace. But I use the tools that God provides for me. Fight you one to one? Perhaps they call the wrong person mad, hmm?" He waved the revolver. "This gun scares you, doesn't it?"

How do I answer that? Bobby thought.

He didn't have to, as Bryant continued, "It doesn't frighten me." He made a motion with his left arm that encompassed his three victims and the hole in the ceiling. "Five shots, two in our friend Russell. One shell left in the chamber." To illustrate, he broke the cylinder and allowed both of them to see the single round in the circle of five empties. He snapped the gun shut. "They certainly were afraid of this." He spun the cylinder across his let forearm. "Watch."

"God!" Tracey gasped.

Bryant placed the muzzle to his head.

Kill him! Bobby prayed silently. Please, kill him!

The sharp click broke through the crystallized air of the room more loudly than the continuing typing of the notes from the printer. Almost as loudly as a shot. Tracey and Bobby released their breaths together.

The expression on Bryant's face was angelic. He lowered the gun. "Did you see it? God won't let me die, and this proves it. Only a true man could pass the trial." He sighed with deep contentment. "Now we have the other matters to deal with."

"One pull?" Preston demanded, desperate to postpone those "other matters."

"If I had been ordained to die for taking an innocent life or disobeying in any way, the hammer would have struck the shell."

"One pull of the trigger for three bodies? What are you, a queer?"

"I'm a man!"

"Three kills, three pulls!" Bobby responded with equal shrillness.

"You don't think I will?"

Bobby caught his own fear and anger and held them in check long enough to whisper, "I think you're shitting your pants right now."

In Calvin Bryant's skewed vision of the world, there was only a single response to that. He prepared to roll the cylinder again.

"Oh, no, spinning the chamber before every pull doesn't prove your bravery or the protection of your god. It only shows us the effects of statistical averages," Bobby said.

Bryant's eyes glowed with hatred for him. He nestled the gun against his temple again.

"Do it, do it," Tracey goaded him.

His entire face seemed to radiate his madness. He squeezed the trigger. Another empty snap.

"Damn you!" Tracey cried.

"You can't kill me!" Bryant jabbed the revolver at Montgomery's corpse. "He couldn't kill me! Satan in all his infernal power couldn't kill me! I am a protected instrument of the light!"

"Three kills, Calvin," Preston said in as even a voice as he could produce. His guts were rolling. His life, Tracey's . . . everything rested on one more pull of the trigger. "Two means nothing."

"You will not be convinced, will you?" Bryant said in wonder. "I could do this all night, I could squeeze this trigger until Doomsday arrives to cleanse the Earth, and not a drop of my blood would be shed."

"Three."

There was a flicker behind the eyes of the Prince of Darkness. It was gone in less than a second, but it told Bobby everything. Bryant's mad faith was cracking.

Not yet, man, just hold on to that craziness a few moments more.

By a strange irony, Bryant had already passed his own twisted test of faith and manhood, since he'd already killed just one person in that room. So far.

"Your god must not be so powerful after all," observed Bobby, "if you have doubts."

The gun jumped to Bryant's head as if on strings. There was a difference this time, however. As much as he would have denied it, the murderer knew the truth. The gun began to tremble.

"Don't you understand?" He was pleading and uncertain, as if he truly couldn't see why he was hated. "Don't you know why it had to be done? To help you, to help the world . . ."

"If your god lives, he will protect you and allow you to prove your worthiness," Preston said in a low and comforting tone. "Show us, Calvin."

Their eyes locked.

"The next pull goes against your forehead," Bryant promised.

A sane man would have turned the revolver on Bobby and then used the gun on his belt to kill Tracey.

For the third time, Bryant squeezed the trigger.

The eruption of sound caused them all to scream.

Two dead men lay in the small office, their brains mingled in a red muddle next to the chattering printer. Another man and a woman lay gravely wounded nearby, but one of the nation's finest hospitals was less than one hundred yards to the east.

Tracey found the key in Perkins' coat and unlocked the cuffs from Bobby's wrists before helping him to lever the filing cabinet off of his badly twisted right leg.

She was numb. None of this was real. Nothing like this could be real.

"The damned crazy son of a gun did it," Bobby repeated to himself as, with Tracey's help, he painfully climbed to his feet. "I knew he was way gone, but to think that he would actually pull the trigger, jeez." He gingerly tested his right leg, and pain screamed all the way into his hip. He chewed on it.

"Bobby!" His suffering seemed to be the first shard of reality to pierce the shock that was wrapping Tracey.

He hopped to a chair and eased himself into it. "No, no, I'm okay! Get to the phone and call for help before they bleed to death."

"It'll be all right, I promise it will," she assured him with tears streaming down her cheeks.

He rubbed her arm gently. "All right, baby, it's all over now. Just call for help, okay?"

"Yes." She stood for a moment as if unable to recognize the office in which she'd worked for years. Then she saw the phone on her desk next to the still operating computer printer and opposite the table that held the lifeless form of Russell Montgomery. Calvin Bryant lay on the floor before it.

Stepping as if she were avoiding quicksand, Tracey walked around the bodies and picked up the receiver. The touch of a button gave her a direct line to the front desk of the medical operations portion of the Center.

"This is Tracey Lund, next door in the Records department," she said with an urgency that still retained a sense of unreality. "There's been . . . a situation here. We have three seriously injured people and two dead. Get some help to us. Hurry." Though the other end had disconnected the call by then, she still held the receiver to her ear as if unable to return her attention to the awfulness that surrounded her.

Her eyes wandered from the grotesque remains of the man in charge of capturing Calvin Bryant and fell on the computer screen. It continued to roll out its retrieved information from Dr. Heywood's program like the graph paper in a lie detector.

"Bobby," she began in a small voice that rose with each syllable, "it says—oh, my God, Bobby!" And then she couldn't speak anymore.

Epilogue

The gas station attendant waited until the car had pulled all the way out of the sun and beneath the shade of the wide canopy above the pumps and stopped before he forced himself to leave the cool office. In June in Utah, it is best not to challenge the blistering heat any more frequently than absolutely necessary.

There were no other cars awaiting his attention, which was good, since he was on duty alone; but he approached this one with disguised caution. The attendant had never been robbed while employed by the station, but as he spent much of his time alone out here in the middle of nowhere, he had occasional unpleasant daydreams about it.

The guy who left the driver's side of the car even before the attendant cleared the office did nothing to ease his apprehension. He wasn't particularly large or muscular in appearance, but there was something in the way that he moved and stood. The mirrored sunglasses and beginnings of a thick black beard added to the image.

"Help you, mister?" the attendant asked.

"Yeah, fill it up with premium." The man sounded harmless enough.

"Cash or charge?"

"Cash." The man bent into the open door and spoke to the other person in the front seat, "You want something cold?"

"A Coke if they have one," answered the second person. The attendant noticed with appreciation that she was a good-looking woman with deep brown eyes. He flipped down the tag and began pumping fuel into the car.

"Think we should wake her?" the man asked.

The attendant peeked discreetly through the rear window to find a second woman sleeping in the backseat. From what he could see, she was a real looker, too, with beautiful red hair.

"No," said the first woman, "let her sleep. She's all worn out from the park tour. She probably won't wake up until it's time to eat again."

The driver looked at both women with an affection that was recognizable even with the glasses hiding his eyes. "Yeah." He began to walk toward the soft drink machine with a pronounced limp.

He still looked like a dangerous dude to the attendant.

Inside the car, Tracey Lund rolled down her window to catch what breeze there might be inching across the vast flat land about her. They had been on the road for a long time, and she was tired in every muscle of her body; but this was Utah, and the end of the journey was in sight. One more night in a motel and then home to a place she'd never visited before.

What waited for her in California? The rest of her life.

She checked on Nonnie, who was breathing evenly as she slept. It had been more than a month since that terrible night at the Center. In another month, everything that had happened while she lived in Virginia would be lost in Nonnie's porous and slowly recovering memory. She wouldn't even recall how Ansel Heywood had changed her face and body and then attempted—without informing her—to wipe away all knowledge of him and his activities through the techniques of what amounted to mental rape.

She would never be Leslie Jane Preston again, but like her brother Bobby and Tracey herself, she at least had a real opportunity to make a new start. Bobby had made the connection that night in his bed when Tracey told him of Nonnie's insistence that she was a writer. When he had left Tracey so abruptly, that was where he had gone, to rouse Nonnie and Carla Pollock from their beds past midnight in a desperate attempt to find out if she was his sister.

Tracey knew within herself that nothing would have happened differently had he remained and the two of them gone to her office together. Delia and Bryant and Montgomery would still be dead.

The Prince lay now in an unmarked government grave, at peace following too many years of suffering, if you believed the official story. If not, he had become parts somewhere in the bowels of the National Board of Physical and Psychological Research and Implementation. Depending upon how you looked at it, he had been either the victim of an immoral experiment conducted by a man Tracey had once loved or Dr. Heywood's crowning achievement.

She had heard that Russell Montgomery had been taken to Boulder, Colorado, for burial. Her emotions were mixed when she considered the man. On the one hand, he might have avoided so much pain and tragedy had he gone public from the beginning and told Tracey and the Madison police what they were dealing with rather than opting to use her as bait for the monster. On the other, he'd done the most that could have been asked of him, he'd given his life in the service of his nation.

Tracey shook her head sadly.

Michelle Fallows and Ivan Perkins were still recovering from their wounds. On her last visit to see the detective in the hospital, he had told her that he intended to take early retirement once he was released. The lifestyle of a policeman had been destructive both to his family and his health long before his encounter with the Prince of Darkness, and he wanted to use the years he had before him in an effort to recoup his losses, perhaps to explore new vistas that wouldn't reactivate the obsessive personality that he had allowed to eat so much of his body and soul.

It seemed like a good idea to Tracey, but she would have taken bets that he wouldn't be completely retired and satisfied until he'd tied up those two or three cases that had eluded closing so far.

Delia McKenzie rested in a small cemetery outside of Peekskill next to her parents. Tracey would always feel responsible for drawing her into the nightmare by her mere presence in the Rosewell Apartments. It would take a long time to learn to live with that.

The attendant topped off the tank and wandered about to her window after replacing the cap and the tag.

"Anything else I can do for you folks?" he asked.

She saw Bobby returning slowly with the soft drinks. "No thank you."

"I see by the tag that you're from Virginia," the young man stated. "Where you headed?"

"California," she replied. "Venice Beach, at least for a week or two."

The man grinned. "Would you believe that I've never been that far west myself?"

A part of Tracey that she'd come to understand only in the last month laughed in response. Would you believe that I'm not who I believed myself to be almost all of my life? this portion of her asked.

She was taken back to that indelible moment in her office when, with Bryant and Montgomery lying dead and Michelle, and Perkins bleeding their lives away, she had been forced to take the time to read the computer printout of Heywood's files. It was then that she had discovered that there really was no Tracey Gale Lund.

She had been born Susan Elaine Mathis twenty-five years ago, and for the first four years of her life that was who she had remained. Only when her father had been established to be one of the most efficient money launderers in the entire national crime syndicate and been forced to roll over on his employers had she ceased to be little Susan.

The Federal Witness Protection Program had assured

Harold Mathis and his family complete protection from reprisal, but not even the leaders of that agency had realized what Ansel Heywood had in mind for them. His cruelly thorough system had been to establish new identities from the mind outward. The torturous days that Tracey recalled as having been spent in the hospital recovering from the accident that killed her sister actually had resulted from the plastic surgery and the surgical, chemical, and psychological tactics employed to clean her brain of her real self and put this manufactured person in its place.

"Brown Eyes." That probably wasn't even her original eye color.

She hadn't been responsible for the death of her sister Shannon simply because she had never had a sister named Shannon. That real child had once been the daughter of the also real Chance and Willa Lund, and she had been a little girl dead before the W.P.P. had brought Susan/Tracey to them in order to break up the Mathis family and more effectively hide its members. But she could never replace the Lunds' own daughter. The stories of Tracey's responsibility for Shannon's death had been merely their own small degrees of daily crucifixion of her.

Naturally, this knowledge provided a great source of relief for Tracey in one sense, even as it opened whole dimensions of doubt and fear in others. Now she knew that she had a real father and mother, two brothers, and a sister out there in the world somewhere, none of whom she had seen in over twenty-one years or could remember at all. Should she try to find them?

Why?

They wouldn't know her any more than she would recognize them. Their minds had been subjected to the same invasive procedures as hers. What right would she have to complicate the lives they now regarded as real and original to them?

Still, it was a possibility that Tracey found herself unable to give away completely. All of these wild discoveries bouncing around inside of her head had to represent one of Newton's Laws, the one about equal and opposite reactions. Maybe she would find the answers on Venice Beach.

"Here you go." Bobby handed her a deliciously cold and wet bottle of Coca Cola. The bottles tasted so much better than the cans. He limped to the front of the car, where the attendant joined him. "What's the damage?"

After paying for the gas, Bobby slid behind the wheel and eased the car back into the gorgeous afternoon sunlight. Tracey was rolling up her window when the smiling attendant tipped his cap and called to her, "Good luck in California! A lot of people claim that they found out who they really are out there, you know?"

Even though the car was pulling away by then, the young attendant was able to see the eerie half-smiles that passed between the man and the woman when they heard that, those strange expressions that seemed to combine a real sadness with hope for the lives they were going to meet.

He stood and watched the car until it was a glinting spot in the sunlit distance.

THE MOON POOL
MAX McCOY

Time is running out for Jolene. She's trapped by a madman, held captive, naked, waiting only for her worst nightmares to become reality. Her captor will keep her alive for twenty-eight days, hidden in an underwater city 400 feet below the surface. Then she will die horribly—like the others....

Jolene's only hope is Richard Dahlgren, a private underwater crime scene investigator. He has until the next full moon before Jolene becomes just another hideous trophy in the killer's surreal underwater lair. But Dahlgren has never handled a case where the victim is still alive. And the killer has never allowed a victim to escape.

BODY PARTS
VICKI STIEFEL

They call it the Grief Shop. It's the Office of the Chief Medical Examiner for Massachusetts, and Tally Whyte is the director of its Grief Assistance Program. She lives with death every day, counseling families of homicide victims. But now death is striking close to home. In fact, the next death Tally deals with may be her own.

Boston is in the grip of a serial killer known as the Harvester, due to his fondness for keeping bloody souvenirs of his victims. But many of those victims are people that Tally knew, through her work or as friends. Tally realizes there's a connection, a link that only she can find. But she'd better find it fast. The Harvester is getting closer.

THE FIFTH INTERNATIONALE
JACK KING

Stan Penskie is an FBI agent working as the legal attaché of the American Embassy in Warsaw. Robert Sito, an officer of the Polish Secret Service and an old friend of Stan's, needs to talk to him right away. He's found some pretty incredible information regarding various intelligence agencies around the world. But Robert never has a chance to go into detail . . . before he is killed.

Stan knows it's up to him to find the killer and uncover the truth. But as Stan digs deeper, more people are murdered and Stan himself becomes the primary target. Can one man battle a clandestine organization comprised of the most powerful people in the world? Can one man expose the hidden agenda of . . . *The Fifth Internationale*?

NOWHERE TO RUN
CHRISTOPHER BELTON

It's too much to be a coincidence. A series of computer-related crimes from different countries, all linked somehow to Japan. Some are minor. Some are deadly. But they are just enough to catch the eye of a young UN investigator. As he digs deeper he can't believe what he finds. Extortion. Torture. Murder. And ties to the most ruthless crime organization in the world.

It's a perfect plan, beautiful in its design, daring in its execution, and extremely profitable. No one in the Japanese underworld has ever conceived of such a plan and the organization isn't about to let anything stand in its way. Anyone who tries to interfere will soon find that there is no escape, no defense, and...nowhere to run.

ABDUCTED

BRIAN PINKERTON

Just a second. That was all it took. In that second Anita Sherwood sees the face of the young boy in the window of the bus as it stops at the curb—and she knows it is her son. The son who had been kidnapped two years before. The son who had never been found and who had been declared legally dead.

But now her son is alive. Anita knows it in her heart. She is certain that the boy is her son, but how can she get anyone to believe her? She'd given the police leads before that ended up going nowhere, so they're not exactly eager to waste much time on another dead end on a dead case. It's going to be up to Anita, and she'll stop at nothing to get her son back.

JOEL ROSS
EYE FOR AN EYE

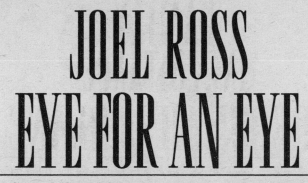

Suzanne "Scorch" Amerce was an honor student before her sister was murdered by a female street gang. Scorch hit the streets on a rampage that almost annihilated the gang, but it got her arrested and sent away. That was eight years ago. Now Scorch has escaped. The leader of the gang is still alive and Scorch wants to change that.

The one man who might be able to find Scorch and stop her bloodthirsty hunt is Eric, her prison therapist. Will he be able to stand by and let Scorch exact her deadly vengeance? Or will he risk his life to side with the detective who needs so badly to bring Scorch back in? Either way, lives hang in the balance. And Eric knows he has to decide soon. . . .

- -

FAMILY INHERITANCE
DEBORAH LeBLANC

The dark, impenetrable bayous of Louisiana are filled with secrets that can never be revealed and mysterious forces that can never be understood. Jessica LeJeune left Louisiana, but she brought some of those mysterious forces with her—and now she's being called back home to her Cajun roots to confront a destiny she could not escape and a curse she might not survive.

Jessica's younger brother, Todd, has descended into a world of madness. His shattered mind is now the plaything of an unimaginable evil. But Jessica is not alone in her battle to save her brother's soul. For deep in the misty bayous, in an isolated wooden shack, lives the person who is their only hope....

FOR THE DEFENDANT
E. G. SCHRADER

Janna Scott is a former Assistant State's Attorney with a brand new private practice. She's eager for cases, but perhaps her latest client is one she should have refused. He's a prominent and respected doctor accused of criminal sexual assault against one of his patients. It's a messy, sensational case, only made worse when the doctor vehemently refuses to take a plea and insists on fighting the ugly charges in court.

Meanwhile, a vicious serial killer who calls himself the Soldier of Death is terrorizing Chicago, and it falls to Janna's former colleague, Detective Jack Stone, to stop him. Body after body is found, each bearing the killer's gruesome trademark, yet evidence is scarce—until a potential victim escapes alive. . . .